TARGET RESPONSE

TARGET RESPONSE

WILLIAM W. JOHNSTONE
with J. A. Johnstone

P

PINNACLE BOOKS
Kensington Publishing Corp.
www.kensingtonbooks.com

PINNACLE BOOKS are published by

Kensington Publishing Corp.
119 West 40th Street
New York, NY 10018

PUBLISHER'S NOTE
Following the death of William W. Johnstone, the Johnstone family
is working with a carefully selected writer to organize and complete
Mr. Johnstone's outlines and many unfinished manuscripts to create
additional novels in all of his series like The Last Gunfighter, Mountain Man, and Eagles, among others. This novel was inspired by Mr.
Johnstone's superb storytelling.

All Kensington titles, imprints, and distributed lines are available at
special quantity discounts for bulk purchases for sales promotions,
premiums, fund-raising, educational, or institutional use. Special
book excerpts or customized printings can also be created to fit spe-
cific needs. For details, write or phone the office of the Kensington
special sales manager: Kensington Publishing Corp., 119 West 40th
Street, New York, NY 10018, attn: Special Sales Department; phone
1-800-221-2647.

This book is a work of fiction. Names, characters, businesses, organ-
izations, places, events, and incidents either are the product of the
author's imagination or are used fictitiously. Any resemblance to
actual persons, living or dead, events, or locales is entirely coincidental.

PINNACLE BOOKS and the Pinnacle logo are Reg. U.S. Pat. & TM Off.

ISBN-13: 978-0-7860-2266-3
ISBN-10: 0-7860-2266-3

First printing: July 2010

10 9 8 7 6 5 4 3 2 1

Printed in the United States of America

ONE

Jungle hell.

Kilroy had survived and thrived in some of the world's worst:

The upper reaches of the Amazon where the borders of Brazil and Venezuela blur into each other in a steaming green inferno whose denizens had long ago traded curare-tipped poison darts for shotguns and machetes.

The Suud, that near-impassable morass of hundreds of square miles of reeds and marshland where the White Nile flows south toward the desert flats below Khartoum.

The emerald forests deep in the interior of New Guinea where tribal folk still follow the practices of cannibalism and head-hunting.

The bamboo thickets and teak forests of Myanmar's Shan State where Burmese warlords and their private armies war incessantly for control of the lucrative opium and heroin trade.

From the Congo to the Philippines, from

the Solomon Islands to the Florida Ever-
glades, in some of the planet's wildest places,
Major Joseph Kilroy, U.S. Army, had plied his
peculiar trade and come out not only alive but
victorious.

Kilroy—the killer.

Now a strange destiny whose source lay in
the corridors of power in Washington, D.C.
and the corporate boardrooms of Manhattan
had led him here to a deadly showdown in the
swamplands of the West African coast.

It was in the fan-shaped Niger River delta
where that great watercourse flows into the sea
by a hundred nameless tributaries. Here, well
east of the port city of Lagos, in one of the innu-
merable mangrove swamps dotting the coastline, Kilroy prepared to make his breakout.

He'd been penned in the swamp for three
days and three nights, hunted and harried by
his foes. He'd have made his break long ago
if he'd been alone. But he had a partner.

When the enemy first struck their treacher-
ous blow, Kilroy had fled into the swamp with
Captain Bill Raynor. He and Raynor were the
sole survivors of a ten-person Defense Intelligence Agency (DIA) team on a covert investigative mission to Nigeria. The clandestine
operation required them to pose as civilians.

The other eight members of the team had
perished when an explosion destroyed their
plane in midair shortly after taking off from a
Lagos airfield. They were homeward bound to

deliver the results of the fact-finding mission to their handlers in the Pentagon in Washington, D.C.

The hidden bomb that blew them and their aircraft to bits had also destroyed the evidence they'd amassed during their probe. Damning evidence that incontrovertibly proved that a leading global corporation had conspired against vital national security interests of the United States.

Sheer chance had prevented Kilroy and Raynor from being on board the doomed flight. They'd been scheduled to depart with the others but a last-minute change in plans had resulted in their separating themselves from the team to follow up a hot investigative lead that took them to the Vurukoo oil fields.

Raynor was an investigator, a veteran sleuth from the U.S. Army Military Police's Criminal Investigation Division, on loan to the DIA for the Nigerian probe.

Kilroy was no detective. He was a specialist, a trigger-puller supreme. A troubleshooter. His motto: "When I find trouble, I shoot it."

He was a member of the Army's ultrasecret assassination arm, the Dog Team.

In the secret vaults where the Army's black ops files were kept, Kilroy held the rank of major. He outranked Captain Raynor, but was content to outwardly play an unassuming subordinate role as part of his cover. His assignment was to keep Raynor alive.

The two of them had been in their tent in

the Vurukoo oil patch when they had learned by radio that their DIA teammates had been blown out of the sky.

Moments later, the enemy had struck.

They had come in the form of a company of well-armed Nigerian troops, an elite unit of hand-picked soldiers from the capital who'd each sworn a loyalty oath to Minister of Defense Derek Tayambo. One of the most powerful and dangerous figures in the government's ruling cabinet in Lagos, Tayambo was a key player in a continent-spanning terrorist conspiracy.

There'd barely been been time for the two Americans to grab some arms and provisions and flee the oil fields before the attackers swooped down on them in force. Blocked from the land route, the duo fled into the swamp.

Now Kilroy and Raynor had two deadly threats to contend with: their pursuers and the swamp itself.

The swamp was rank marshland half flooded by overspill from the Rada and Kondo branches of the Niger River in oil-rich Vurukoo province. It knew two states of being: gloomy daylight and darkness.

The scene could have been from earth's primeval dawn hundreds of millions of years ago:

Twisted mangrove trees writhed in eerie shapes, their snaky boughs intertwining to form a canopy of foliage that kept the swamp below locked in a perpetual daytime dusk. Contorted roots formed a gnarly woodwork web that floored land and water. Patches of solid ground were few and far between. Black stinking mud was everywhere.

Weed-tufted islets were honeycombed by slow-flowing channels that frequently pooled into ponds and lagoons. A layer of jade green scum topped dark stagnant water. Here was the haunt of crocodiles, snakes, and insects.

The heat was seething; the humidity, stifling. A murky haze overhung the steaming water. The air was thick with swarming clouds of flying insect pests. Stinging mosquitoes, biting flies, and noxious gnats that flew into eyes, mouths, and nostrils.

At the height of the pursuit, there must have been 150 troops fanning out into the swamp and environs in search of Kilroy and Raynor.

The swamp at least was impartial. It was hostile to all human trespassers in its domain, be they transplanted Yankees or homegrown Nigerians.

Nigeria's population is 55 percent Muslim and 45 percent Christian. The traditionalist Muslims of the dry northern uplands and the dynamic, business-oriented Christians of the south have a long history of bitter rivalry.

Most of Minister Tayambo's company of loyalist troops were Muslims from the arid north. The others were mostly city and town dwellers from the coast. The swamp fought and hindered them as it did the Americans they hunted.

No human antagonist but rather a lethal

swamp dweller was to spell doom for Bill Raynor. It got him at midday of the second day that he and Kilroy were in the marsh.

The previous thirty-six hours had been a nightmare ordeal of hunger, thirst, fatigue, privation, and harrowing danger for the two men.

They'd managed to scrounge up a single canteen of fresh water and a couple of handfuls of foil-wrapped Meals, Ready-to-Eat (MREs) before taking it on the run. Kilroy was armed with an AK-47 with a single banana clip containing about thirty rounds, a .44 Magnum handgun, and a wicked foot-long survival knife in a belt sheath.

Raynor had an M-16 with a single clip and a 9mm Beretta semiautomatic pistol with one clip loaded and a couple of spares in his pockets.

The initial attack had come swiftly, without warning. Only the chaos and confusion of its opening moments had allowed them to grab those minimal armaments and rations before cutting a hole in the rear of the canvas tent they'd been occupying in the camp and fleeing for their lives as hostile troops invaded the oil fields.

Even so it had been a close-run thing, with enemy bullets nipping at their heels as they disappeared into the brush at the edge of the swamp.

Since then Kilroy and Raynor had been playing a murderous game of hide-and-seek with their pursuers. The hunt was relentless, going on day and night. By the second day the ordeal was seriously taking its toll on the fugitives.

The swamp water was undrinkable, a hell-broth of deadly germs and impurities. Kilroy and Raynor strictly rationed the precious store of clean water in the single canteen they shared, limiting themselves to a single mouthful each every few hours. Despite which, the water level in the canteen declined with alarming rapidity.

It was a losing game. They sweated out more fluid than they took in—the threat of dehydration loomed. There could be no boiling of the swamp water to purify it. They couldn't risk betraying their position to the hunters with telltale fire and smoke.

Hunger, too, made its inroads on their dwindling reserves of strength and energy. Between them they had about a half dozen MREs. They stretched out their food stores, making them last. Their mostly empty bellies were knotted with want.

No less pressing was the lack of ammo. They evaded the troops as best they could to preserve what limited rounds they had. Sometimes there was no getting around a clash. When discovery by one of the roving bands of hunters seemed imminent, the fugitives opened fire.

Kilroy was a dead shot. Each time he pulled the trigger, he killed a man. Raynor was a marksman but nowhere in Kilroy's league. Kilroy was world-class. Trouble was, he had too few bullets.

By Day Two the thirty-round banana clip of

his assault rifle had been cut in half, with a dead Nigerian trooper for every expended round. His high-powered .44 had a greater reserve of ammo to draw on. Kilroy wore the long-barreled revolver on a belt holster and the gun belt sported about twenty loaded cartridge loops.

He now wore the gun belt over his shoulder, with the holstered .44 hanging butt-out under his left arm. He'd rigged the weapon that way to keep it dry during the many crossings of waist-high water he'd had to endure.

Even when wielded by an expert such as he, though, a handgun was no match for the enemy's assault rifles and small machine guns. Kilroy had no desire for working that close to the foe.

He and Raynor had killed about two dozen of the opposition since the pursuit began, but at no time had they been able to get close enough to the dead to scavenge their weapons, food, or water. They were constantly forestalled by the nearness of other packs of manhunters, who at the sound of gunfire gave out a hue and cry and closed in to resume the chase.

The fugitives had a simple plan: lose their pursuers, break out of the swamp, and then steal a ground vehicle or boat and beat it back to Lagos.

The goal seemed a long way off. So far it had taken their best efforts merely to stay alive and keep ahead of the foe, a course that had resulted in driving them deeper into the swamp.

Disaster struck on the second day.

Infrequent breaks in the canopy of foliage overhead revealed a heavy, overcast sky. A pale disk of sun smoldered behind gray clouds. The dusky gloom deepened as the steamy heat increased.

Kilroy and Raynor were approaching the ragged edge of exhaustion. The night before, they'd managed to grab several fitful hours of sleep, doled out in small doses when the pursuit slackened.

Soldiers sought them by night, bearing flashlights and flaming torches. Some came on foot, others in small boats.

During the intervals when they'd temporarily outdistanced their pursuers, Kilroy and Raynor took turns, one standing watch while the other snatched a portion of troubled sleep.

All too soon, a glimmer of light, a shouted voice, a splash or crash in the underbrush warned that the hunters were nearing. The fugitives would flog their fatigued bodies into motion, plunging deeper into the swamp as the chase began again.

Now, at midday of the second day, Kilroy and Raynor continued to push their way onward, stumbling along like automatons.

They came upon a rare stretch of solid ground, a low rise covered with thigh-high reeds that opened into a glade. Kilroy thought to himself that they'd finally caught a break, if only for the moment. Hard ground instead of muck to stand on, and a respite from the relentless pursuit that dogged their trail.

Raynor lurched forward, staggering, almost falling. He reached out, resting a hand on a gnarled tree trunk to support himself. He paused for an instant, left arm extended straight from the shoulder, clutching vine-wrapped tree bark, heavy head bowed, looking down as he labored for breath.

Suddenly he cried out in surprise and pain, pulling his arm back as though it had been burned. The cry echoed through the trees.

A black, ribbonlike wriggler clung to his bare forearm.

At first Kilroy thought Raynor had been bitten by a snake. The swamp teemed with them, most of them venomous. Kilroy had already had more than one close brush with green mambas. He'd given the grass-green reptiles a wide berth, knowing the mamba for one of the world's most virulent and aggressive species of poisonous snakes.

No serpent had battened onto Raynor, however. He'd been bitten by a foot-long black centipede.

Features contorted with pain, breath hissing through clenched teeth, Raynor used his free hand to grab the segmented crawler.

"Don't!—" Kilroy began, but he was too late. Raynor tore the creature free from his arm, threw it down on the ground, and stomped it, crushing it beneath his boot sole.

Kilroy went to him. "Ain't that a bitch?" Raynor said, mustering up a sickly grin.

Kilroy examined the other's arm. The centipede's head was still attached to it. It had buried twin pincerlike mandibles deep into Raynor's flesh, where they clung so tenaciously that when Raynor had tried to free himself from their biting grip, its segmented body had torn loose from its head.

The walnut-sized head had a smooth, shiny, helmetlike black carapace. The centipede's primitive but tough nervous system kept its severed head alive even though separated from its body.

"Fucker doesn't want to let go," Raynor said, making an effort to keep his voice flat, even-toned. He reached for the head to pry it loose but Kilroy stopped him.

"You don't want the jaws to break loose and stay in your flesh," Kilroy said.

"I'm not going to keep its head for a souvenir," Raynor gritted.

"It'll have to be burned off," said Kilroy.

There was no place to sit but on the ground—and who knew what else might be lurking in the weeds. This was prime snake country, and with the abundance of black-water channels, crocodiles were never too far away, either. Better to administer the treatment with Raynor standing up.

Kilroy unbuttoned the flap of the left breast pocket of his safari-style shirt and took out a cigarette lighter, a heavy-duty metal job with a nonreflective matte black finish. "This'll hurt," he said.

"It already hurts, so go ahead," Raynor said.

Kilroy flicked on the lighter, a trusty model that had served him well in the past. It did not fail him now but burned with a steady yellow flame. He liked his cigars, and if he'd had one available he would have lit it and applied the hot end directly to the centipede's head. But he didn't, so he used a broken twig instead. The twig was sodden with dampness and took a bit of time to ignite. When he got the pointed end of it going he blew on it, fanning it into a glowing orange red ember.

He pressed the tip against the centipede's head where it butted up against Raynor's flesh, right at the midpoint of the black helmeted carapace where its clawlike mandibles were buried in the muscle of the forearm.

There was a hissing sound as the twig's hot point met ebony exoskeleton. A line of nasty-smelling smoke rose from the area of contact.

The creature's eyes were a pair of shiny black beads on opposite sides of its globed head. They rolled wildly during the burning. Its severed head twitched and jerked.

Raynor's body was taut, quivering. Veins stood out on his face, his neck cording. His skin was sallow under its bronze tan, misted with a sheen of cold sweat.

Blind instinct caused the centipede's head to retreat from the stimulus of the burning point applied to it. Its curved mandibles retracted partway, wickedly barbed tips still penetrating the flesh.

Kilroy touched the flame once more to the

point of the twig, reheating the fading orange tip before applying it to the centipede's head again.

Raynor groaned. With a final wriggling spasm the mandibles pulled free and the centipede's head fell to the ground with a soft plopping sound. Raynor let out with a gasp the breath he'd been holding.

The job was only half done. Like most denizens of the swamp, the centipede was toxic. It injected venom along with its bite.

Kilroy freed his knife from its belt sheath. He ran the lighter flame along the razor-sharp edge near the tip of the blade, sterilizing it as best he could.

His free hand gripped Raynor's wrist, steadying the other's arm. The bite was on the top of the forearm. The area was already swollen into an egg-sized red bump. Kilroy made an X-cut over the affected area. Raynor bit down on the edge of his shirt collar to keep from crying out. There was a smell of scorched hair and flesh.

Kilroy knew better than to try to suck out the venom. That would risk poisoning himself. No, that doctrine was exploded. His fingers gripped the flesh around the bite area and squeezed, expelling globs of blood streaked with brown mucouslike veins, spilling it to the ground. He was careful not to get any of the stuff on him.

Raynor shuddered like a wet dog shaking itself dry.

The metal lighter grew too hot to handle.

Kilroy paused for a moment until it cooled off. He then held the flame against the flat of the tip of the blade, heating it until it took on a dull red glow. He pressed it against the wound, cauterizing it.

Raynor's legs started to fold at the knees. Kilroy got an arm around him, holding him up until the spasm passed.

"I'm okay," Raynor rasped, his voice a croak. He didn't sound okay.

Kilroy cut a long strip from the bottom of his shirt and used it as a makeshift bandage to wrap the bitten area of Raynor's forearm.

"Stupid of me," Raynor said, shaking his head. "I put my hand on the tree without looking and the damned thing got a piece of me."

"Look at the bright side—at least it wasn't your gun hand," Kilroy said.

"Yeah, sure . . ."

"Take a drink of water," Kilroy said, indicating the canteen hanging from a strap around Raynor's neck and across his shoulder.

Raynor shook his head. "That's all right. Let's get going."

"Doctor's orders. It'll give you a boost and you need one now."

"No—"

"Quit fucking around and do it. You can play hero later."

Raynor unslung the canteen and screwed off the cap, which was secured to it by a tiny length of chain. He held the canteen to his lips and tilted his head back, taking a mouthful.

He swirled the water around in his mouth before swallowing, the muscles of his throat working painfully.

He held out the canteen to Kilroy. "Not thirsty," Kilroy said.

"Now who's playing hero? Cut the shit," Raynor said.

Kilroy accepted the canteen, taking a small swig from it. The water was warm, almost hot, but the wetness was refreshing. He screwed the cap back on and reached toward Raynor to return it.

"You keep it," Raynor said.

Kilroy made a face. "Aw, for chrissakes—"

"You'll be doing me a favor. It's one less thing for me to worry about."

"All right, but only because it's easier than arguing about it. We've wasted enough time here already," Kilroy said. He fitted the strap over his head and slung the canteen down along his side.

A faint noise behind him caused Kilroy to glance back over his shoulder toward the far end of the glade, the way they'd come. There was a rustling in the brush and a flicker of motion in the bushes about thirty yards away.

A Nigerian soldier in olive drab fatigues parted the foliage and stepped into view in the open. He saw Kilroy and Raynor as he entered the glade. He froze for a beat, then shouted something and reached for the rifle strapped over his left shoulder.

Kilroy already had his AK-47 raised, shouldered, and swinging toward the newcomer. The selector was set for single shots. He squeezed the trigger. The rifle barked.

The trooper fell backward, dead. The space that he'd been occupying opened up, affording a view of several more soldiers positioned in single file along a trail reaching back through the brush.

Kilroy shot the next man in line. The others jumped to the sides, taking cover.

Angry shouts and shots erupted along the trail. A racketing clamor of autofire erupted. The soldiers weren't aiming at anything they could see—they were just shooting into the glade in the direction from which the gunfire had come.

Other shouts sounded in the near distance, coming from the right and left of the trail, the voices of other hunting bands calling out to their comrades under fire.

Hot rounds zipped through the air, smacking tree limbs and cutting down branches. They all fell wide of the mark, but once the troopers got their bearings and augmented their numbers with reinforcements, they'd zero in on their targets.

Kilroy's expression was rueful. If he only had a tenth of the ammunition they were so prodigally expending, he could clean house. But he didn't, so—

It was time to move out.

"Here we go again," he said sourly.

Crouching low, he and Raynor scrambled into the brush on the near side of the glade, disappearing behind a tangle of green.

The chase was on again.

By midafternoon they seemed to have lost their pursuers. One thing that couldn't be outrun, though, was the poison in Bill Raynor's system. Raynor had been favoring his left arm, the limb that had been bitten by the black centipede, holding it close to his side, using it as little as possible.

He and Kilroy were making their way through a patch of dense scrub brush. Kilroy was a few paces ahead, blazing the trail. The ground was spongy underfoot, the tangled foliage bunched up close.

Raynor stumbled, bumping into a low, shrub-like tree with his left side. He gasped, trying to regain his balance. He grabbed a tree branch with his right hand, steadying himself.

Kilroy looked back. Raynor stood frozen, eyes squeezed shut, face a mask of agony. Kilroy caught a glimpse of Raynor's left arm. The forearm was swollen to twice its normal size.

Raynor opened his eyes; it took several beats before they came into focus. Kilroy went to him. "Let me see that arm," he said.

"It's nothing," Raynor said.

"What affects you affects me. So let's see."

The arm was deep red from elbow to wrist. A paler red blush extended into the bicep area and the back of the hand, outriders of the crawler's toxic contagion. Kilroy touched Raynor's bare arm, careful to rest his fingertips well away from the bandaged area of the bite. The skin was hot to the touch.

Raynor's glassy-orbed gaze met Kilroy's clear-eyed appraisal without flinching. "It is what it is. Nothing to be done about it. It hasn't reached my legs, so let's keep moving. Cover as much ground as possible while it's still daylight," Raynor said.

Kilroy nodded. "You ready?"

"Lead on."

Kilroy turned, resuming his forward progress. Now that his face was turned where Raynor couldn't see it, his expression was worried. Not for himself but for Raynor.

Kilroy trudged onward, the other following. He caught himself listening for the sound of Raynor's footfalls, to make sure he was keeping up behind him. Were they making progress?

Yes, of a sort, if progress was defined as putting some distance between them and the hunters. But their course was taking them not out of the swamp but ever deeper into it.

Kilroy glanced over his shoulder, back along the trail. "If you need a break, sing out," he said.

"Don't worry about me. I'll walk your ass into the ground," Raynor said. His face was sallow, strained. He did not so much walk as stagger.

The slog into the morass continued. The two men didn't talk much. They needed to save their breath for the hike, and besides, when they opened their mouths to speak, gnats flew into them.

The air was so heavy, so humid, it was as moisture-laden as it was possible to be without actually raining. Kilroy longed for a rainfall. It would give them a chance to slake their thirst and refill the canteen with fresh rainwater.

Distant thunder rumbled, but no drop of rain fell. Tortuous miles grew as the day lengthened and the gloom deepened.

They came to a basin, a shallow hollow several football fields in length. The boggy ground was a maze of dozens of small ponds linked by twisty creeks and threaded by narrow lanes of solid ground. There had been a fire here once, possibly caused by a lightning strike during the dry season. The basin was studded with skeletal remains of dead trees killed by the blaze. Most stood upright but a number of them had fallen, forming impromptu walkways and bridges.

Kilroy halted. "What are you stopping for?" Raynor demanded.

"I'm going to climb a tree and take a look around," Kilroy said.

"Oh—sorry. Thought you were stopping on my account . . ."

"Don't think so hard."

Raynor sat down on the trunk of a fallen tree. He looked like hell—filthy, haggard, and exhausted—but so would any man who'd spent a day and a half in the swamp.

Kilroy figured he looked the same. What worried him was the haunted, feverish look in Raynor's eyes and the way the bones of his skull showed beneath taut, yellowish skin. His face was taking on the semblance of a death's head. And his left arm—it wasn't good. The swelling had reached his hand and the red flush was stealing up into his shoulder.

Kilroy unslung his rifle and set it butt down on the ground, leaning it against the fallen tree.

He crossed to a nearby tree that he'd picked to use for his vantage point. It showed a number of limbs that had broken off close to the trunk, forming ladderlike handholds. The green fought to reclaim its fire-blighted hulk, wrapping it with a mass of flowering lianas and dangling vines.

Kilroy reached for a low-hanging limb that looked sturdy enough to support him and tested his weight against it.

It held, so he pulled himself up, knees and thighs gripping the trunk as he reached for the next handhold. He wedged a booted foot in the crotch where a branch joined the trunk, affording him a steady platform. He groped for the next handhold and mounted higher.

In this fashion he scaled the tree. His ascent was not without incident. More than once, a branch that he tested snapped off under his hand and fell to the ground. That's what testing is for. When it happened he was braced and ready with a solid perch beneath him. But it always came as an unpleasant discovery.

The noise was the worst part, for a dead tree limb breaks with a sharp, sudden crack like a rifle report, and it sounded dangerously loud in his ears. The first time it happened, it started a sudden flight of birds from a nearby tree. They took to the air as one, scattering in all directions. Kilroy worried that the sound or sight would draw the attention of nearby spotters.

He did not climb straight up the tree. The branches were not uniformly steady enough for that. He followed a spiraling course up and around the trunk. When he was fifty feet above the ground he stopped. That was high enough. None of the branches above him looked able to hold his weight.

In his treetop perch Kilroy took his bearings. Heat, haze, clouds, and the long shadows of falling day all conspired to obscure his vision and blur the view, hemming in the horizon.

Below, swampland extended in all directions out and away from him. No structures, no signs of human habitation showed as far as the eye could see. A pale sun disk hung about thirty degrees above the western horizon, floating amid towering gray clouds.

Nearer, a quarter mile west of the basin, a branch of the river wound and coiled its way down from the north, sluggishly flowing south. The water was so brown it was almost black, the color of coffee murky with coffee grounds.

Kilroy and Raynor had come down from the

northwest, striking a roughly southeasterly course. Kilroy scanned the northwest quadrant, searching in vain for some sign of the derricks of the Vurukoo oil fields rising above the treeline. An unbroken vista of swampland unrolled toward the north.

East of the basin lay a vast tract of flooded forest, masses of gray-green foliage held in a web whose strands were channels of stagnant water.

South, the swamp extended to a low ridge that stretched east–west along the horizon. Beyond it, a tantalizing sliver of silver emptiness wavered at the limits of visibility. It glimmered like a mirage, winking in and out of sight.

That razor line of open space could be the Kondo, the big river into which all the watercourses of the swampland ultimately drained. An avenue of escape to the coast, the goal that he and Raynor sought.

That would make the water west of the basin the Rada River, which flowed southwest to meet the Kondo somewhere beyond the ridge.

Kilroy's spirits lifted.

They received a swift check from a glimpse of motion on his right.

A boat rounded a bend of the Rada and came into view. A long, open bargelike boat with a stern-mounted motor. In it were about eight to ten men—soldiers armed with rifles.

The boat came downriver, creeping along at several miles per hour. There was something ominous in its slow, steady advance. It rippled the water's surface with an arrow-shaped wake. Its stern was tailed by a thin, fan-shaped plume of blue-gray exhaust from the motor.

Now Kilroy could hear the engine's stuttering putt-putt. He squirmed around on his perch, putting the tree trunk between him and the boat. The troops betrayed no sudden excitement or alarm, fired no shots. He guessed they hadn't seen him.

On the far side of the river, a line of soldiers inched into view, marching south in single file on a path that ran along the top of the west bank. There was something about them suggestive of a column of ants.

Kilroy was unable to see the Rada's east bank, hidden from him by an overhanging canopy of foliage. Was there a second column of soldiers prowling the river's near side?

He didn't intend to stick around and find out. He started his descent, covering behind the tree trunk as much as possible to screen himself from the hunters on and along the river.

He looked east, beyond the basin rim where a flooded forest was webbed by dozens of waterways. Several of the widest channels were speckled with objects floating on the surface. At this distance they were mere blurs, but they could have been small boats filled with more hunters.

Kilroy climbed down as quickly as he dared, careful to avoid breaking any branches, whose sharp cracking sound would alert the troops. About halfway down to the ground, he stepped onto what he thought was a sturdy branch—only to have it move underfoot.

Recoiling, he looked down. Coiled around the branch below was a huge snake, a python twenty feet long and as thick around as his thigh. Its scaly hide was brown with dark brown bands.

It writhed, its sinuous body one giant muscle. It lifted a massive, boxy head, yellow eyes glaring. Jaws gaped, baring a fanged maw and wicked forked tongue, as it hissed a warning.

Kilroy's heart felt like it jumped up into his mouth as he was seized for an instant by primal fear. Adrenaline flooded him.

His nerve returned. He drew the survival knife from his belt sheath and brandished it, holding on to a branch with his other hand.

The python was curled around the branch below so that its swaying head was at the far end of the branch. A long upswooping curve of its neck raised its heavy head, bringing it to Kilroy's eye level.

Kilroy knew that the python kills not by its bite but by constriction, wrapping its muscular coils around its prey and crushing the life out of it. Lethal or not, though, a bite from those curved and gleaming three-inch fangs would be no picnic. The python also uses its hard head as a club to stun its victim into insensibility.

He and the python were eye to eye. "I'll cut your fucking head off," Kilroy rasped throatily. He wasn't sure he believed it, and he didn't think the python did, either.

The python hissed in response, a sound like the venting of a steam engine.

Steadily eyeing the serpent, Kilroy squirmed away from it, circling to the other side of the trunk. One foot extended, he felt around with it until he found a lower branch opposite that wasn't occupied by the python.

Clenching the flat of his blade between his teeth to free his hand, Kilroy hastily climbed from his perch, scrambling down the side of the tree. Coming to a branch twelve feet above the ground, he gripped it in both hands, extended his arms full length beneath it, and hang-dropped to the earth below. Soft, marshy soil cushioned his fall, which he took on bent legs.

The python remained where it was on the branch, looping its head around the trunk to follow Kilroy's progress. Kilroy scrambled out from under the tree.

Raynor was on his feet, holding the M-16 in one hand, muzzle angled toward the serpent. Kilroy sheathed his knife, securing the butt strap that held it in place. "Don't shoot—he's harmless."

Raynor laughed without mirth. "That must be why you got down that tree so fast."

Kilroy grabbed his rifle. The python made no move to pursue. Kilroy gave the snake a dirty look. "You're lucky I didn't turn you into a pair of cowboy boots, you prick," he said to it.

The python seemed unimpressed.

"What'd you see up there? Apart from your new buddy, that is," Raynor asked.

"One of those good news, bad news deals," Kilroy said. "The bad news is that there're troops a quarter mile west of us. There's a river there—the Rada, I think. They've got a boat looking for us. Ground troops, too."

"How many?"

"A shitload. There's a flooded area to our east. Looked like there were boats out there, too."

"And the good news?"

"There's a big river to the south. The Kondo, the one that'll take us to the coast."

Raynor showed his teeth in a forced grin. "How far, Kilroy?"

That was the question. On foot through the swamp, while being sought by a small army? And Raynor with a skinful of poison, his condition worsening by the hour?

"How far?" Raynor repeated.

"A day's march," Kilroy said, not sugarcoating it, giving it to him straight. Raynor's face fell, his expression one of defeat.

"Or a couple of hours by boat," Kilroy added quickly.

"We don't have a boat," Raynor said. "Why not wish for an airplane while you're at it?"

"We'll steal one or hijack it from the Nigerians. If it comes to it, we can build a raft and float downstream on it by night."

"It's a plan, anyway." Raynor's tone was bleak.

He and Kilroy resumed their trek, crossing south across the basin. Not much of a hike if they had been able to move in a straight line.

But the swamp offered few straightaways and no easy routes.

It was a journey of constant detours, zigzagging between isolated spans of solid ground too soon interrupted by marshy bogs, impenetrable thickets, and channels too deep to ford.

Several hours passed before they neared the basin's south rim. The way was barred by a belt of black muck some fifteen feet wide.

Kilroy used his knife to cut off the branches of a slender sapling, trimming it down to an eight-foot pole. Toeing the edge of the black belt, he probed the mud with the pole. The stuff was deeper than a man's height.

Not quicksand, but quickmud.

Twenty yards away, a fallen tree stretched across the black belt at right angles. It had once stood on the far side but had toppled toward the near side, forming a natural bridge that spanned the quickmud. The trunk was largely bare of branches where it crossed the obstacle; it was three feet in diameter, its rounded upper surface partly covered by patches of moss.

Raynor handed Kilroy his M-16. "You take it. My sense of balance is a little shaky. I wouldn't want to fall in and foul it."

"You won't," Kilroy said, but he took the weapon, slinging it over his left shoulder.

Raynor went first, stepping up onto the fallen tree.

"Easy," Kilroy said. "Take whatever time you need."

"The longer I stand here dicking around, the more likely I am to fall," said Raynor.

"Cross it on hands and knees if you have to."

Raynor shook his head. "My best chance is to scoot across." He stood sideways, leading with his left side. His legs were spread wider than shoulder width apart. "Here goes nothing," he said.

He edged across the tree like a basketball player moving sideways downcourt. He lifted his left foot, moving it forward, planting it securely before lifting his right foot and advancing it. A mechanical style but it seemed to be working for him.

He reached the midpoint of the tree before his foot slipped. He cut off a choked cry, fighting for balance. He regained his footing and sidestepped quickly, hurrying to the far side.

Raynor had reached the opposite bank when he pitched forward, falling headfirst toward the serpentine tangle of dirt-encrusted roots that spread umbrella-like from the base of the downed tree.

His right arm flailed around seeking a handhold to arrest his fall, not finding one. He fell heavily on his left side. Gnarled roots cushioned his fall. Still, he shrieked with pain.

His outcry pierced the thick, oppressive air.

A troop of monkeys clustered in a nearby tree fled, startled, loosing a chorus of shrillings and chatterings as they scrambled to the tips of the boughs and flung themselves through empty space to a neighboring treetop.

Kilroy nimbly crossed the tree bridge to the

opposite side. Raynor lay still, unmoving, tangled in brownish-white root work. His eyes were squeezed shut; pencil-thick veins stood out on his forehead.

"Bill. Bill!" Kilroy said in a hoarse stage whisper, gripping the other's right shoulder.

Raynor stirred, groaning. His eyelids fluttered, opening on pain-dulled orbs. "Huh? . . . Must've blacked out for a second," he muttered.

Kilroy helped Raynor extricate himself from the mass of roots. He held him under the arm, steadying him. Raynor shivered. Kilroy guided him to the tree the monkeys had quitted, easing him down so he sat with his back propped up against the trunk.

The monkeys swarmed the upper boughs of a nearby tree. They were small creatures, each measuring about eighteen inches long from head to toe pads, with long, thin, curling tails. They had short brown fur, black snouts, and gray bellies. Still agitated, they howled and screeched down at the human intruders.

Dusk was falling fast; shadows thickened in the basin's gloom. In the thinning light Kilroy eyed Raynor.

Raynor's bitten left arm was grotesquely swollen from fingertips to shoulder. His hand was thick and clumsy as if covered by a gardening glove, with fingers the size of sausage links. Beyond the arm itself, the creeping red flush denoting the poison's progress had spread to his neck and the top of his chest.

Kilroy started at what sounded like distant

shouts. They were hard to distinguish over the monkeys' clamorings.

Alert, intent, he listened for a repetition of the shouting. None came, and he'd almost convinced himself that his ears had been playing tricks on him when there came the sound of a shot.

A dull, flat cracking report that came from a good distance away, but all the same, a shot. A few beats later, a second shot sounded, as if in response to the first.

With no visual referents it was hard to determine from what direction a sound emanated, but it seemed to Kilroy as though both shots had come from somewhere to the west, beyond the basin.

The reports further stirred up the monkeys, sending them into fresh screams of outrage and abuse.

"We're in for it now," Raynor said. "Sorry."

"Can you walk?" Kilroy asked.

"Sure. Give me a hand up."

Kilroy gripped Raynor's right hand and helped him to his feet. Raynor swayed, then recovered his balance.

"I'm useless. Take off while you've still got a chance," Raynor said.

"Don't talk stupid," Kilroy said.

"Face the facts—I'm done."

"Hell, if you can stand, you can walk. If you can't, I'll carry you."

"You've already carried me long enough, Kilroy. Too long."

"Don't throw in the towel now, Bill, not when we're so close to the river."

Raynor shook his head. "Alone, you can make it. Not with me. The poison bite's getting to me. . . . It'll finish me off soon anyway."

"Guys have lived through worse than that and so will you," Kilroy said. "Hey, I'm supposed to be bodyguarding you. What're you trying to do, make me look bad by dying on me?"

Raynor forced a smile. It was pretty ghastly— Kilroy could see the skull behind that smile.

"Do I have to carry you out of here? Because we've got to go and I ain't leaving you behind," Kilroy said.

"You hardheaded bastard. All right, I'll stick for now. You can let go of me," Raynor said.

Kilroy released his grip on the other's arm, standing ready to catch him if it looked like he was going to fall. Raynor lurched, steadying himself by taking a wider stance. "Okay, I'm all right. I may just be able to do you some good yet. Give me the weapon," he said.

"Now you're talking," Kilroy said, grabbing up the M-16 and handing it to Raynor. Raynor slung it over his right shoulder.

A lot of dead wood littered the ground. Kilroy found a likely-looking branch and picked it up. It was three feet long, solid, mostly straight, with a knob at one end. He tested his weight against it; it seemed sturdy enough.

"Here, use it as a cane," he said.

Raynor shook his head. "Don't need it."

"Maybe you don't need it now but you might

later. What the hell, when you run out of ammo you can throw it at the enemy," Kilroy said. Raynor took it.

Twigs and pieces of rotten fruit from above began pelting the ground around the two men.

"The monkeys are throwing them at us. Let's get out of here before they start throwing something else," Kilroy said.

He and Raynor started up the long, shallow slope leading out of the basin. It was a relatively dry spot of ground, watery mud oozing up to only the tops of their boot soles with every step.

After a few tentative strides Raynor began using the makeshift cane to brace himself. He lurched along like a drunken man but kept moving.

The slope was covered with spindly ten-foot-tall trees whose interlaced boughs formed a thin but more or less continuous canopy. The duo slogged to the crest of the slope, the southern rim of the basin.

It was a low elevation but still provided a vantage point of sorts. Ash-gray shadows pooled in the hollows of the landscape, thickening and thrusting east. Through a gap in the trees a stretch of the river could be seen.

On the far side of the crest, a short downgrade slanted into a broad valley whose low point was cut by a sluggish blackwater channel that ran roughly east–west.

At the west end of the valley it joined the river bordering the rim of the basin, the Rada

River, upon which Kilroy had earlier seen the barge and on its far bank a column of troops. Neither were now in view.

"We'll go downhill and follow the creek to the river," Kilroy said. Raynor grunted assent. He was saving his breath for walking.

He and Kilroy descended into the valley. The hillside was covered with the same type of spidery, stunted trees that covered the inner wall of the basin.

At the bottom of the hill the ground leveled off into a muddy field thick with knee-high weeds. The spidery trees thinned here, giving way to tangles of scrub brush that screened off much of the surroundings, forming a kind of maze.

The foliage ended near the channel, leaving a five-foot-wide strip of bare earth bordering the edge of the north bank. The strip was a game trail, its muddy surface marked by the hoofprints and paw marks of the creatures that used it.

The bank ended suddenly, dropping three feet straight down to the water below. That explained why the trail was bare of the basking crocodiles that sunned themselves on river-banks where the water was easier to access.

Kilroy and Raynor paused under the foliage at the edge of the tree line. Shadowy stillness was broken by the gurgling sounds of slow-running water.

Kilroy reached out to part the bushes. Raynor's good hand clutched the other's shoulder.

"Kilroy," he began, soft-voiced, "if I don't make it—"

"You will," Kilroy said.

"If I don't, when you reach Lagos, don't trust Thurlow," Raynor said.

Ward Thurlow was the CIA agent who'd been the primary liaison with the Pentagon's investigative unit, the team of which Kilroy and Raynor were now the only two survivors.

"You'll make it. But why Thurlow?" Kilroy asked.

"I've done plenty of thinking since we took it on the run, turning the facts over in my head and trying to make sense of them. I keep coming to one conclusion: it had to be Thurlow who fingered the team to Tayambo," Raynor said.

"I never had much use for the guy, but how do you figure him for the Judas?"

"Process of elimination. That the others were flying back to Washington yesterday was a closely held secret. So was the fact that you and I were nosing around at the Vurukoo fields. But only Thurlow was in a position to know both."

"Well . . ." Kilroy was doubtful.

"There's more," Raynor said quickly. "I was suspicious of the extent of Thurlow's contacts in the Lagos power structure. He was too chummy with the Tayambo crowd at the Ministry of Defense, always trying to steer the investigation away from them," Raynor said, sounding short of breath.

"You're the detective. I'm just a trigger-puller. If that's your theory, I'll buy it."

"Listen, Kilroy. When you get clear of this mess, drop out of sight. Don't use any of the usual channels to get out of the country. Our system here is compromised, rotten. Drop off the radar and go black. Not just the agency's radar, the Pentagon's radar, too. That way you might have a chance of getting out alive."

"I've got contacts in Lagos and alternate ways out. We'll use 'em both," Kilroy said. "But first we'll roast Thurlow over a slow fire and get some answers out of him before feeding him to the crocs."

"I'm looking forward to it," Raynor said, smiling wanly.

"I'll go first, scout along the trail. Wait here till I tell you it's all clear," Kilroy said.

He parted a couple of leafy branches, stepping out onto the trail. He stood in a half crouch, rifle leveled, looking, listening. He nodded to Raynor, who was watching him from behind the screen of brush.

Kilroy faced west and began moving forward. The valley was thick with gray gloom, giving it a feeling of unreality. A ribbon of open sky showed above the channel. Heavy clouds hung low over the treetops.

Kilroy advanced twenty, thirty yards. The hush was intense. Even the insects had momentarily fallen silent.

A flock of flying things suddenly burst out of

the trees, the flapping of their wings seeming unnaturally loud as they broke the silence.

They flew in a rising spiral, winged shapes swirling upward in a rushing whirlwind toward the open sky above the channel. Jagged black silhouettes were outlined against the backdrop of gray clouds.

They were not birds but bats. Bats! Hundreds of them. Something had spooked them from the boughs they clung to while waiting for the coming night.

Gunfire crackled on the trail behind Kilroy. Raynor shouted, "It's a trap!"

Kilroy threw himself into the foliage bordering the path. His limbs got tangled up in a mess of vines, hampering his freedom of movement. Writhing, thrashing, he fought to break free and bring his weapon into play.

The scene came alive with shots, shouts, action.

Across the channel, on the south bank, a flashlight beam blazed into being. It lanced through the dusk, sweeping along the trail Kilroy had just quitted, searching for him. It swept east along the trail where a fusillade of gunfire sounded.

The beam picked out the scene of a deadly confrontation. A band of armed men maybe a dozen strong materialized on both sides of the creek about twenty yards east back of where Kilroy had left Raynor.

Ambushers!

Raynor's cry of pain when he had fallen

earlier must have alerted the troops scouring the riverbank to the west. They'd sent an advance guard east into the valley to close it off.

Now they were in motion, sealing the trap. But they'd moved too soon, alerting Raynor, who opened fire on them.

Raynor stepped out into the open on the north bank, facing east. He stood swaying, holding the butt of the M-16 braced against his right hip, firing it one-handed at the soldiers charging at him on his side of the channel.

A round tagged a Nigerian trooper in the middle, chopping him down. Several more rushed forward to take his place, firing wildly. Their assault rifles were on autofire, racketing like jackhammers.

Raynor pumped out single shots from his M-16 into them, one by one.

Another soldier shrieked and fell sideways, toppling off the bank and falling into the water with a splash.

Troopers on the far side of the creek opened fire on Raynor. Raynor's form jerked and shuddered as rounds ripped into him.

He turned toward them, squeezing off more shots. His weapon fell silent—out of ammo. Empty.

Muzzle flares sparked on both sides of the creek as more ambushers got Raynor into their sights, streaming lead into him.

He jerked this way and that as the slugs

impacted him. The M-16 fell from his hand. He fell to his knees, head bowed.

There was a lull in the shooting as three troopers closed on him. The flashlight beam fell on the tableau like a spotlight, illuminating it.

One of the Nigerians wielded a panga, the local equivalent of a machete. With a wordless shout of triumph he raised it high over his head, swordlike blade poised for a vicious decapitating downstroke.

Kilroy, now free of the weblike vines that had netted him, thrust the muzzle of his assault rifle through the bushes and shot the panga wielder.

The meaty thud of a round drilling flesh was accompanied by the sight of the panga man falling over backward out of sight.

Kilroy's shot suddenly set the west side of the valley boiling with the figures of a horde of armed men pouring into it, racing east along both sides of the channel. They were part of the main body of the troop column, of which the dozen ambushers east of Raynor had been an advance guard.

Many booted feet stamped and thundered over the ground in double time. Branches broke and brush rustled as hidden lurkers poured out of their places of concealment.

Where Raynor knelt, the panga wielder had been closely trailed by a pair of riflemen. They had fallen back in alarm as their fellow had been cut down by Kilroy's snap shot. Recovering from the sudden fright, they now swung their rifle muzzles toward Kilroy.

Raynor's good right hand moved, drawing his 9mm Beretta from its holster and firing into the duo looming over him. The pistol barked, its muzzle flares underlighting the agonized faces of the two troopers as bullets opened up their middles.

The remnants of the advance guard, seven shooters, all let rip at once at Raynor. Slugs poured into him, shredding him ragged.

Raynor fell down dead.

The flashlight beam now swept west over the trail, searching for Kilroy. The light was held by a trooper on the other side of the channel not far opposite from Kilroy. Several riflemen were grouped around him, ready to open fire when the beam picked out Kilroy.

Kilroy shot first, firing in the prone position from behind a fallen log. A howl of pain sounded from across the channel as the light-bearer was tagged. The flashlight dropped, falling to his feet. It did not break but remained lit, rolling on its side back and forth in a small, tight arc.

Gunfire erupted from the riflemen grouped nearby as they sprayed the woods in Kilroy's direction.

The Nigerian troops pouring into the valley from the west began shooting, too. Many guns fired, yellow spear blades of light stabbing from rifle muzzles. Bursts of automatic fire crackled, tearing into tree trunks and branches.

The attackers couldn't see what they were shooting at but that didn't stop them.

The valley was an arena of mass chaos. Soldiers shot without looking. Some of them shot at each other.

A nasty little firefight broke out between skirmishers from the main body of troops and the handful of the ambushers still left alive in the east. Bodies piled up before the combatants realized they were trading shots with their comrades in arms.

The confusion suited Kilroy just fine. It turned what could have been a death trap into a first-class clusterfuck. Noise, gunfire, squads of troops running this way and that—all combined to hide him from his pursuers.

As silent as smoke Kilroy faded back into the brush, slipping away from the hunters. The deepening darkness of oncoming night was his ally, cloaking him with its sheltering shadows.

Raynor? Nothing to be done for him. No man could have survived the merciless final fusillade that had all but shot him into pieces.

Kilroy was alone now. The western end of the valley was filled with troops. He went northeast across the basin's outer slope, swinging a wide detour around the few ambushers still alive in that area. Unaware of his passage and concentrating on not being shot by their fellow troops, they were easily evaded.

Leaving them far behind, Kilroy crossed the creek, wading through listless, waist-high waters that were as warm as blood. After climbing up onto the south bank, he followed its winding course due east, into the recesses of the flooded forest.

In the distance, bursts of gunfire still sounded.

"Joseph Kilroy" was a war name assumed by he whose birth name was Sam Chambers. He'd never known his real father but he knew of him.

He was the bastard son of Terry Kovack, the supreme warrior in the Vietnam-era Dog Team. That particular cadre of elite Army assassins had been disbanded in the war's sorry aftermath of national defeatism and antimilitary agitation.

Terry Kovack had soldiered on to fight without banners or bugles for lost causes he considered right in a succession of conflicts in global hot spots, ultimately making the supreme sacrifice in a bloody last stand in a dirty brushfire war here on the African continent.

Would history repeat itself and doom his son to a similar fate?

"Not if I can help it," the man called Kilroy vowed to himself.

TWO

The swamp was thick with green mist; the mist was thickest in the flooded forest. Banks of greenish haze drifted through clusters of dripping trees.

The swamp by night was a noisy environment. It rang with shrill cries of animals and birds, growls, grunts, hisses, and bloodcurdling shrieks. Adding to the unrest was a constant counterpoint of splashes, drippings, creaks, and groans. All sounding against a steady background of the insect chorus: buzzing, chirping, humming, droning.

It was night of the third day. The hunt was still on.

East of the Rada River the flooded forest was fitfully lit by a number of flickering phantom lights. The ragged globes were beads of brightness widely scattered through the sprawling vastness of the morass. Fireballs that hovered over the watery avenues honeycombing the area.

One such light appeared in a winding channel at the southeast corner of the drowned jungle, floating about four feet above the surface of sluggish black water.

The channel snaked its way through the marsh, twisting and looping, filled with blind curves and sudden turnings. It was never more than fifteen feet across at its widest; its average width was ten feet and in some tight spots it narrowed to barely eight feet. Its depth varied between five feet and eight feet, with everywhere a soft, mucky bottom. No earthen banks bordered its sides.

Such was the nature of the drowned forest. A vast bowl filled with tall, straight trees, it had become submerged in recent years when a feeder stream of the Rada had carved a new channel into what had formerly been boggy marshland, totally flooding it.

The tall trees were unable to survive the constant immersion and quickly succumbed. Their cores rotted, their branches refused to put forth new leaves, and the trees died. Many of the slim, straight trunks remained standing, rising from the black lagoon like the pillars of a flooded cathedral.

But the swamp was a crucible of creation, teeming with green, pulsing life. Plants that had previously led a marginal existence thrived in the new aquatic environment, swarming it with masses of vegetation.

A variety of trees took hold in swamp water: mangroves, cypresses, and water oaks. Not tall and slender, they were stunted, dwarfed, and gnarly, with serpentine root and branch systems. Spiky.

Shaggy vines, flowering lianas, and cablelike creepers draped the dead tree columns, wrapping them with an elaborate three-dimensional webwork that screened out the sky.

Now, a ghostly light rounded the bend and came into view, hovering in midair. No will-o'-the-wisp or luminous mass of marsh gas this, but rather the crackling head of a flaming torch fixed to the bow of a boat.

Like the surrounding plant life, the boat, too, was designed to flourish in the wetlands. A slim wooden dinghy, it had a pointed bow and squared-off stern. Its low sides, flat bottom, and shallow draft fitted it for the shallows of the swamp.

A small outboard motor was attached to the transom board at the stern. The shrouded engine drove a long, slim shaft about four feet long that extended like a metal stinger from the back of the boat. The shaft was fixed so that it lay almost horizontal several inches below the surface of the water. The tip of the shaft sported four small, propeller-like fins. The motor turned the finned shaft, providing propulsive power.

The near-horizontal extension of the driveshaft and its minifinned propeller allowed it to operate in shallow water while minimizing the risk of snagging. Should the fins become fouled by reeds or underwater plants—

a frequent occurrence in the swamp—it was relatively easy to clear them.

Two Nigerian soldiers manned the boat.

Ojo the steersman occupied the stern seat, operating a tillerlike handle attached to the motor housing. The motor was mounted on gimbals that let it traverse a free arc of movement away from the stern board. By moving the tiller to the right or left, the steersman altered the position of motor and driveshaft, allowing him to control the direction in which the craft was heading.

The second man sat at the bow, serving as spotter. Rasheed held a six-foot-long pole that he used to ward off floating logs and the like, break up tangles of vines or creepers, and push the boat away from obstructions pressing it too closely on either side.

Ojo the steersman was round-faced, fleshy, heavyset. A coastal dweller born and bred, he was no stranger to the marshy river deltas of the Nigerian southlands, but this miserable manhunt in the swamp had long ago begun to get on his nerves.

Not so much the surroundings but the quarry they hunted had thrown a shadow over his soul.

The spotter, Rasheed, was one of Ali Abdul Mukhtar's militia men recruited into Minister of Defense Derek Tayambo's elite corps of bodyguards. His hawklike features and lean body type marked his origin in the arid northern region.

These seething swamplands were doubly alien and oppressive to one accustomed to the bonedry, desertlike plains of the north. But what Rasheed lacked in affinity for the swamp he made up for with the ferocity of his fanaticism.

He was a Believer, a Muslim jihadist who'd sworn fealty to warrior-imam Mukhtar's holy crusade to turn Nigeria into an Islamic state governed by the tenets of ultraorthodox sharia law. The purity of his hate for the infidel allowed him to transcend the bodily and psychic discomforts of the marsh.

As for Ojo, he was a swampman and its hardships were second nature to him. He had no liking, though, for the haughty northerner Rasheed with whom he'd been partnered.

And even less liking for this grinding hunt for the elusive American . . .

Lighting the way forward was the torch, a wandlike length of wood whose knobbed head had been dipped in tarry pitch and set aflame. Its base was wedged into a metal ringbolt at the tip of the prow, securing it in place. It thrust forward at a tilted angle away from the boat.

It was torchlight that created the illusion of a phantom fireball drifting above the swamp.

At least a half dozen other such flickering fireballs coursed through the flooded forest this night, each one shed by a torch fixed to the bow of a similar boat coursing the waterways in search of one lone man.

Man? Devil, more likely, thought Ojo.

The American was an implacable enemy

haunting the swamp, at least in the minds of the Nigerian troops who had been seeking him in vain for three days and nights. No ghost he, but a creature of flesh and blood—of that there could be no doubt.

The proof was in the ever-mounting toll of bodies of slain comrades found floating face-down in a blackwater channel or sprawled in a heap on solid ground. They had been shot, stabbed, clubbed, and even strangled to death.

Human prey had become predator, targeting isolated individuals, stragglers, and others who'd become separated from the main body of troops.

A shot would ring out somewhere in the swamp and when the hunters came to investigate, they'd inevitably find another of their number dead with a bullet in the head or heart.

A shriek would sound in the night—or in daylight—from behind a patch of brush and a victim would be discovered with his throat cut or his middle ripped open to let his guts out.

Worse, though, to the living, because so unnerving, was the death that came wrapped in silence.

A line of soldiers would be filing along a trail when suddenly the next-to-last man in line would glance over his shoulder to pass a remark to a comrade who was bringing up the rear only to find that that man had disappeared.

A search along the back trail inevitably would reveal the vanished one not too far behind the nearest bend, slain in some singularly unpleasant fashion.

This slow, steady attrition of their numbers was dispiriting—demoralizing. The troops would have been glad to declare that the American had perished somewhere in the swamp and taken themselves back to the barracks at their home base in Lagos.

Alas, it was not to be. Their commanding officers would not have it so. They took their orders from two white men, the South African mercenary Krentz and the Yankee spy Ward Thurlow. This pair of outlanders were favored associates of Defense Minister Tayambo, the supreme leader to whom all members of the elite bodyguard corps had sworn unquestioning allegiance.

Truly the ways of politics—like fate—were strange, thought Ojo, shaking his head. One thing was sure, however: the manhunt had gone sour. It might well be cursed.

The fierce joy experienced by the hunters on the second day when one of the Americans was slain and the other fled into the flooded forest had long since dissipated, eaten away by the rising body count of their own.

Surely the other American would soon be taken, if not by the troops then by the swamp itself. The swamp was a mankiller, and this man was a foreigner, an outlander infidel soft with the corruptions and weaknesses of the Great Satan U.S.A.

So argued the optimists in the ranks. Instead,

the reverse had happened. The lone American seemed to thrive in the difficult environment, while the manhunters continued to fall victim to him.

Each setback, each freshly slaughtered corpse, further enraged the company commanders. Of course, the officers stayed safely out of the swamp, remaining behind on riverboats or in the camp pitched on the point at the junction of the Rada and Kondo Rivers.

Nothing would do but that the rank-and-file troops must continue the quest day and night, even to this midnight hour of the third day, when a half dozen boats prowled the flooded forest to rout the quarry from his hiding place.

Better to be riding on a motorboat than prowling the land areas of the swamp on foot, thought Ojo. Even with such uncongenial company as Rasheed.

The northerner sat perched on the bow thwart holding the pole lengthwise across the tops of his thighs, his back turned to Ojo. Rasheed's stiffly held neck and upright posture radiated the innate arrogance that Ojo found so offensive.

The steersman was careful to suppress all signs of dislike, however. Rasheed was touchy and quick to take offense, especially at a real or imagined slight from one like Ojo, who was not one of his jihadist coreligionists. And he was ever ready to avenge such slights.

An enormous panga in a leather sheath was worn strapped diagonally across Rasheed's back, with the hilt protruding within easy reach behind the top of his left shoulder. His assault rifle lay behind him, propped muzzle-up where the middle thwart met the starboard gunwale.

Ojo's rifle stood in a similar position, leaning against the near side of the middle thwart where it joined the port gunwale. Several inches of water in the bottom of the boat prevented its occupants from laying their rifles flat there.

The engine puttered away, venting a cloud of blue-gray exhaust. The channel wound through what seemed like an endless tunnel whose walls on either side were pillared by dead tree trunks and veiled by trailing tangles of vegetation.

Torchlight added to the eeriness of the scene, throwing murky shadows into ceaseless, restless motion.

The passage once more began to narrow. Stands of mangrove trees bordered it on both sides, extending their massive, intricate root system into the water. Branches intertwined overhead, forming an archway.

Ahead, a sturdy bough crossed the channel at right angles, stretching out about eight feet above it. A thick branch abundant with foliage.

Ojo eyed it with unease. Such overhangs could be dangerous. Leopards liked to take their prey from above, lurking on a sturdy tree limb to pounce on the unwary victim below, fastening powerful fanged jaws on the back of the prey's neck and breaking it. Their preferred method of making a kill.

Ojo shrugged off the thought. He well knew that the flooded forest was barren of leopards. The big cats—leopards, cheetahs, lions—all shunned this forlorn swamp.

Even the carrion-craving jackal, that none too fastidious cousin of the dog, gave it a wide berth.

No, the danger here came not from feline predators but from reptiles; namely, crocodiles and snakes.

The boat neared the overhanging limb. Some bits of tree moss dropped off the branch to fall plopping into the water. The limb creaked as if under some heavy burden.

Rasheed looked up, tilting his head back. Something moved up there—

A lightning bolt detonated in the cramped space of the channel. Simultaneous with the lightning came a booming thunderclap.

Blasted out of the bow thwart, Rasheed fell backward into the bottom of the boat.

Ojo had time to register the thunderbolt that struck down Rasheed. That was all. Defying the maxim that lightning never strikes twice in the same spot, a second such thunderbolt struck Ojo.

The top of his head exploded and he ceased to exist.

The boat continued its slow forward course. The big leafy branch shook as a pair of hands gripped it and a massive form swung down into view. The nightcomer dropped into the boat as it passed beneath him. He was mindful of the danger of swamping the craft or putting a booted foot through its bottom. He landed lightly in the beam of the boat, its widest part, touching down easily in a muscular crouch.

His weight caused the shallow-draft dinghy to sink deeper into the water, for an instant sinking it so that black water rose dangerously close to the tops of the gunwales. He rode out the disturbance like a surfer on a board, minutely adjusting his position and maintaining his balance until the boat rose and righted itself.

He was . . . Kilroy.

Kilroy piloted the boat farther along the channel, whose switchback course ultimately wound toward the west.

A night and a day, and half a night again had passed since the ambush that killed Raynor and saw Kilroy flee into the depths of the flooded forest.

He had evaded his pursuers by the simple strategy employed by most successful fugitives— by being willing to take the chase to more extreme limits and endure more unremitting hell than those who were hunting him were willing to undergo.

A heavy rainfall on the night following Raynor's death had allowed Kilroy to slake his thirst and fill his canteen with fresh water.

With Raynor gone, Kilroy had enough MREs to last for several days.

Plastering his flesh with handfuls of black mud, smearing it over every inch of exposed skin, had won Kilroy some relief from plaguing insect pests. He had caught a few blessed hours of fitful sleep wedged into a treetop.

Daybreak. He'd expended his assault rifle's last rounds escaping the ambush in the valley. No matter. He still had his .44 Magnum handgun and survival knife to take the war to the enemy.

The flooded forest was ideal for bushwhacking; it made it so easy for lone troops to become separated from their fellows. A hand from behind clapped over a foeman's mouth to stifle his cries, a razor-edged knife blade cutting a throat—and the deed was done.

The first Nigerian soldier he'd slain had furnished him with a rifle and ammunition to further fuel the ongoing fight. As the long, murderous day had worn on and their numbers decreased, the men of Tayambo's elite bodyguard had grown unsure of who was hunting whom.

Night fell, and with it had come teams of torch-bearing boatmen to ply the flooded forest and bring him to bay. Kilroy had welcomed their advent; a motorized dinghy was his ticket out of the swamp.

Hours had passed before the proper opportunity to strike presented itself. A lone boat separated from its fellows, taking a course that would deliver itself into his hands.

He had raced to get ahead of it and intercept it, jumping from matted tussocks to gnarled mangrove root works, climbing trees and crawling out to the ends of their branches to leap to his next solid stepping-stone through blackwater channels. He had lost a rifle along the way.

But he had reached the critical junction point ahead of the boat, whose bow-mounted torch glowing fuzzily through green mist heralded its arrival from a long way off.

Kilroy had scaled a mangrove tree, climbing out along a branch that overhung the channel. It had groaned with creakings and sagged dangerously under his weight but held. Crouched on a crooked limb, hidden by masses of leafy boughs, he had waited with drawn gun and a hunter's terrible patience for the boat to arrive.

As it neared, he had drawn a bead on the spotter in the bow and shot him in the heart. A second shot had taken the steersman above the eyebrows . . . and the boat was Kilroy's.

He now moved to take control of the boat, a type familiar to him. It was the same basic model of slim, shallow-draft craft used in swamplands around the world, from Central Europe's Pripet Marshes to the archipelagoes of Malaysia.

The engine was about the size and horsepower of a lawn mower motor. The tiller was fitted with a handgrip throttle controlling the rate of fuel flow.

The boat nosed against a cluster of half-submerged mangrove roots, bumping into them. Kilroy's form unfolded, moving aft.

Ojo the steersman sat slumped against the stern's square-edged transom, dead hand still clutching the tiller. A .44 slug had taken him above the eyes, blowing off the top of his skull. His head was tilted back over the top of the stern board, shattered cranium oozing blood and brain matter into dark waters.

Kilroy pried open the steersman's fingers, unwinding them from the handle of the tiller. He elbowed the corpse to one side, careful not to upset the boat.

The bow was snagged in a knotted tangle of mangrove roots, its progress temporarily halted. The motor idled, sputtering, laying down a plume of blue-gray exhaust that mixed and merged with the green mist.

Kilroy made quite a sight. His shirt was in rags, and his baggy pants were in little better condition. Strapped across his upper body was a shoulder harness with a holstered .44 under his left arm. He still retained his sheath knife and canteen.

From head to toe his body was covered with a coating of stinking black mud, protection against the hordes of omnipresent swarming insects. Without it they would have eaten him alive or driven him mad.

As it was he was perhaps not at the moment what could have been called entirely sane.

The mud pack also provided good camouflage. Only the whites of his eyes, his teeth bared in a snarl, of which he was unaware, and the palms of his hands and undersides of his fingers broke the dark uniformity of his mud-daubed form.

Using Rasheed's pole, he pushed off from the mangrove roots, freeing the boat's snagged bow. He steered it into the middle of the channel.

The throttle was already set low; Kilroy left it alone, fearing to throttle down any farther lest the motor stall and he be unable to restart it. He pushed the tiller handle downward, causing the engine to tilt forward and raise the driveshaft and propeller clear of the water.

The boat now drifted forward, drawn solely by the sluggish current. The two shots with which he had downed the boatmen had sounded with thunderous crashings.

In their aftermath, the cries and howls of the swamp had become muted and stilled. Even the ferocious whirring and buzzing of the insect swarms had temporarily subsided to a hush.

Kilroy listened for the answering call of man-made sounds: gunshots, shouts, or boat motors. Anything that would indicate the nearness of other boatmen searching for him. No such noises were to be heard.

It seemed he had slipped pursuit for the moment.

He turned out the steersman's pockets but found nothing of value. He hoisted the body over the side, easing it into the black water.

The corpse bobbed around, rolling so that it floated facedown, its shattered skull upturned. An arm got snagged on a mangrove root.

The drifting boat began to pull away and presently left the cadaver far behind. Kilroy took note of the two assault rifles on board and eagerly examined them. They were dirtier than he liked but nonetheless in decent working order. With them he also found a canvas ammo bag filled with spare magazines.

Kilroy thrilled to rising exultation. Armed with this much firepower, he'd raise merry hell breaking the ring with which the opposition had encircled him.

Careful to avoid disturbing the balance of the low-sided boat, Kilroy moved forward.

Rasheed the spotter lay faceup with his back on the bottom of the boat and his long legs tangled up in the bow. His eyes were open; they'd rolled back in the sockets so only the whites showed. His mouth gaped open. Flies were already buzzing around inside it. They really flocked to the hole that the .44 slug had punched through his chest.

Kilroy hooked his hands under the dead man's arms, hoisting him up and draping his upper body across the port gunwale. He drew the panga from its sheath, holding it up to the torchlight and eyeing it. The long blade was a well-tempered piece of steel with a keen edge. He could put it to good use should the occasion arise. He decided to keep it, and the sheath, too. He worked the scabbard and straps free of the body.

The corpse he didn't need. It would follow the steersman's into the water.

Kilroy wrestled around with it, positioning it preparatory to dumping it overboard. Hard work, made doubly difficult by the need to take care to avoid tipping the boat, forcing him to expend a lot of energy he could ill afford to spare.

The placid waters of the channel began to swell and seethe with agitation. The boat swayed from side to side.

Something bumped against the bottom of the hull, nearly causing Kilroy to tumble overboard. He saved himself by gripping the gunwales. For an instant he thought he'd collided with a submerged log or rock. The turbulence increased, whipping up the surface of the water.

Suddenly something emerged from below, thrusting an enormous wedge-shaped snout into view.

The snout divided in two, opening on the fulcrum of a massive pair of jaws, revealing a stinking, gaping maw whose upper and lower halves were lined with double rows of jagged teeth. Each tooth was roughly the size and shape of a flint arrowhead. Topping the far end of the snout were two golden, glittering orbs.

Crocodile! Kilroy had dodged plenty such during his time in the swamp but this brute was one of the biggest he'd yet seen.

It closed its jaws on the head and shoulders of Rasheed, hauled him over the side. The boat tipped hard to port, nearly capsizing before the corpse came free of it. Rolling its massive bulk to one side, the crocodile submerged, dragging the body underwater. The wave generated by its movements rocked the boat again.

Kilroy lunged for the stern, gripping the tiller and levering the driveshaft and propeller into the water—not too deep, for fear of disturbing the thrashing crocodile in its feeding frenzy.

Opening the throttle, Kilroy powered the boat away from the croc and its prize and out of rough waters.

THREE

The command gunboat sat in the Kondo River near its junction with the Rada River. It was the dead-night hour between midnight and dawn.

Measuring thirty feet long from stem to stern, the low-slung motor launch carried a crew of six men. The sleek, trim craft was powered by a pair of powerful inboard motors.

The black-hulled launch had white-topped gunwales and a white foredeck. A name on the stern transom had been hastily painted over. The coat of paint obscured but could not totally hide the word beneath it:

MYRMEX.

This was not the boat's name but rather the name of the company that owned it. MYRMEX was a private security firm that specialized in supplying auxiliary support and infrastructure to the armed forces of various countries that contracted its services.

It was a Non-Governmental Organization,

one of the privately owned NGOs that in recent years had come to perform services previously handled by national military establishments in war-torn areas, such as handling construction projects, supplying food and fresh water to the troops, providing private armed guard security for embassies and corporate regional operations, and the like.

Originally U.S. based, MYRMEX had relocated its corporate headquarters to the tiny principality of Lichtenstein to evade congressional investigations into massive fraud, corruption, and graft in its dealings with the Pentagon's efforts in Iraq, Afghanistan, and certain pro-American Gulf emirates.

MYRMEX was deeply involved in Nigerian political intrigue. And why not? Nigeria's 36-billion-barrel oil reserve made that country a power player on the global chessboard.

Some MYRMEX operations were more sensitive than others. Its dealings with Nigerian Defense Minister Derek Tayambo were best kept clandestine. That's why the MYRMEX logo had been painted over wherever it appeared on the gunboat. The launch's identifying registry numbers had also been painted over.

However, the haste with which the boat had been pressed into service had resulted in a sloppy job. In moderate light, the black block letters spelling out MYRMEX in various places on the boat could be seen through the thin coating of paint covering them.

This was of no great concern to the boat's

masters, however. The nature of the launch's current assignment was such that the only individuals who might have been able to make use of the fact that this was a MYRMEX operation were the very persons at whom that mission had been targeted:

Kilroy and Raynor.

A third of the way aft from the bow the launch's foredeck gave way to a rectangular open compartment. At its head two bucket seats faced an instrument panel. One was for the boat's pilot, the other for its forward gunner. The pilot sat on the left, the gunner on the right. They could see over the foredeck to the way ahead. A clear Plexiglas windscreen curved across the foredeck, shielding the control cockpit from any water spray kicked up by a rapid transit.

A .50 caliber machine gun was mounted on the foredeck with its handle-mounted trigger buttons and cartridge belt loading mechanism within easy reach of the gunner. It was set on a swivel post that raised the barrel above the top of the low, curving windscreen, allowing a clear, near-180-degree traverse.

A second such machine gun stood at the stern, mounted on a vertical post that required the operator to stand while using the weapon.

Sandbags were secured by lines to the tops of the gunwales to provide some protection against enemy fire.

The gunboat was not under fire now. Or in action. It lay at anchor in the middle of the Kondo River.

After being joined by the Rada, the Kondo flowed southeast for several miles before curving due south to empty into the sea. The Kondo was broad, sluggish, muddy, and murky. The water was about fifteen feet deep in midstream where the gunboat was anchored.

The launch stood tethered to the river bottom a hundred yards or so east of where the Kondo was joined by the Rada, to avoid the mild chop and turbulence generated by the junction. The boat commanded a view of both rivers and their surroundings.

The company of Nigerian troops was encamped on a point of land on the right, east bank at the mouth of the Rada. The lights of their campfires showed as patches of blurry red and yellow glare flickering behind a screen of the river's greenish mist.

This was the main base of Minister Tayambo's elite bodyguard corps. Much of the force was on night duty patrolling the perimeter and interior of the swamp.

A number of small, squat, shallow-draft, fiberglass-body motorboats with squared-off bows and four-man crews coursed up and down along the shoreline. Their searchlights were lances of brightness spearing through the steamy darkness of the night. They paid special attention to the channels and rivulets flowing out of the swamp into the Kondo and Rada.

Squads of foot soldiers were posted along the shoreline. They were supposed to be on patrol, but at this late hour most of them were either drunk or sleeping on duty.

The gunboat's searchlights were now dark. The launch was lit by lines of running lights, their glow augmented by several kerosene lamps hung around the compartment to provide some illumination.

From here Ward Thurlow directed the manhunt for Kilroy. He didn't handle the nuts and bolts of the operation, not really; that chore was left to his executive officer, Colonel Krentz.

Also on board the boat were Nigerian bodyguard corps members Sergeant Diki Ajani and the gunboat's permanent crew of Sesto, the boat pilot; Hamid, the forward gunner; and T'gai, the stern gunner.

Thurlow made his home in Alexandria, Virginia, and had never missed it more heartily than he did now. Officially assigned to a minor post at the American embassy at Lagos and thereby protected by diplomatic immunity, he was in reality a CIA agent and field operative, one of the agency's up-and-coming bright young staffers.

Oil-rich Nigeria was an important posting, its attractions steadily increasing as Washington's current administration's power and prestige steadily sank around the world.

The toxic combination of a weak, feckless, indecisive president and a do-nothing Congress, compounded by a dismal economic climate brought about by the malfeasance of an unholy alliance of corrupt politicians, bankers, and Wall Street speculators, had brought a once great nation to its knees.

Distrusting an American chief executive whose word and will were as feeble as the declining dollar, the petroleum producers of the Middle East were increasingly receptive to the blandishments of the People's Republic of China—Red China, currency-rich in no small part due to the funds of U.S. corporations outsourcing vital manufacturing jobs from America to the PRC.

Has history ever witnessed such a blatant example of the shortsighted greed of a few being allowed to destroy the vital sinews of a rich and dynamic nation?

Ward Thurlow thought he knew which way the wind was blowing and had trimmed his sails accordingly, forsaking his loyalty to his native land and the CIA, which employed him, to covertly sell his services to the corporate globalists and financiers who literally and figuratively were selling the United States short.

That was why Thurlow was enduring another miserable night in a boat on the Kondo, spearheading a seek-and-destroy mission against two men who had dared to defy America's would-be hidden masters.

Ward Thurlow, thirty, was slim, boyish, with short dark hair and a clean-shaven, fine-featured patrician face. Three days and nights out in the field in the Vurukoo delta had left him somewhat the worse for wear.

His face was now drawn, haggard. He needed a shave. Most of all, he needed a bath. He stank. His sweat-damp clothes hung on him like wet laundry. They stank, too. At least out here on the water the insect population was slightly less pestiferous than on land, he told himself.

The time was a few minutes short of three a.m. By all rights Thurlow should have been fast asleep in the comfort of his coolly air-conditioned quarters at the American embassy compound. A soft mattress, clean sheets—

Thinking of the comforts presently denied him, he sighed. Here he was in the cramped quarters of a crowded launch, suffering what he thought of as unspeakable torments.

Simply because one U.S. Army son of a bitch named Joseph Kilroy didn't have the common sense, the decency, to lie down and die the way he was supposed to.

Ward Thurlow looked around, surveying his surroundings with eyes accustomed to the wanly lit interior of the boat.

Sergeant Ajani sat wedged in the portside quarter of the compartment, head bowed, eyes closed, snoring. The big bastard had the professional soldier's ability to sleep anywhere, anytime. Thurlow would have liked to have kicked him awake, but he didn't dare. Truth to tell, he was afraid of Ajani.

The man was a stone killer who radiated the threat of imminent menace, despite—or possibly because of—his outward seeming affability and good humor. Even Colonel Krentz, the cold-blooded South African mercenary who served as Thurlow's intermediary, relaying the rogue CIA agent's orders to the Nigerian troops that Minister Tayambo had put at his disposal, was careful to address the huge, hulking sergeant with studied politeness.

Ajani's true character was shown by his attitude toward the metal cannister secured opposite him. The others on board, cold-blooded Colonel Krentz included, gave it a wide berth, studiously avoiding it whenever possible.

Not Ajani. The cannister and its contents bothered him not at all. That was why he was able to sleep and snore peacefully despite its nearness to him in the stern.

The drum-shaped metal container was about the size of a five-gallon can, with a lid on top and a pair of handles at the side. It was secured in place by a length of rope that ran through the handles and was lashed in place to a metal cleat mounted on the side. Its tightly sealed lid could not contain the foul smell that emanated from the can.

The flies liked it, though. They weren't as thick here in the middle of the river as they were on land, but the cannister—or rather its contents—drew them like a magnet. They swarmed around it, buzzing and droning, vainly seeking an entryway into the can.

Just as well, though. If the flies hadn't been drawn to the cannister, they would have turned their attentions to the crew, biting them.

Sesto and Hamid had positioned themselves as far away from the metal cannister as it was possible to be while still staying in the boat compartment and not climbing on the foredeck.

The boat pilot and forward gunner occupied the bucket seats in the control cockpit. Sesto sat leaning back in the left-side pilot's seat, bare feet perched up on top of the instrument panel's console and planted on either side of the wheel. He, Hamid, and T'gai, the three crewmen, all went barefoot on board the launch, claiming that there was less risk of slipping and falling than if they wore shoes.

A shapeless canvas hat was pulled down covering Sesto's eyes. Whether Sesto slept or not, Thurlow couldn't tell, nor did he give a good damn.

Hamid sat in the right-side seat, swivel chair turned to the starboard facing the junction of the Kondo and Rada and the base camp on the point. He had a long, sharp-featured face, heavy-lidded eyes, and a wispy, goatish mustache and chin whiskers. He chain-smoked hand-rolled cigarettes, wreathing his head in a halo of nasty-smelling smoke that seemed to have some success in keeping the insects away.

T'gai, the stern gunner, sat amidships with his back propped up against the portside bulwark. His legs were bent at the knees. Folded arms rested on top of his knees, pillowing his head.

Colonel Krentz stood at the starboard side,

using a radio handset to communicate with various river- and land-based elements of the Nigerian troops. He conducted a running dialogue with varied bursts of squawking gibberish emanating from the handset.

Gibberish to Ward Thurlow, that is, who, despite a prolonged posting in Lagos, had failed to master more than a few phrases in any of the several major dialects spoken throughout the land. But that was why Krentz was here, to serve as interlocuter between Thurlow and the Nigerians.

Part of the reason, anyway. Krentz was a contract employee of MYRMEX, which, like Thurlow, had good reason for wanting the liquidation of the man called Kilroy, last surviving member of the DIA team that had been probing their mutually illicit and now demonstrably treasonous alliance.

Krentz was in his late forties, a few inches above medium height, compact and dense textured. He was balding, with a horseshoe ring of hair, and had a spade-shaped face with a dark goatee.

Krentz was a career mercenary, a South African Boer in self-imposed exile from his homeland due to several outstanding warrants for his arrest for conspiring to overthrow the government. For two decades and more he had plied his trade in a series of brushfire wars and revolutions throughout the continent.

His rank of "colonel" was one he'd awarded to himself; he'd never advanced higher than lieutenant in any conventional military force, Thurlow knew. As far as the CIA agent was concerned, Krentz could call himself anything he liked as long as he got the job done.

And quick.

Krentz was fluent in various major northern and southern dialects of the Nigerian tongue, enabling him to communicate with the troops now combing the swamplands for the fugitive.

Thurlow gave the orders and Krentz carried them out. Knowing next to nothing of military matters, Thurlow was content to leave strategy and tactics to Krentz, whose orders by now could be boiled down to the simple imperative:

Get Kilroy!

Krentz finished speaking and slipped the handset into a hip pocket of his cargo pants. He went to Thurlow, who stood leaning up against the portside gunwale.

"What news from the front?" Thurlow asked.

"All quiet," Krentz said. He spoke English with an accent. "Nothing to report since that outbreak of shooting an hour ago."

"Any details?"

"One of the riverboat patrols reported hearing some shots coming from somewhere at the western edge of the swamp."

"That's it? No follow-up?" Thurlow pressed.

"Nothing else to report. Some shots were heard, that's all we know. It could have been Kilroy or it could have been some of the boys shooting at a croc."

Ordinarily Krentz would have referred to

the troops as "kaffirs," a highly uncomplimentary term. But he was wary of using the word around Sergeant Ajani, who might or might not have been sleeping and certainly would have taken offense at the term. It was a mark of the respect bordering on intimidation that the hulking noncom generated in those around him that even his nominal superior Colonel Krentz was wary of incurring Ajani's dislike.

"None of the dinghies in the swamp have radios; there're only so many to go around. Most of them went to the riverboats. One of them heard some shots and called it in. That's all for now," Krentz said.

He shrugged, waving a hand in dismissal. "It means nothing. After three days and nights in the swamp the boys are ready to shoot at their shadows—or each other, for that matter."

"For once I don't blame them. This hellhole would get on anybody's nerves."

"Including yours, Ward?" Krentz snickered. "You've got it easy. The Kondo is a paradise compared to the swamp. As you'd know if you set foot there."

"I don't see you going in there either, Krentz."

Krentz smiled bleakly, without warmth, white teeth shining palely in the dirty yellow glow of a kerosene lamp.

"That would be improper distribution of labor. There's nothing I could do there that the boys can't do better," he said. "Besides, somebody's got to stay here with you and coordinate the hunt."

Krentz took a cigar from his breast pocket. It looked like a brown twig, long, skinny, and crooked. "Smoke?" he offered.

"Christ no! Those ropes you smoke taste like shit," Thurlow said.

"The very best dried dung. They use it here to stretch out the tobacco," Krentz said, chuckling. He bit off the end of the cigar, spat it overboard. He used a lighter to set fire to the end of it, puffed away.

Smoke clouds blanketed him, undisturbed by the still, heavy air. Even out here on the water there was barely the breath of a breeze.

"If you ask me, we're wasting our time here. The swamp's probably gotten your man," Krentz opined.

"Our man," Thurlow corrected. "Your bosses at MYRMEX want him just as badly as I do."

Krentz nodded. "Point taken."

"He was still alive today. Alive enough to slaughter another squad or two of the troops. He's terrorizing them. Picking them off one at a time, cutting their throats. Strangling them and leaving their bodies hanging from vines on the trail," Thurlow said, his voice taking a petulant, whining tone.

"He's lasted longer than I thought he would," Krentz said. "Who is this Kilroy anyway? I never heard of him—and I should have, the way he handles himself. I know all the big players in the killer elite on this continent."

"He's not from this continent. He was U.S. Special Forces or something, I don't know."

"If you don't, who does? Didn't your spook friends back at Langley give you any background information on him?"

Thurlow shook his head, his expression peevish. "Just the routine handout. Kilroy's an action man, a shooter. Tours of duty in Iraq, Afghanistan, the usual itinerary."

"Whoever he is, he's a jungle fighter. The boys should have done him. If they didn't, the swamp should have," Krentz said.

"There was nothing in the record to indicate that he was worth more than a passing notice. I didn't think he was worth further investigation."

"Now you know better, eh, Ward?"

"I couldn't pry too closely. Didn't want to show an undue interest in him or any others in the DIA team. My 'friends' back at agency headquarters, as you call them, wouldn't be my friends for too long if they knew what I was really up to in Lagos."

"A very uninformed intelligence agency."

"They only know what I tell them, Krentz. Washington's a long way off. But that's not who I have to keep happy. My bosses back home—my real bosses, not the agency—won't be happy until the job's finalized and Kilroy is dead," Thurlow said.

"It'll get done. It's only a matter of time. He's just one man," Krentz said. "Go back to Lagos and leave me and the troops here to finish the job. It'll all be over in another day, two at the most." Indicating the swamp, he added, "No lone man can last long in that hell."

"There's nothing I'd like better than to haul ass out of here," Thurlow said feelingly. "I'm dehydrated. My bowels are starting to act up on me. The heat and the bugs and the stink are driving me crazy. Lagos is the shithole of the world. I never thought I'd miss it. But compared to this godforsaken swamp . . . At least back at the embassy compound there's air-conditioning and clean sheets, hot meals and cold beer, a bath—"

"So go back. I'll stay out here and kick the butts until the job is done. That's what they pay me for."

Thurlow shook his head. "Not that I doubt your abilities, Krentz, but I don't like to leave any loose ends. More important, my bosses don't like them. I'm not leaving without tangible proof that Kilroy is dead."

Krentz gestured toward the cannister lashed in place in the stern of the boat. "Proof like that, you mean?"

"That's another story. All I need is a confirmed kill. I don't like this business of collecting trophies," Thurlow said.

"It's not a matter of what you like or I like, Ward. In this case it's a matter of what Minister Tayambo likes," Krentz told the other.

"You don't have to remind me. What a fucking ghoul! What the hell is his problem anyway?" Thurlow asked.

Krentz's eyes narrowed, looking sly. "It's

juju," he said. "Magic. Tayambo's got a couple of tribal witch doctors on his payroll. Most of the big men in the palace cadre do. It builds their confidence and unnerves their enemies."

"What does Tayambo do with his . . . trophies?" Thurlow's voice dropped to a hoarse whisper.

Krentz's shrug was eloquent. "Who knows? Maybe he gives them to his devil doctors to use in their cauldron of blood to brew up potent black magic spells. Maybe he collects them. A generation ago, Ugandan dictator Idi Amin used to eat the hands and hearts of his enemies."

Thurlow swore.

"Ritual cannibalism, you know. A widespread practice throughout the continent, then . . . and now. Eat your enemy and you absorb his power," Krentz went on, enjoying the other's evident discomfiture.

"You've got to be philosophical about such things, Ward. Minister Tayambo is an important man. If he craves such keepsakes, who are we to tell him no?"

Thurlow grimaced, visibly steeling himself. "Well, at the embassy the ambassador is always telling us to be mindful of building good relations with our hosts. And nothing succeeds like gift giving."

"There you are. Be guided by the ambassador and you can't go wrong," Krentz said cheerfully. "But have you considered the possibility that we might never be able to confirm Kilroy's death? The swamp is big, with lots of places for a body to disappear. Kilroy might be at the bottom of a quicksand patch or in the belly of a crocodile."

"I doubt it. That son of a bitch is proving uncommonly hard to kill," Thurlow said sourly.

Krentz flicked his cigar snipe overboard, its glowing ember describing a meteoric arc until it hit the water and blacked out.

The radio transceiver in his pocket started squawking. Krentz hauled it into the light. Excited shouts came crackling from it.

"What the devil?" Thurlow said.

"I don't know what it is, I can't make it out." Krentz depressed the TRANSMIT button and in the local language demanded to know what was going on. The excited-sounding squawking continued unabated. "Bloody kaffirs! Don't know enough to stop transmitting all at once—"

The radio was of a type that allowed only one user on the transceiver to transmit at a time. Until the present speaker took his finger off the transmit button, the circuit would be monopolized and no other transmission could get through.

Popping sounds crackled somewhere upstream on the Kondo. The sound carried far over open water.

"What's that? Shooting?" Thurlow asked.

The others in the boat stirred, coming to wakefulness. Sesto took his feet down from the top of the instrument board, placing them on the deck flooring. Hamid swung his swivel chair around toward the bow and began busying himself readying the machine gun. T'gai stood up, hands balled into fists.

Sergeant Ajani rose, opening pop eyes whose corneas were as yellow as old ivory. Pleased by the prospect of action, he smiled, showing a mouthful of crooked teeth.

The boat's occupants looked upriver toward where the shooting was sounding. A shriek sounded through the transceiver before being abruptly cut off. "Aaaaiiieeee—!"

The scream was accompanied by the release of a TRANSMIT button, clearing the circuit. Krentz took advantage of it to jump in and send his message, shouting for all other units to shut up so that he could arrange for an orderly succession of reports from the various handset users.

Commotion showed in the camp on the point of the southeast shore of the Rada, with antlike blurs of troopers running to and fro, backlit by campfires.

Flames flared into being on the Rada near the shore.

"What's that?" Thurlow demanded.

Krentz peered into the dimness to see better. "Something is burning—"

A dull crumping sound was followed by a vivid orange and red flash.

"My God, one of the patrol boats blew up!" Krentz said.

Pieces of burning wreckage floated on dark water. A puff of smoke telescoped outward from the blasted vessel, growing, climbing skyward.

Searchlight beams crisscrossed upriver, scissoring as several boats tore back and forth across the Rada, searching for the cause of the commotion. Shafts of white light skimmed over land and water.

The base camp was in an uproar, figures running about shouting wildly to no purpose except to menace each other.

A sputtering sound neared as a patrol boat broke loose from the pack and plowed downstream away from the others.

"It's one of ours—why doesn't the idiot turn on his light?" Krentz wondered aloud.

Sesto started the engines. They labored roughly for an instant, coughing, choking, sputtering, then suddenly came alive with a dual, full-throated rumble of power.

Hamid manned the aft machine gun, unlimbering it, unsnarling the cartridge belt so it would unwind freely from the ammunition box within which it lay coiled.

T'gai took up a stance at the stern machine gun and set about readying it for action.

Its searchlight dark, a square-bowed, flat-bottomed patrol boat came zipping downstream like a rock skimmed across the surface of the water. It cut a dirty-white wake across black water as it swung toward the gunboat to approach it at right angles to its starboard side. It came head-on at full throttle.

"My God, they're going to ram us!" Thurlow cried, backing away from the starboard side.

Krentz was excited. "This is what we've been waiting for! The breakout!"

"What?!—"

"Action at last, Ward! Now we can make an end here!"

The flat-bottomed boat closed fast, arrowing toward the starboard beam amidships.

Hamid was unable to get his forward machine gun into play; the line of fire on the attacker was too acute for the weapon's transverse sweep.

T'gai stood at the stern machine gun post, grinning wolfishly as he swung the muzzle into line with the oncoming boat.

Sergeant Ajani hefted his assault rifle, leveling it at the motorboat.

Krentz hefted a fire ax. "I'll cut the anchor line—"

The flat-bottomed boat suddenly switched on its bow-mounted searchlight. A white beam of brilliancy stabbed across the narrowing water at the gunboat.

Behind the glare could be seen the outline of two human forms. They sat rigidly upright in the pilot's and passenger's forward seats, motionless, unflinching. From behind and between them erupted a stream of rifle autofire.

Rounds cut the air above the gunboat. Krentz dropped the ax to take hold of a searchlight by its handles, swinging it around on its stand to pin the attacker.

A line of slugs ripped into the searchlight, shattering the lens and snuffing out its beam. Krentz cried out, cursing as his face and hands were sprayed with broken glass, and he fell back.

"They're going to ram us—shoot!" Thurlow yelled.

Sergeant Ajani opened fire on the nearing boat.

T'gai gripped the stern machine gun's handles, thumbs depressing the firing studs. The machine gun let rip with a racketing blast. The weapon ate up the cartridge belt, spewing empty brass cartridges into the air.

Tracer bullets, part of the ammo load, appeared as hot-yellow-white streaks clawing the darkness as they reached across the water. T'gai used them to sight in on the charging patrol boat.

Fifty-caliber rounds chewed up the bow, disintegrating the figures at the front of the craft. Still it came on, its speed not slackening, following a course as straight as a torpedo running hot.

Thurlow, frantic, all but danced in place. "What keeps it going? Why don't they die?" He shook his fist at the square-bowed boat. "Die, damn you, die!"

T'gai, unflappable, kept pouring it on, streaming lead into the foe. The oncoming boat abruptly swerved to starboard.

Something went over the port side into the

water, unnoticed by those on the gunboat in their excitement.

The patrol boat's engine choked, stuttering. Gas leaked from it.

Tracer rounds poured in. Fire leaped up. The patrol boat became a fireball, coming apart in a shattering blast. Flaming debris spewed on the waters.

The night bloomed bright, blazing for an instant before fading to dark.

Its forward movement arrested a stone's throw from the gunboat, the burning wreckage of the patrol boat sank beneath the surface. Steam hissed, raising pale white clouds as the hulk was swallowed up by the Kondo.

Giant ripples expanded outward from it in concentric circles like when a rock is dropped into a pond.

Krentz sat up in the bottom of the gunboat, pawing at his face. Shards and needles of broken glass jutted from the backs of hands that had protected him when the searchlight was shot out. Droplets of blood like red sweat oozed from a dozen places on his cheeks and forehead where minute glass particles had stung him.

Thurlow hovered over him. "Are you all right, Krentz?"

"Yes—none of the glass got in my eyes, thank God. . . ."

"That was close, too close! But we got him, though—we got Kilroy!" Thurlow said. He rose to his feet, standing on trembling legs. "Nice shooting, T'gai. You too, sergeant. There's a bonus in this for you, for all the crew!"

Thurlow stood at the starboard side, resting his forearms on the sandbags lashed to the top of the gunwale, putting his weight on them. He was still a little weak in the knees.

The others grouped around him, looking at where the motorboat had gone down. A couple of fire-charred bodies bobbed in the water.

"So much for Kilroy. His breakout . . . was broken," Thurlow said with deep satisfaction.

"No trophies to take back to Tayambo, I'm afraid," Krentz said, laughing shakily.

"I don't know, a couple of bodies are still floating around."

Krentz cut a side glance at the other. "You'll have trouble picking out Mister Kilroy now that the fire's gotten to all of them."

"It's worth a look. I'd hate to disappoint the minister," Thurlow said, cool eyed, with a bland smile.

"Better move quick then, Ward, before the crocs get them," Krentz cautioned.

"We'll bring them alongside with a gaffing pole."

Something came out of the water and hauled itself up the port side of the gunboat.

Sergeant Ajani was nearest to the interloper. He turned to face it, just in time to see Kilroy clamber up a line and over the side.

Kilroy crouched on folded legs on the gunwale, dripping rank river water, clutching a panga. Gripping the hilt in both hands, he raised his arms high and brought them down in a blur of motion.

The machete-like blade came down square in the middle of the top of Ajani's head. It struck with a ripe chunking sound, like a melon being sliced in two.

The blade came down at an angle, burying itself in Ajani's skull to the eyebrows, which were lifted in surprise. Ajani's pop eyes bulged as though they were going to burst from the sockets.

Kilroy tried to wrench the blade free, but it was planted so deep in the other's cranium that it was temporarily stuck in place. Ajani backpedaled, tree-trunk legs buckling at the knees. The panga went with him, wrenching free of Kilroy's hands.

Kilroy launched himself from the gunwale in a headfirst dive, slamming into Ajani and shoving him to the starboard side of the boat.

Ajani was a big man weighing more than 250 pounds. His dead weight crashed into Thurlow and Krentz as they turned to face the newcomer.

Ajani toppled, knocking down Krentz and Thurlow in a tangle of thrashing limbs.

The impact jarred the panga loose and it fell clattering to the bottom of the boat. Ajani's massive head wound spewed a fountain of blood.

Kilroy snatched up the panga by the handle.

Krentz, cursing, wriggled clear of Ajani's massive inert form, shoving it toward Thurlow. Having almost extricated himself from the noncom's dead weight, Thurlow was once again destabilized and knocked off balance, slipping and falling, his lower body being pinned under Ajani's corpse.

Krentz's hand plunged toward the sidearm holstered on his right hip, drawing a squat, stubby Walther PPK.

The pistol cleared the holster just as Kilroy slashed down with the panga, severing Krentz's hand at the wrist.

Still gripping the pistol, the hand dropped into the bottom of the boat. The pistol did not fire.

Krentz held his maimed arm in front of his face, goggling at it as gore geysered from the end of his wrist, where it had parted company with his hand. He started screaming.

T'gai snatched up Ajani's assault rifle.

Hamid picked up the fire ax. He wanted to get into the action but the others were between him and Kilroy, blocking him. He moved to scramble around them.

Ward Thurlow slithered out from under Ajani, pulling a flat black .32 semiautomatic pistol from his pocket.

Kilroy snap-kicked Thurlow, driving the ball of a booted foot against Thurlow's jaw. Thurlow jerked the trigger as he fell back, firing a shot from his pistol that went wild. He fell back, banging the back of his head against the side of the boat. The pistol slipped from his hand, skittering across the boards.

Kilroy lunged toward T'gai just as T'gai began to swing the rifle around to bring the muzzle in line with his assailant.

They came together with a crash, Kilroy thrusting the panga deep into T'gai's soft belly just below the breastbone. The panga ran T'gai through, its pointed tip emerging out of his back.

Kilroy pulled the rifle from T'gai's nerveless hands before the other dropped. Hamid charged, both hands holding the ax raised above his head. He slipped on blood, losing his footing.

Kilroy squeezed the trigger of the rifle, firing a three-shot burst into Hamid's middle at point-blank range, nearly cutting him in two. Hamid spun like a top, falling to one side.

Krentz was still on his feet, his good hand gripping his maimed arm, blood gushing from the end of it. Kilroy shot him, putting him out of his misery.

Sesto, frozen into immobility throughout the sudden, savage clash, now came alive with a shriek and threw himself overboard.

Thurlow, dazed, raised himself to a sitting position with his back against the side of the boat. He moaned as Kilroy pointed the rifle at him, smoke curling from the muzzle.

Kilroy could have been the living incarnation of some fearsome folkloric swamp devil. The river had washed off some but not all of

the mud coating him, leaving his body tiger
striped with dark smeared streaks alternating
with bands of paler flesh. Wild eyes blazed in a
devil-mask face.

"We meet again," he said.

FOUR

Kilroy had finally made his breakout. It hadn't been easy. He had to fight all the way.

Earlier he'd piloted the dinghy to the western edge of the swamp. A flat-bottomed patrol boat with four Nigerian troopers in it stood guard where the channel Kilroy had been following out of the flooded forest and through the swamp emptied into the Rada River.

The patrol boat's searchlight was trained on the mouth of the channel, covering it. Its occupants weren't paying much attention to their duties. The hour was late; they were alone in the boat with no superior officer to monitor them. Two of them were sleeping and the other two were passing a bottle of palm liquor back and forth.

Kilroy was running dark. The searchlight could be seen from a long way off, deep in the recesses of the swamp. Catching sight of it shining through the trees, vines, and hanging moss, Kilroy plunged the torch at the bow of the dinghy into the water, extinguishing it.

Immediately he throttled down, shutting off the motor. He waited for a reaction from the patrol boat.

None came.

The searchlight held its original position with no deviation. If the patrol boat had spotted his torch or heard his engine, it would have responded by sweeping the beam in and around the channel to locate the newcomer and starting its engine to move into action.

There was no such response, indicating that he was as yet undetected.

In the bottom of the dinghy lay a pair of flat-bladed oarlike paddles, an emergency recourse in case of engine failure. Kilroy picked one up and dipped it into the water.

Once outside the flooded forest, the sluggish channel current had increased somewhat. It carried the dinghy forward at a rate of several miles per hour, its speed increasing as it neared the Rada.

Kilroy used the paddle mostly for steering and occasionally to push the boat back in the middle of the channel when it drifted too near one of the banks. The channel did not proceed to the Rada in a straight line but followed a winding course. That was a help since he was able to get close to the channel mouth before having to worry about being seen in the light.

The dinghy silently crept close to the end of the channel. One last turn separated the channel from the river. A spit of land on Kilroy's left stood between him and the exit—and the patrol boat.

Kilroy selected a likely spot from which to make his move. The finger of land on his left thrust out into the Rada. It had a slight elevation of several feet, solid ground, and a matted tangle of vegetation for cover.

Kilroy readied to make his move. He selected the cleaner, better-maintained assault rifle of the two in the dinghy. It was loaded with a full clip. He slung the canvas ammo bag over a shoulder.

He'd already appropriated Rasheed's panga, adjusting the straps to fasten the scabbard diagonally across the flat of his back with the blade's hilt in ready reach behind his left shoulder.

Stepping onto the bank, he wedged the dinghy's bow deep in a tangle of mangrove roots that reached into the water.

He started up the engine. It fired up with a cracking noise that sounded loud in the still of the swampy night. The driveshaft and propeller were raised out of the water to avoid giving the engine any propulsive power. It was the noise of the motor that he needed.

As a lure.

He climbed up onto the bank, making a nest for himself amid a tangle of twisted dwarf trees and brush.

The sudden eruption of engine noise produced the desired effect. The river patrol boat wasn't idling anymore. From it came shouts. Its engine started up.

Its searchlight swung into action, sweeping back and forth across the finger of land. The powerful beam was unable to penetrate the dense tangle of foliage where Kilroy had made his nest. The beam swung overhead through the trees. A change in the engine's tempo indicated that the patrol boat was in motion.

The boat swung around into the river, rounding the point and entering the channel. Its searchlight swept from side to side, scanning both banks of the channel. Greenish banks of mist rolled across the scene, partially obscuring it.

The beam flitted across the dinghy, fastening on to it. The swamp boat's engine sputtered away, laying down a cloud of gray-blue exhaust.

The patrol boat came up the channel cautiously. One of the men inside shouted something, hailing the dinghy.

From his place of concealment Kilroy could now see that the square-bowed boat held four soldiers, two in front, two behind. Like the dinghy, the patrol boat was powered by a stern-mounted outboard motor, although a larger and more powerful engine, to be sure.

The pilot sat on a stern seat, working a tiller to steer the boat. Except for the pilot, the other three troopers had their rifles trained on the dinghy. One of them used one hand to train the bow-mounted searchlight on the empty boat with the active motor.

The patrol boat cut its engine, letting momentum carry it to the dinghy. The searchlight beam flooded radiance on the dinghy, illuminating it in a white-hot glare. It left untouched the shadowed canebrake where Kilroy lay cloaked in darkness.

The patrol boat came alongside the dinghy to investigate. Kilroy opened fire on the soldiers grouped together in the square-bowed boat.

He squeezed off a quick succession of rapid-fire bursts, wreaking mass slaughter. He was careful to place his shots so none of them would accidentally hole the bottom of the boat. That would be a hell of a note, he told himself.

Within seconds three dead bodies lay sprawled in the patrol boat. The fourth trooper had fallen overboard when hit and now lay floating facedown in the channel.

Kilroy rose from his bushwhacker's nest, making his way down the channel's left bank to the water. He stepped into the dinghy and shut off the engine. Pushing away from the bank, he paddled to the patrol boat.

Carefully, he climbed out of the dinghy into the larger craft, stepping on the bodies littering the bottom of the boat. He took hold of the tiller handle protruding from the motor, turned the throttle handle to lower the engine's output to a low, throaty purr.

He collected the rifles and spare ammo, inspecting each weapon to make sure that it was locked, loaded, and in good working order. He set the booty within ready reach.

He hefted one of the bodies and dumped it over the side. The corpse had concealed a coiled length of rope beneath it. He'd planned to throw the other two bodies overboard but now decided against it. He'd have a use for them later.

The channel water began to churn and thrash. Crocodiles, attracted by the scent of blood in the water, coursed toward the site.

"Eat hearty, boys," Kilroy muttered.

The boat rocked with unease but was bigger and more solid than the dinghy, less likely to be upset by the crocs' agitation. The saurians fastened their jaws on various limbs and then rolled around in the water until they tore them off.

Kilroy used his survival knife to cut off various lengths of the coiled rope. He used them to tie the two remaining bodies upright in the pair of forward seats. They presented a macabre spectacle as they sat sagging against the ropes, heads lolling, open mouths gaping, eyes open and staring.

Kilroy reversed the engine, turned around in the channel so the boat pointed downstream. He switched off the searchlight. The blessed darkness was his ally.

He stayed in place for some time, engine idling, as he allowed his eyes to once more get accustomed to the lack of light. When his night vision returned, he got ready for the big breakout. He sat on the stern seat, hand on

the tiller, an assault rifle laid across the tops of
his thighs.

"Let's take 'er for a little spin, fellows," Kilroy
said to the corpses lashed to the forward seats.
He was perhaps not entirely sane at this point
but it was working for him.

The patrol boat coursed downstream, making
for the Rada.

Nearing the river, the channel widened, its
banks fanning outward away from each other.
The trees thinned; there was more open space
and air. Dark clouds pressed down, lowering
the ceiling, hemming in the scene.

To the south, lights could be seen through
the brush, the lights of the soldiers' camp on
the point thrusting into the Kondo.

Kilroy entered the Rada, the current flowing
south. A pair of widely scattered lights showed
on the water, the lights of other patrol boats.
One cruised a quarter mile north on the Rada;
another stood downstream.

Kilroy swung the boat south toward the junction with the Kondo. He steered downstream,
coursing south along the Rada's west bank. A
square-bowed patrol boat similar to the one in
which he was riding stood guard, barring the
way where the river poured into the Kondo.

Beyond, in the middle of the Kondo, a gunboat rode at anchor, its form dimly illuminated
by its running lights and by several lanterns
strung along it.

The gunboat was his meat, Kilroy decided.
Its superior size identified it as the flag vessel

of the enemy's river craft, the command seat from which the water search was directed.

It would do no good to make a mad dash for the Kondo without neutralizing the gunboat. Otherwise the larger, better-armed craft would easily overtake his smaller boat and shoot it to pieces.

No, the situation called for a bold stroke, one that would leave Kilroy holding all the marbles if he succeeded. And if he failed?

No matter, for then he would be dead and beyond caring.

Time to lighten his load. The panga was essential to his plan and must stay with him. His boots would be a hindrance later but he wasn't getting rid of them, not when there was a possibility that he might have to once more resume his desperate trek on land. But the big .44 handgun had outlived its usefulness and would have to go.

He hated to do it. It was a good gun and deserved better. But what choice did he have? When he made his play, the .44 would be one more encumbrance and might spell the difference between success and failure. Besides, once wet it would be more danger than deliverer; there was no trusting wet cartridges that might splutter and fail.

After wrapping the holstered handgun with its shoulder straps, he raised it to his lips and reverently kissed it good-bye.

"Adios, amigo," he murmured. He let it slip

from his hands into the water, mourning the loss of one good gun.

"Here we go, fellows," he called to the two corpses forward.

Kilroy opened up the throttle, making for the patrol boat downstream. He approached at a moderate clip, throttling down as he neared the other.

He crouched down on the stern seat so that he was partially covered by the two corpses up front. They would create the illusion of live men as long as they were not examined from too close up—he hoped.

He drifted toward the patrol boat, coming at it broadside. In it were four men, one of whom hailed his boat.

Kilroy rose from his seat, leaning forward to reach between the two men tied upright in their seats. He switched on the searchlight, pointing it at the other boat, lighting it up.

He took them by surprise, his assault rifle streaming lead into the figures massed in the boat. They threw their arms up in the air, wailing and howling as they were cut down.

The rifle emptied. Kilroy set it down and picked up another, continuing the process. An unnecessary exercise—everyone on the other boat was dead.

He grabbed the tiller and steered away from the patrol boat. Leaking fuel and hot lead combined to set the boat on fire.

Kilroy opened up the throttle and roared past it. He pointed his bow at the gunboat anchored in the middle of the Kondo and charged, intending to ram it amidships. The gunboat's searchlight pointed at the newcomer, illuminating the two corpses tied to their seats.

Kilroy let go of the tiller long enough to shoulder a rifle and shoot out the searchlight.

Collision was imminent.

Machine gun fire chewed up the front of Kilroy's boat. The dead men writhed and jerked as machine gun slugs slugs tore into them.

Kilroy abandoned ship, throwing himself over the port side in a low headfirst dive. The water hit him with a hammering blow, as if it were solid, not liquid. Open hands held in diving position over his head cleaved the water's surface and he knifed through it, going deep.

For an instant he feared the impact had torn the sheathed panga free from his body. He felt for it, was reassured to find that it was still there. So was the knife worn at his hip.

He swam underwater toward the gunboat, angling toward its stern. His lungs felt close to bursting.

When he could stand it no more he broke the surface, popping up to gulp a breath of air. The wake that had been torn through the water by the speeding patrol boat in its last few seconds helped hide his head.

He immediately ducked back underwater and continued swimming toward the gunboat. His boots were heavy, weighing him down, slowing his forward progress, but he kept moving, kicking and stroking.

The patrol boat he had quit burst into flames, curving to starboard now that no one was steering it.

It blew up.

The impact was a dull concussion that slammed and battered Kilroy. He was far enough from the blast for its effects to be minimized, but it still gave him a hell of a pounding.

His head broke the surface, he gulped air, then submerged. Using the breaststroke and frog kick he neared the gunboat, slanting past the stern. The murky water was warm, enervating. Thinking of crocodiles helped speed Kilroy along.

He reached the gunboat's port side. Its occupants had all turned their attention toward the starboard side, watching the final destruction of the patrol boat.

Noiselessly Kilroy stroked to the port quarter at the gunboat's stern. A rope line securing the sandbags to the gunwale provided a ready handhold. The space between the waterline and the top of the gunwale was not so great that his arms couldn't span it.

Wrapping both hands over the edge, he hauled himself up out of the water. He heaved himself up, throwing his middle over the gunwale, pulling up his legs and getting his feet under him.

He drew the panga from its sheath, raising it.

Ajani turned to see what was making the commotion.

Kilroy brought the panga down. . . .

FIVE

Kilroy was now in command of the gunboat. Krentz, Ajani, Hamid, and T'gai went over the side to feed the crocodiles. When last seen, Sesto was swimming madly for shore; darkness swallowed him and Kilroy never knew if he made it to the safety of dry land or not. Nor did he care.

The patrol boat he'd seen earlier upstream on the Rada stayed there, showing no inclination to come downriver to investigate what had happened. If it did, the gunboat's .50 machine guns would make short work of it.

The troops encamped on the point were no threat; they were too far away for accurate shooting and had no boats with which to take up the chase.

Kilroy stepped on something fleshy and yielding: Krentz's severed hand.

He pried open its fingers, freeing the gun they held. He kept the gun and tossed the hand into the water.

He held the Walther up to the lamplight. It was a good piece, clean, oiled, with a full clip ready for action. Kilroy stuck the gun into the top of his waistband, wearing it butt-out over his left hip for quick access.

Ward Thurlow sat on the bottom of the boat with his back against the sidewall, legs extended in front of him. A raw red scrape centering a massive purple-brown bruise on the side of his jaw marked where Kilroy had kicked him. He held his face in his hands.

But peeked between his fingers.

He uncovered his face. It was pale, drawn, and frightened, the dilated blacks of his pupils showing like a pair of dots pasted to his eyeballs. He cleared his throat.

"I can get you out of this, Kilroy," he began.

"After getting me into it," Kilroy said. "Suppose you tell me why I shouldn't feed you to the crocs a piece at a time."

"Money."

"Well, that's something, anyhow," Kilroy said after a pause.

Thurlow took that as encouragement. He stood up, rising creakily on quaking legs. He clutched a sandbag atop the gunwale for support.

"There's money, plenty of money. It's yours. Only don't kill me," he said. "I can get you out of this country and back to the States. You'll be a rich man. You'll never have to work again."

"Who's paying for it? You?" Kilroy asked. "Or MYRMEX?" he pointedly added.

Thurlow rubbed his face as though trying to stroke some feeling into it. Accidentally fingering the bruised area where Kilroy's kick had landed, Thurlow winced, gasping.

"So you know about MYRMEX," Thurlow said.

"Everybody in Lagos knows that Krentz was on the MYRMEX payroll," Kilroy said. "It's all starting to come together now. It takes an outfit with the money and manpower of MYRMEX to go against Uncle Sammy and blow up a DIA investigative team. Even an old Army dogface like me can figure that out, even without the benefit of an Ivy League education like yours."

Thurlow ignored the sarcasm and nodded vigorously, head going up and down like a bobblehead doll's. "Then you know you can't buck the MYRMEX combine and live."

"I'm doing all right so far," Kilroy said.

"For how long? Once you're on MYRMEX's shit list, they won't rest until you're dead. But I can get you off the hook, Kilroy. A word from me in the right ears and you'll go on the payroll, with more money than you ever dreamed of. Otherwise, you'll never get out of Lagos alive."

"You forget one thing, Thurlow. You're the only one besides me who knows that I'm alive," Kilroy said, smiling thinly.

Thurlow held up a hand palm out, as if in appeal. "Think, Kilroy. Just stop and think before you do anything stupid that you'll regret. I'm your ticket to riches and freedom," he said.

Kilroy rubbed his chin thoughtfully. "Funny

thing, Thurlow. I've been watching you for some time now and something struck me: You've been looking around every which way on this boat except for one direction. You make a point of not looking at that tin can back there that's drawing all the flies. Why is that?"

Thurlow's pallor deepened, taking on a green tinge. "I don't know what you mean."

"You're still not looking at the can. Maybe I'd better investigate," Kilroy said.

"You're wasting time you could be using for your getaway."

"What a pal. Concerned about my safety, are you? That's okay, I can spare a minute or two."

Kilroy went to the stern, went down on one knee beside the cannister lashed in place in the corner of the starboard quarter. He positioned himself where he could keep an eye on Thurlow at the same time.

He used his belt knife to cut the lines securing the round five-gallon can. The pommel of its hilt served to hammer open the lid. Kilroy popped open the top. The foul odor returned.

"Well, what have we here?" he said.

The can was filled almost to the brim with a crystalline white powder.

"Dope? Cocaine, heroin?" he mused. "In this part of the world, more likely heroin, though you couldn't grow opium in the swamp. . . ."

He dipped a fingertip into the powder, coating it with white grains. He touched the very tip of his tongue to the stuff, tasting it.

"Salt," he said. He frowned, thinking. "Odd . . . Why salt?"

He tilted the can on its side, pouring the salt on deck. As its level dropped, it revealed an object that had been buried in the stuff:

A human head. Freshly severed at the neck.

The hair was too short to get a grip on. Kilroy gripped the head by the ears and hauled it out, holding it up to the lantern light.

Its features were frosted with caked salt. Kilroy brushed them clean to better make them out. Recognition brought a sad, sweet smile to his lips.

"How about that? It's my old buddy Bill Raynor," he said softly. "Hey, Bill, how you? Never thought I'd see you again."

Kilroy looked up from Raynor's face to Thurlow's. "Just goes to show you, life is funny."

Thurlow held out both hands in front of him, making a placating gesture. "That's none of my doing, Kilroy. It was Krentz. Krentz did it, not me. I didn't want any part of it," he said quickly.

"What business did Krentz have with poor ol' Bill's head?"

"Tayambo wanted it, the sick fuck. What for, I don't know. He collects them like trophies, I guess."

Kilroy mulled it over, his face expressionless. "Head-hunting, eh? And the salt acts as a preservative, especially in this hot weather, hmm?"

A nervous tic started in the corner of Thurlow's

mouth. "I swear, Kilroy, I had nothing to do with this atrocity—"

"Don't swear, it ain't polite," Kilroy said mildly. He put the head back in the can and closed the lid. "Well, he'll keep. Talk to you later, Bill."

Kilroy rose. The Walther was in his hand, pointed at Thurlow. "You don't look too bad off yet," he said. "Here, have one on ol' Bill."

Thurlow shrieked. "For God's sake, don't!—"

Kilroy shot him once, in the right knee. Thurlow collapsed in a heap.

"Once the shock wears off it'll really commence to hurting," Kilroy remarked conversationally.

Ward Thurlow didn't hear him—he had passed out.

Kilroy went forward. Leaning over the side, he took hold of the taut line angling into the water and heaved, freeing the anchor from where it had snagged its steel flukes into the river bottom. He hauled it in, depositing the anchor with a thunk on the gunboat flooring.

Thurlow was awake now, babbling and sobbing.

Kilroy sat down in the pilot's seat, familiarizing himself with the instrument panel and controls. He was a ground pounder from way back and not a sailor, but over the years he'd learned plenty about boat handling, enough to pass for a pretty fair mariner.

He started up the engines. Taking the wheel, he eased the dual throttles forward. The gunboat lurched forward, surging, following the Kondo's southeasterly course downriver toward the sea.

Dawn.

Not so much of a sunrise as it was a general lightening in the east, the sun's naked orb hidden by a heavy overcast and steamy mists.

The gunboat was anchored above the mouth of the Kondo where it emptied into the sea. Beyond, following the coastline on a westerly course, Lagos lay a few hours away.

Kilroy had paused to take care of some unfinished business.

On the boat's starboard side, about twenty yards away, lay a long, flat beach of sticky black mud.

It was carpeted with crocodiles, scores of them. Big ones, medium ones, small ones. They wallowed, basked, lolled, and from time to time snapped at each other. They grunted, snorted, and bellowed.

Kilroy fashioned a sliding loop at the end of a rope line whose opposite end was secured to a cleat on the gunwale.

The loop went over Ward Thurlow's head and shoulders and under his arms. Kilroy pulled it taut, snugging it.

Thurlow was in pretty sad shape. He could have passed for a corpse, so pale and stiff was he, except for sick, pain-dulled eyes and a continual moaning that escaped from his slack-jawed mouth.

He'd had information Kilroy needed and the latter hadn't been too particular about how he got it. Thurlow had spilled his guts once Kilroy had gone to work on him. It hadn't taken much. The bullet in his knee had ruined the rogue CIA agent. There wasn't much of him left.

Soon there would be a whole lot less.

Kilroy had squeezed him for facts, leaving behind only the rind and the pulp. Now he had to hold Thurlow up as he propped him against the gunwale.

Thurlow swayed, pain-dulled eyes heavy lidded, almost closed.

"This is where we say good-bye," Kilroy said, slapping Thurlow on the back.

Thurlow forced his eyes open; they went in and out of focus. "What . . . whaddya mean?"

"Last stop. I wasn't fooling when I said I was going to feed you to the crocs," Kilroy said.

Thurlow screamed, "No!"

Kilroy shoved him over the side into the water.

Thurlow hit with a splash. The rope halter pulled him up short, keeping his head and shoulders above water.

Kilroy played out the line, causing Thurlow to drift toward shore. Thurlow found new reserves of energy as he thrashed about screaming. And that was just from being in the water. His arms and legs were free, so he could splash around pretty good, making quite a stir. Blood from many cuts and scratches oozed into the turbid waters.

Thurlow swam back to the boat. He clawed at its sides, trying to pull himself up out of the water, a feat he lacked the strength to accomplish. He was babbling now, pleading, choking on river water that poured into his screaming mouth.

Kilroy used a long gaffer's pole to push Thurlow away from the boat.

Thurlow's thrashing agitation in the water acted like a dinner bell to the crocodiles.

Singly at first, then in pairs, then groups, they waddled down the black mud of the beach into the river. Once in the water they moved fast, converging on Thurlow.

Massive jaws gaped, closing on his arms and legs. The beasts struck and rolled, tearing him limb from limb.

Thurlow's fancy cell phone had a built-in digital camera. Kilroy used it to make a record of the carnage.

Red clouds swirled in muddy brown water that churned and boiled from the feeding frenzy.

Even as an armless, legless trunk, Thurlow still kept on screaming. Right until a crocodile's steaming, voracious maw clamped shut on his head.

Kilroy raised his knife to cut the line tied to what was left of Ward Thurlow but he didn't have to. A croc's dagger teeth had already parted the rope.

While late-coming crocodiles fought over the scraps, Kilroy raised anchor. He took the wheel, piloting the boat out of the estuary and into the open sea.

On to Lagos!

SIX

The Palace of Government in Lagos, Nigeria, was a massive pile of stucco-covered masonry painted pink with white trim. It had arched windows, a massive domed roof centered with a pointy tip, and corner turrets. Its Arabian Nights roofline was spoiled by an array of spiky antennas and satellite dishes.

The fantastic structure was fronted by a spacious courtyard. The extensive palace grounds featured elaborate gardens with rows of palm trees, hedges and shrubs, marble statuary, and a network of paved walkways.

The site was bordered by a ten-foot-high black iron spear fence and guarded by patrols of soldiers armed with small machine guns.

A boulevard lay beyond the towering, stone-pillared main gate and at right angles to it. The thoroughfare was four lanes wide. A median lined with lofty palms divided the roadway into two, two-lane strips, each strip bearing traffic in an opposite direction.

The time was late afternoon. The boulevard was clogged with traffic: trucks, taxis, beat-up old cars, motor scooters, motorbikes, pedicabs, bicycles—a teeming profusion of variety of wheeled transportation.

The air was heavy with a pall of exhaust fumes. The traffic, chaotic and noisy, was further enlivened by collisions and near-collisions. The air rang with a din of horns honking, tires screeching, and unmuffled engines racketing.

Across the boulevard, on its far side, lay a row of newly built apartment and office buildings, a pricy and much prized new addition to the cityscape.

It was a hot, sweltering day with a hazy, gray-white sky. Behind an overcast of clouds and brown smog, the sun was a broad, blurred smear of sullen, simmering yellow-white heat.

The palace's main gate opened on a broad paved drive as long as three football fields laid end to end, leading to the fantastic structure housing the seat of government and key ministerial offices.

An open courtyard paved with massive tan flat stones fronted the palace. A wide white stone staircase angled upward to the columned front entrance, with its multidoors set in a two-story-high rounded archway.

A half dozen or so official vehicles were parked in the courtyard. Most were shiny air-conditioned limousines reserved for the use of important government officials. Pride of place was held by the showiest and most important official vehicle of all, a limousine belonging to Minister of Defense Derek Tayambo.

A shiny stretch limousine as long as a cabin cruiser, this ornate land yacht was purple with gold trim. Real gold.

Here was no creampuff, however. The custom-made machine was sheathed in armor plating hidden beneath layers of a glossy, mirror-finish purple paint job. Windshield and windows were made of bulletproof glass several inches thick. Under the hood was a sixteen-cylinder diesel engine.

The undercarriage, springs, and suspension were specially reinforced to bear the weight of all that armor. The tires were made of solid rubber to bear the heavy load without bursting. Which also hardened them against bullets.

The interior was customized with genuine leopard-skin upholstery. Exterior roof and side panels were covered in special leopard-skin-print vinyl. They would have been covered with real leopard skin had the genuine article been able to withstand the rigors of the capital's steamy, seething climate.

Tayambo's personal chauffeur, the brother of his second wife, was more smartly uniformed than most of the soldiers on duty, and they were an elite palace guard. He sat in the shade with some of the soldiers, smoking and chatting.

Off to the side where they wouldn't block the coming and going of high-powered officials and VIPs were several sand-colored

Hummer-type vehicles assigned to the security forces. With all the heavily armed troops stationed on the grounds, the palace was better guarded than many state military posts.

On the palace's third, top floor, a row of glassed-in French doors opened onto a tan stone balcony with a waist-high balustrade. The glass doors were banded with strips of black iron grillework. Above them was a high, arched, plate-glass window. Doors and windows were closed, sealed tight.

Within lay an impressive ministerial conference room. Here was where the president met with his cabinet. A meeting was now in session.

Brightness flooded into the room through the French doors and arched windows. A long mahogany table stood at right angles to the balcony windows, parallel to the room's long axis. At the far end, seated at the head of the table in a high-backed throne chair, was Minister of Defense Derek Tayambo.

The seat was normally reserved for the president, but the chief executive was a sickly man, ill and aging, who rarely attended cabinet meetings—or, for that matter, properly oversaw the orderly operation of the country's executive governmental functions.

Power, like Nature, abhors a vacuum, and in the absence of strong (or any, really) leadership from the president, Minister Tayambo had taken up control.

The administration's ostensible Number Two man, Vice President Johnny Lisongu, was seated way down at the foot of the table, far from the august presence of the high-and-mighty Tayambo.

The defense minister, in his midforties, had a soccer ball–shaped head and a pair of jug handle ears. His head seemed as wide as it was long. His scalp and cruel, thick-featured face were clean-shaven. His eyebrows came to points in the centers, giving him a satanic look. Perched atop his shining skull at a jaunty angle was his trademark leopard-skin fez.

Tayambo wore a custom-tailored khaki uniform whose knife-edged creases were kept in place with ironing and plenty of starch. It was no mean feat to look sharp in Lagos's sultry climate beyond the palace's coolly air-conditioned confines.

The defense minister wielded a bamboo-handled horsetail fly whisk. The palace was more or less free of flies; the whisk was a traditional symbol of authority. When crossed or irked, Tayambo was wont to slash the whisk across the face of the offending party.

Seated below him on both sides of the long conference table were eleven lesser ministerial officers, along with the vice president.

About half of the functionaries wore military uniforms; the others wore civilian clothes. Of the latter group, some wore Western-style suits and ties, and the rest wore more traditional folk-loric garb, dashiki shirts with colorful prints.

"The next order of business is the matter of the new port facility being built on the coast by the MYRMEX group," the cabinet secretary announced, reading from a printed roster of the day's issues at hand.

"The matter is decided," Tayambo said. "The port will be sold to our good friends from the People's Republic of China."

His flat declaration left little to no room for discussion. Several ministers of other departments exchanged glances and stirred uncomfortably in their seats, but none seemed inclined to dispute the matter.

Tayambo thrust his head forward on the end of a thick bull neck, gimlet eyes scanning both sides of the table, searching for dissent.

The few restive officials in the room sat stone-faced and very still.

Vice President Johnny Lisongu nervously cleared his throat. Tayambo glared at him.

"Excellency, might it not be more prudent to lease the property to the Chinese, rather than sell it outright?" Lisongu ventured to ask.

"No! There is no new port facility unless the Chinese continue financing the construction, and they won't do that unless they hold title to the land," Tayambo said, in a harsh, no-nonsense tone.

The vice president sat too far away for Tayambo to hit him with the fly whisk and Tayambo feared that he might miss if he threw it. Instead, he went off on a tirade.

"It's a good site, an excellent natural harbor," Tayambo said. "It will make an ideal transshipment point to offload our shipments of oil.

We'll run a pipeline to the refinery and storage tanks, all of which will be built by MYRMEX and paid for by our Chinese friends.

"They have the resources. Most of all, they have the funds. China is the coming world leader in the next generation and MYRMEX is their chosen instrument in this sector. China and MYRMEX combined, who can withstand their power?"

From outside the room came a dull crumping sound, a heavy thud. Nothing major but enough to make the assembled dignitaries glance away and turn toward the windows overlooking the courtyard.

A beat or two later came a tremendous booming blast. It shook the windows and doors. Had they not been made of thick plate glass and been so solidly set in their black iron frames, they might have been jarred loose.

The conference room also shook. Water pitchers and glasses on the table jumped into the air. The chandelier suspended from the ceiling on a chain jingled, swayed pendulum-like.

A column of smoke and fire uncoiled in the courtyard, thrusting skyward.

"Palace coup! The army has turned against us!—" one of the ministers said, voicing the great omnipresent fear of them all, including Tayambo, who as Minister of Defense well knew that the military was well stocked with ruthlessly ambitious colonels eager to seize supreme power. The generals were at the top of the heap and not inclined to rebel—it was the colonels who presented the main threat.

Thrown up with the column of smoke and fire were squares and slabs of purple metal.

Some of the more venturesome or curious went to the French doors, peered downward at the courtyard from whence the disturbance had arisen. Several spoke at once:

"What is it?"

"What's happened?"

"Minister Tayambo, it's your car!"

"What?" Tayambo pushed back his chair, jumping to his feet.

"It's been blown up!" someone said.

The sky rained down scraps and shards of purple metal on the courtyard square.

Outrage mastered caution. Tayambo, stung, raced for the far end of the room overlooking the courtyard. Short stubby legs churned like pistons, carrying him to the glassed-in French doors.

"Don't go outside, Excellency. It could be a trap," a uniformed official warned.

The relevant part of the courtyard could be seen from inside as the men looked through the glass doors and over the balcony railing to the square below. The courtyard was a scene of chaos and confusion. Armed troops ran this way and that. But with no tangible foe to close with, they could do nothing more than run around aimlessly.

The epicenter of the disturbance lay at the base of the pillar of oily black smoke wreathed with red flames that mounted upward ever higher. Flames burned brightly there, a yellow-red fireball at whose heart laid the boxy outline and skeletal framework of what had once been a magnificent automobile.

The blast had blown off the roof, hood and trunk lids, armored fenders, and side panels. Blazing tires melted into molten black pools, sending out prodigious volumes of black smoke.

Even as Tayambo goggled in stunned disbelief, a purple metal fragment the size of a car door, which had been blown higher than the palace roof, now fell back to earth, crashing into the basin of the fountain in the landscaped center square.

"My car! Treason! They'll pay for this!" He had no idea who "they" were at the moment but he was certain it had to be a plot. One aimed at him, hitting him where it hurt.

That magnificent machine with its signature leopard-skin-print vinyl roof and side patterning was inextricably associated with him. When it drove around town everyone knew to get out of the way. It said, "Tayambo's coming!"

To strike at the car was a mortal insult to the mighty minister of defense.

The author of that insolence was far away, across the boulevard from the palace drive, out the main gate. He was in place on the rooftop of an office building a good 350, 400 yards away from the palace.

He was Kilroy. He wore a blue jumpsuit with the logo of a repair company blazoned on the front and back. He lay prone near the front edge of the roof operating a .50 caliber sniper rifle.

The building was a rectangular slab twenty stories tall, its narrow face fronting sidewalk and boulevard. It towered over its neighbors.

The flat rooftop was covered with tar paper studded with countless small pieces of white gravel. In its center was a concrete cube with a peaked skylight and a solid gray metal door in one side that accessed the rooftop.

The rooftop was tangled with lines and squares of sheet-metal conduit ducting, bundles of pipe and tubing, all centered around a boxcar-sized air-conditioning unit. The horizontal layout was punctuated vertically by ventilator-housing shafts.

Kilroy had gained admittance earlier by posing as an air-conditioner repairman. Many such mechanical specialties were handled by foreigners, so he did not excite any undue interest or notice from the building manager. The building had never been flagged as a potential threat by security forces due to its distance from the palace.

The manager had delegated the superintendent to escort Kilroy to the top of the building. The duo rode to the top floor in an elevator and climbed a flight of stairs to the roof. It was hot and the superintendant saw no need for broiling out in the sun when he could be in the building's air-conditioned interior. He left Kilroy in place and hurried back inside.

Kilroy toted an oversized red metal toolbox. Once he was alone on the roof, he gimmicked the door, locking it from the outside. Barring access from within, so no one could surprise him at "work."

The roof was bordered by no retaining wall, no parapet. It just ended on all four sides with a straight two-hundred-foot drop. That was no bother to Kilroy, who had no fear of heights.

He set up near the rooftop's front edge, going down on one knee and opening the lid of the toolbox. Concealed in it in specially made brackets were the components of a disassembled .50 sniper rifle. He quickly put it together, mounting it on a bipod stand.

He stretched out prone on the flat roof, oblivious to the sharp-edged white pebbles that dug into his flesh.

He was no less oblivious to his ordeal in the Vurukoo swamps, his escape by the gunboat, his covert return to Lagos, and the complicated intrigue and series of maneuvers in contacting an underground network of spies, crooks, and patriots who had enabled him to establish himself in a safe house and ultimately acquire the hardware and forged documents that would allow him to complete his mission.

His thoughts were focused only on carrying out his self-appointed task.

He mounted a telescopic sight on the sniper rifle's top rail, adjusted the optics, sighting it in. From here he had a clear sight line looking down across the long palace grounds to the courtyard and the third-floor conference room.

The .50 rounds were each as long and as thick as his index finger. He loaded one and assumed the prone firing position, unconsciously controlling his heart rate and breathing.

The scope's crosshairs were aimed at the rear of Tayambo's limo.

A great, intent stillness came over Kilroy, the aura of total concentration. With the gentlest of pressures, almost a caress, his finger squeezed the trigger.

Firing an armor-piercing, high-explosive round into the car's gas tank.

The high-velocity round punched through armor plate and blew up inside the gas tank. The ensuing havoc and destruction was spectacularly satisfactory.

Kilroy reloaded, waiting for a break in the roiling smoke clouds that temporarily obscured the courtyard. When the gap showed, the rifle was pointed at the glassed-in French doors of the palace's third-floor conference room.

Defense Minister Derek Tayambo stood there with his face pressed to a glass pane, staring incredulously down into the courtyard at the blazing ruin of his imperial automobile.

As Kilroy knew he would be. It was a matter of basic human psychology.

No mistaking Tayambo for anyone else, not with his signature leopard-skin fez topping his shiny head.

Kilroy centered the crosshairs on Tayambo's head above the eyebrows and fired a high-velocity round through it.

The target exploded in a halo of pink mist, sure proof that the round had struck its target and vaporized brain material.

Tayambo wasn't the only one who knew something about head-hunting.

Kilroy did, too.

SEVEN

"So this is Crestfield!" Steve Ireland said.

"Yes. What do you think of it?" Skye Moray asked, her face alive with interest and excitement.

Steve thought about it for a moment before answering. "Nice place for a murder," he said.

"You're teasing me," Skye said, frowning. Then she laughed. Her laughter was musical.

The two of them sat their horses on a rise overlooking the Crestfield manor and grounds. It was three o'clock on a Saturday afternoon in mid-March.

Crestfield was a rich and spacious estate sited on the flat-topped summit of a high Hessian Hill in Rampart County in the Blue Ridge Mountains of Virginia. The property occupied several square miles of fields and woods.

Its centerpiece was several acres of cleared grounds and the manor house that sat amid them, dominating the scene. A broad expanse of rolling fields was dotted by occasional lone trees and isolated stands of timber. Short, tufted yellow-brown grass was hard-packed against the ground. The turf showed the signs of having endured a long, hard winter. It lay dormant, awaiting the quickening of spring.

At the center of the fields was the manor house. A massive pile of stones and timber, it fronted north, its long axis running east–west. The stones were the color of milk chocolate and the timbers dark chocolate. It had wings, additions, turrets, gables, dormer windows, and buttresses. The roof was covered with gray slate tiles.

A paved driveway rose up from out of a stretch of woods, curving in front of the house. It split into branches connected to a multicar garage and a stable. Steve's dark green Chevy Suburban was parked to one side of the main drive along with several other vehicles.

Steve Ireland, thirty, was tall, long-limbed, athletic. He had short jet-black hair, dark blue eyes, and a rawboned clean-shaven face. The black hair and blue eyes were a genetic heritage from his forebears, who were genuine Black Irish. His strong features were not unattractive in a grim, hard-bitten way.

He wore a blue winter jacket, black sweater, faded blue jeans, and dark brown hiking boots. He was mounted on a pale gray mare with an English-style saddle.

Skye Moray was in her early twenties. She had it all: youth, beauty, health, and riches. She had a fine-featured vixenish face, shoulder-length auburn hair, yellow eyes, and a ripe, red-lipped mouth. Her hair was tied back in a ponytail. Her slender physique was full-breasted and long-legged.

She wore a tobacco-colored three-quarter-length cloth coat with black velour collar and cuffs, a cream-colored scarf, a heather turtle-neck sweater, and tight gray-tan twill riding breeches tucked into knee-high dark brown leather riding boots. Hands fitted into thin, tight, wrist-length dark brown leather gloves gripped the reins of her mount, a chestnut gelding.

It was a raw, blustery day. A heavy gray sky hung low, pressing down on the landscape. Occasional chill winds blew from the north-west. It had rained earlier; from the look of things it could rain again, or maybe snow. The air was heavy, moisture-laden. The tempera-ture was about forty degrees Fahrenheit but felt colder due to the damp, bone-chilling cold and thinner air here high atop the hill.

It was a dark day. Lights showed in various rooms of the house; electric lamps blazed over the front entrance.

The manor house's south face gave onto a flagged terrace overlooking a wide, sprawling patch of turf. Southwest of the main building was the stable, a shoebox-shaped structure with a low peaked roof. Not far from it stood the garage, a minimansion by itself, with living quarters above the multivehicle bays of the ground floor.

"So what do you think of our little domicile?" Skye prompted.

"It looks like a haunted house," Steve said, indicating the mansion.

"It was built at the end of the nineteenth century in the Gothic Revival style. I admit it's more Gothic than Revival," Skye said. "So you don't like the Moray family's latest acquisition?"

"I said it looks like a haunted house; I didn't say I didn't like it."

"Do you like it?" she pressed.

"I haven't made up my mind yet. I'll let you know later," Steve said.

"It's not exactly what you'd call cozy, but at least it's got plenty of room. That's important when you come from a big family like mine. At least in a big place like this we're not always tripping over each other," Skye said. "I envy you," she went on. "You live alone. You're not surrounded day and night by aunts and uncles, brothers and sisters."

"Don't you like them?" Steve asked.

Strong white front teeth nibbled a luscious lower lip as Skye thought it over. "I suppose I do. Some more than others. It's not something I give a lot of thought to. They're just there all the time and they've always been there."

"If it's privacy you want, why don't you get a place of your own? From the looks of this spread, I guess you could afford it."

Skye's yellow-gold eyes widened, her mouth forming a smooth O. "Live alone? I could never do that. Ours is a very close-knit family. I couldn't imagine not having them around."

"There you are, then. Or, rather, here you are."

"Do you like living alone, Steve?"

"Yes," he said flatly. Not that he was averse to occasional female companionship, he told himself. Especially when the female was as young, provocative, and vibrant as Skye Moray.

She laughed. "A confirmed bachelor, eh?"

"I travel a lot," Steve said. "I'm out of the country for a good part of the year."

"Oh yes, the international courier service you work for. Sounds exotic."

"It's not. I'm a glorified deliveryman, really."

"Is that government work?"

"For the government and private industry; whoever needs sensitive documents and/or parcels delivered somewhere way the hell out of the way," Steve said. Which was true, as far as it went. It was part of his cover story.

Not that he was undercover now. He was on his downtime between missions, enjoying a few weeks of rest and recreation before his next assignment. His leisure time might well prove enjoyable indeed, he thought, if spent in the company of his attractive new neighbor.

When Steve or Skye spoke, their breath showed as pale white wreaths of mist, due to the cold. The horses' exhalations, too, came as steamy puffs.

Skye rose in her saddle, standing in the stirrups as she surveyed the splendid view of the eastern slope laid out below.

"Hard to believe we're only ninety minutes away from Washington. The mountains, the woods, and countryside. Quite lovely, really," she said.

"It's nice," Steve agreed. He liked the scenery well enough but he was generally a man of few words—an asset in the peculiar trade he followed.

Skye lowered into the saddle. "Sorry I couldn't give you better weather for riding. But you said you like to ride."

"I do. Any weather I can ride in is fine with me. I don't get many opportunities these days to go horseback riding, so this is a treat."

"You ride very well, Steve. I'd say you've spent a lot of time in the saddle."

Steve glanced at her, unsure whether or not her words held a double meaning. Skye's expression was innocent, guileless.

"When I was a boy I spent most of my spare time on a horse. I grew up on a ranch," he said.

"How interesting! Where was it?" she asked.

"Out west," he said, answering vaguely, as his professional aversion to supplying information about his background and past history kicked in. "I'm happy to be here. Thanks for the invite, Skye. As I said, it's an unexpected treat."

"Sometimes those are the best kind," she said, laughing. "You say you like to ride, so . . . let's ride!"

Yellow eyes flashing, Skye turned her horse's head to the right and gave it a touch of her boot heels, urging it forward. The animal broke into a run.

Steve swung his horse around, following, quickly drawing abreast of her. The two rode north, galloping across a straightaway. The property featured plenty of open acreage for the horses to run in free and unconstrained.

Skye rode well, thought Steve. So did he. He preferred the traditional Western-style saddle but the English saddle gave him no trouble.

It was exhilarating, the pure physical plea- sure of horseback riding: the headlong wind and speed, the animal coursing beneath him in swift forward motion, hoofs pounding the turf.

A quarter mile and the straightaway ended where woods bordered the fields on the north. Skye and Steve reined in, slowing the horses to a halt.

After the run, red spots of color glowed in Skye's creamy cheeks, while her yellow eyes glittered. Her rounded bosom rose and fell from her hard breathing,

"That warmed me up," Steve said.

"So will this," said Skye, taking from a side pocket of her riding coat a silver flask. Or was it platinum? Steve wondered. She unscrewed a cap linked to the flask by a slim shiny chain and offered the flask to Steve.

"Brandy," Skye said.

"Ladies first," Steve countered.

"Who says I'm a lady?" she challenged. "But since you insist . . ." Skye held the flask to her lips, tilted it upward, and took a long pull from it. "Ah."

She held it out to Steve, and this time he accepted it. He sniffed the contents. Rich and potent. He took several mouthfuls, gulping them down.

The liquor drew a line of fire down his throat, detonating in a blossom of welcome heat in the pit of his belly. Its warmth raced through his veins.

"Much obliged," he said, returning the flask to her. She capped and pocketed it.

"I know a place I want to show you. This way," Skye Moray said.

A trail mouth opened in the trees, the dirt path winding back into the depths of the forest. Skye rode into it, Steve joining her. The trail was wide enough so the two of them could ride abreast.

An old fire trail rutted by twin tire tracks of off-road vehicles, it took them deeper into the forest. It was bordered on both sides by a profusion of bare gray trees; patches of mulched brown dead leaves mottled black-brown earth. Patches of snow showed under the trees and on their north sides. The trees acted as a barrier against gusty winds, which shook their tops.

The trail meandered, following the lay of the land, rising, falling, curving one way and then another. The open grounds and manor house were soon lost from view.

The woods were classic Atlantic Seaboard second growth. Groves of furry evergreens, dark, shaggy, and aromatic with resin, even in winter. Bare trees—oaks, maples, elms—shot through with rock outcroppings and threaded with silvery streams.

A quarter hour later, Skye slowed her mount, her eyes scanning the right side of the dirt road. A secondary path branched off from it. She rode into it. It was narrow, so Skye and Steve had to go in file.

Another ten minutes' ride and the trees on either side of the trail fanned out, opening into a secluded glade. The circular enclosure, about twenty feet in diameter, was bordered by a stand of pine trees. In its center stood a gray granite boulder the size of a shuttle bus. Near it lay a fallen tree weathered silvery gray.

Skye reined to a halt, stepped down from the saddle. "We'll stop here for a while."

"All right," Steve said, dismounting.

Skye fastened the reins of her horse to the trunk of a short, squat shrub, securing the animal. Steve did the same, tethering his horse nearby.

"I found this place the first day I went out riding at Crestfield," Skye said. "Wherever I go, the first thing I do is find some place off the beaten path that I can make my own. A place no one else in my family knows about, so I can have some privacy. My private place, a place I can share with my special friends."

Skye reached behind her, freeing the band that held her hair in a ponytail. She gave her head a toss, causing the hair to come loose and spill across her slim shoulders in a glossy reddish-brown curtain.

"Won't you be my special friend, Steve?" she asked.

"Sure. I'm a friendly guy myself."

"Prove it."

Steve embraced her.

"Kiss me," Skye said, leaning into him.

Her riding coat was open, and through her sweater her breasts nuzzled his chest. She tilted her hips, grinding her pelvis against his. Her head tilted back, eyes closed, mouth open, available and waiting.

Steve covered her mouth with his. Skye's full lips were naturally, ripely red. She tasted warm and sweet, meeting him with fierce energy.

Steve kissed her with his eyes open. He caressed her breasts, hips, thighs. He worked his hands under her sweater. She wore no bra; her flesh was warm, firm, smooth.

He was hard, the crotch of his jeans tented out. Skye rubbed him through his pants. Steve unbuckled her belt, opened the top button of her pants. He slid his hand inside, down the front of them. Her pants were very tight. His fingers stole inside her panties, probing inside her. She was hot, wet, and juicy.

Skye's mouth broke away from his, and she eased out of his embrace.

"Do me here," she breathed. "Now."

That's just what Steve intended.

Skye turned her back to him, facing the fallen tree. She looked over her shoulder at him, eyes shining, lips moist and parted. She pulled her pants the rest of the way down. They were tight, forcing her to sway her hips and shake her rounded rear as she worked them down. Pants and delicate, wispy panties were bunched up at her knees, leaving her bare up to the hem of her sweater.

Skye spread her booted feet apart and leaned forward, bending from the waist, shoving her succulent heart-shaped ass toward him. Her naked flesh was pink and shining. Her palms pressed against the top of the tree trunk, bracing her.

"Hurry," she breathed, looking back at him again. Her hair fell across her face, partially veiling it. A glittering yellow eye peered out from between silky auburn strands.

Steve opened his pants and pulled them and his shorts down. Cold air tingled against his bare flesh. He took a condom out of his inside jacket pocket, tore open the packet, and fitted the condom on.

"You lied," Skye said. "You said this was an unexpected treat." She sounded short of breath.

"It is. I just like to be prepared," Steve said, his voice husky.

"You're no Boy Scout."

"No." He came up behind her, gripping his hardness, guiding the head of it between the wet lips of her sex. Her breath caught in her throat.

He eased into her opening, entering her, planting himself in deep, up to the hilt. He put it to her and she met him more than halfway, working out. His hands, strong fingered with veiny backs, wrapped around her wriggling hips, clutching them.

They both were young, strong, eager, and hungry. Their coupling was intense and athletic. Presently their breathing sounded as if they were running a race. This was one race where the object was to delay reaching the finish line as long as possible.

The horses grew restless. From time to time one or the other pawed the ground with a hoof and snorted.

The lovers' breath panted harder and faster. Skye's sharp, polished fingernails clawed the bark of the fallen tree. Steve held back until she reached her finish.

Skye's body went rigid, trembling. She tossed her head back, hair flailing in the air, eyes squeezed shut as she climaxed. From between clenched teeth a single supersonic note escaped her:

"Eeeeeeeeee—!"

Steve let himself go. His face was stony, impassive. A half sigh, half groan sounded from him.

For an instant the scene went slightly out of focus, melting, blurring at the edges of his vision. But only for an instant.

It was said of the famous frontiersman Daniel Boone that whenever he discovered another settler living within sight of his own property, he picked up stakes and moved somewhere even more remote.

Steve Ireland could understand the sentiment. He was that way himself.

When he had learned about ten days ago that he had new neighbors on Hessian Hill, his first feeling was one of unhappiness.

Hessian Hill was one of the foothills in the eastern range of Virginia's Blue Ridge Mountains. In other, less spectacular locales it would have qualified as a small mountain itself, but sited here amid the scenic grandeur of the rugged Blue Ridge range, it had been tagged with the diminutive appellation of "hill."

The Hessian part of the name derived from the historical fact that a detachment of German mercenaries from Hesse serving under the flag of Britain's King George III had forted up on the summit for several years during the American Revolutionary War.

Steve Ireland owned a small, secluded piece of property high on the hill. When he wasn't away on assignment he lived alone in a modest-sized wooden A-frame house on his tract of land.

The mountainous terrain ensured that the area had escaped the sprawl of modern development. A handful of homes built on rock ledges and shelves were scattered across the eastern slope; they were few and far between.

Steve Ireland's patch of land stood on a

rocky outcropping not far from the summit.
Set on a vantage point near the ledge's edge, it
commanded a view of most of the sprawling
eastern slope and the valley below.

In wintertime, when the trees were bare, he
could make out the scant few houses dotting
the hillside. In warm-weather months when
leaves were heavy on the trees, the structures
were hidden by the foliage. He liked it better
that way.

Far below, several thousand feet down, the
silver snake of a river wound across the flat of
the valley. Several small towns stood at the in-
tersection of various roadways crisscrossing the
valley, but they were too far away to disturb
Steve's solitude.

Up on the heights he had the sun, moon,
stars, woods, and rocks. There was plenty of
good hunting and fishing. And few people to
bother him.

He would have preferred a spot even more
remote, more isolated from civilization and its
discontents, where he could live like a hermit
when he wasn't working. But he knew better
than to indulge his passion for isolation.

That would send a warning signal to the handlers who monitored his psychological state to
make sure he was fit for duty.

Captain Steve Ireland, United States Army,
was a member of the Dog Team. One of the
Army's elite cadre of ultrasecret assassins.

He was good at what he did and he liked
the work. But the rare individuals who'd

earned the franchise to kill those foreign and domestic foes deemed a threat to the nation's vital security interests were themselves under constant scrutiny.

They were dangerous men—and women— these select few Dog Team operatives. Dangerous by virtue of their lethal skills and also by virtue of the explosive nature of their assignments.

The fact that the Army maintained a clandestine assassination apparatus that operated both at home and abroad was a secret that must never become a matter of public record.

The hypocritical hyenas of the mainstream media would set up an orchestrated howl of hysterical denunciations and demands that the operation be unmasked and destroyed root and branch. Though that may be a bit unfair— to the hyenas, not the mainstream media.

Working in concert with headline-hunting publicity hounds and deluded bleeding-heart liberals and pacifists in Congress and the federal government, the inquisitors would not rest until they'd eliminated one of the nation's last bulwarks against chaos, anarchy, and ultimate decline.

Dog Team operatives were fine-tuned human precision instruments. The nature of the work was such that it contained numerous pitfalls for the unwary. An operative could learn to like killing too much. Contrariwise, one could grow soul sick from too much slaughter and reach the breaking point.

Temptations abounded. This was a world where expert assassins could command fabulous sums for striking down the masters of society. A skilled Dog Team operative gone rogue could become an incredible destabilizing force.

The team's higher echelon, the Top Dogs who controlled and directed the actual operatives in the field, remained constantly on the alert for the subtle warning signs that an active-duty member was going wrong.

Steve Ireland knew he was under special scrutiny. Several years ago, he'd been seriously wounded by the roadside bomb blast of an improvised explosive device at the conclusion of an assignment in Somalia.

The IED ambush had slain his fellow squad members and sent him to a secret Stateside clinic for many months of painful and extensive healing and rehabilitation. Once fully recovered, he rejoined the team's active-duty roster and returned to his trade of sanctioned killing. He knew without being told that his performance would be monitored more closely than ever.

A serious, life-threatening injury was a milestone in the life of every combat soldier. It could exert a powerful negative influence on the recovering casualty, causing him to become fearful and averse to risk taking in one case, or reckless and careless of harm in another.

That's why Steve Ireland had made his home, such as it was, in the Blue Ridge Mountains of Virginia. It provided him with the rustic seclusion that he craved, while still positioning him within an hour-and-a-half's drive of his home base in Washington, D.C.

He was between assignments during this winter break when his new neighbors moved in around the start of March.

He became aware of their presence during an early morning jog. It was a weekday. He ran several miles daily as part of his rigorous physical fitness regimen.

The sun had been up an hour or so when he finished lacing up his jogging shoes and hit the trail. It was a cold, clammy morning, heavily overcast. Steve wore a quilted utility vest over a gray sweatshirt and sweatpants.

He set out along a hiking trail that ran north from his property. Hessian Hill ran north–south; his place sat not far below the summit.

Sneakered feet padded on bare dirt and dead grass. He ran lightly, soft-footed, making as little noise as possible. A habit of his—and good training, too. He quickly fell into a rhythm, breathing through his nose, arms hanging loose at his sides, leaning forward slightly, feet rising and falling.

The trail slanted upward through woods, leveling off at the ridgetop, a flattened summit several miles wide. Gray mist veiled the dripping trees.

Lights glimmered beyond the woods. Electric lights.

This was new.

The route skirted the open land of the Crest-field estate, a cleared area occupying a prime position on the flat hilltop. Crestfield was where the Hessian force had once been encamped.

It overlooked a splendid scenic view of the eastern slope and the valley below. Its open fields had once provided space for drilling grounds for the foreign troops and a bivouac area. That had been long ago and no trace remained of their presence, not even a historical plaque to mark the site.

In the middle of the nineteenth century, a hunting lodge had been built on the locale, serving as a retreat for congressmen and their influential friends from the muggy swamps of Washington, D.C., in the summertime. At the turn of the century, a tycoon had bought the property, torn down the lodge, and there raised a Gothic mansion.

Since then, various wealthy families had occupied it. At the end of the first decade of the twenty-first century, a declining economy had forced the abandonment of the house and property.

The mansion was boarded up. The property was maintained by a realty agency. A number of spotlights and floodlights were set up in and around the estate; automatic timers switched them on from dusk till dawn. The Realtors apparently did not care to burden themselves with the expense of keeping a permanent watchman on the property.

Every month or so the Realtors' representative

came to inspect the estate for vandalism or weather damage. At autumn's end, fallen leaves were raked up, bagged, and carted away. At the start of spring, landscapers tidied up the grounds; during the warm weather months the lawns were mown, hedges trimmed, and fields weeded.

During the three years that Steve Ireland had lived on the hill, the Crestfield estate had been vacant and unoccupied.

The property was posted NO TRESPASSING, but Steve ignored the stricture to the extent of laying out his morning run so that part of the route took him through the woods at the eastern edge of the property, allowing him to enjoy the glorious sunrise view breaking over the valley.

He slowed to a halt at the woods' edge, gazing across the fields at the mansion. Bright lights burned behind newly unboarded windows. Several cars and trucks were parked on the curving driveway in front of the house.

Crestfield was vacant no more.

Steve Ireland grimaced. A solitary soul, he could find no welcome for the new neighbors. Still, his small house and modest piece of land were far enough away from the estate to ensure that he should suffer no disturbance.

He had no plans to change the route of his morning jog, either. The scenic vista was a payoff for the hard work of exercising and he saw no reason for altering his route. If he lacked the stealth to move through the woods undiscovered by the new tenants, then he was badly slipping indeed. And if there was one quality he had in abundance it was stealth, a necessity in the assassin's trade.

On Friday of that week, he got in his Suburban to make his weekly run down into town to go food shopping and pick up other needed supplies. It was a bright sunny day, cold and crisp.

A dirt road linked his property to Crestline Drive, a paved road running north–south across the summit. It took him past the estate, where he glimpsed more signs of life in the house and on the grounds.

From Crestline he turned right onto Shunpike Road, a strip of two-lane blacktop that switchbacked up one slope of Hessian Hill and down the other side. He drove into MacKinlay, a crossroads town where he did his shopping.

Returning home that afternoon, he saw a moving van parked in front of the Crestfield house; moving men were toting furniture and packing boxes into the mansion.

A week later, Steve was driving east on Crestline to make his run to MacKinlay when he saw a red sports car at the side of the road and a young woman standing beside it. She waved him down.

He slowed the Suburban to a halt and pulled up alongside the sportster. The machine had run off the road and lay nose down in a ditch, its right rear wheel poised over empty space.

The young woman had a clean-lined model-like face, glossy reddish-brown hair, and a slim body that was well rounded in all the places it ought to be. She stood on the Suburban's passenger side. Steve rolled down the window so he could speak to her.

She had high cheekbones; a thin, straight nose; yellow-golden eyes; and a ripe, red-lipped mouth. A helmet of straight, thick auburn hair brushed her shoulders.

"Hello," Steve said.

"Hi. Can I trouble you for a ride? I live a mile or two down the road," she said.

Her voice was nice, too, Steve decided. "Glad to. Hop in," he said, opening the door for her. She got in, closed the door, fastened the safety harness.

"These boots aren't too practical for walking," she said, indicating her footwear, a pair of high-heeled ankle boots. "Otherwise I wouldn't have bothered you."

"No bother at all," Steve said. He put the truck in gear and started forward.

"A mile or two down the road, you said. Would that be the Crestfield place?" he asked.

"Why, yes. But how did you know?" she asked.

"I live on the ridgetop myself, back that way a piece," he said, gesturing a thumb south. "There aren't many places on the hill and I noticed that some folks had moved into the estate. That sports car looks like it'd fit right in at the mansion."

"That makes us neighbors, then. I'm Skye Moray—Skye with an *e* on the end."

"Glad to know you, Miss Moray. Steve Ireland's the name."

"Please call me Skye."

"If you call me Steve."

"All right . . . Steve."

He was enjoying Skye's company and saw no reason to prematurely curtail it, so he drove along at a leisurely place. "Looks like you had a little mishap."

"A stupid thing," she said. "A squirrel ran across the road. I swerved to avoid it and ran into the ditch."

"Hope you weren't hurt."

"Only my pride, Steve." Skye gave a quirked smile. "I forgot my cell or I would have called home for a ride."

"My good fortune that you didn't," Steve said.

The entrance to Crestfield loomed up on the left. The entrance was flanked by a pair of square-sided stone gateposts each eight feet high. Their tops were crowned with freshly installed globe lanterns, now unlit. A broad paved driveway stretched up and back toward the estate proper.

Steve turned left into the drive, following a gently slanting path up into the grounds. The drive crested a rise, mounting a flat-topped summit with its open expanse of fields.

Signs of life and renewal were in evidence all around. Several luxury cars and highline SUVs were parked along the side of the curving drive. The drive and front stone stairs had been swept clean. New drapes were hung over some of the ground-floor front windows. Lights burned behind them.

Steve halted in front of the main entrance. "Here we are."

He got out, went around to the passenger side, and opened the door for Skye. She swung her long legs out of the door frame and dismounted from the truck cab.

"Thanks so much, Steve. You've been a great help."

"My pleasure. Welcome to the neighborhood," he said.

A portable horse trailer was parked farther down the drive near the southwest corner of the house where a paved path split off from the main drive to curve back toward the stable. The rear gate was open, revealing an empty double stall. A ramp connected the rear of the trailer to the paved drive.

"You're keeping horses in the stable?" Steve asked.

"Yes. Riding is one of my passions," Skye said.

Steve wondered what her other passions might be but forbore to inquire. "You should enjoy it; this is good horse country. Plenty of scenic trails hereabouts," he said.

"I'm looking forward to exploring them. Do you ride, Steve?"

"I used to. Not for the last few years, though."

"Please be my guest, then. You and Mrs. Ireland, we'd love to have you."

"Just me—there isn't any Mrs. Ireland," he was quick to say.

"So much the better," Skye said, her face lighting up with a mischievous grin. Merriment danced in her yellow-gold eyes. "You were kind enough to give me a ride. Now I can return the favor."

"I'll be looking forward to it," Steve said.

Skye opened her purse, took out a cream-colored leather-bound notepad with a slim gold pencil attached. She wrote something on a piece of paper, tore it off, and handed it to him.

"Here's my number. Call me soon, Steve."

"What's a good time to call?" he asked.

"Anytime. I'm available," Skye said. She rose on her toes to kiss him on the cheek.

Steve phoned her that same Friday night.

Which is how he came to be riding with her on the next day, Saturday.

EIGHT

An early dinner was served later that Saturday afternoon at the Crestfield manor house. The Moray clan was seated around the dining room table. As guest, Steve occupied a seat at one end of the table.

"For our first visitor here at our new home," had said Jules Moray, patriarch of the family, indicating the place setting. Steve had tried to politely decline the honor but the senior Moray had been insistent.

Jules sat opposite him at the head of the table. He reminded Steve of a Man of Distinction in an ad for an upscale men's clothier or highline brand single-malt Scotch whiskey.

Jules, in his midsixties, was still a fine figure of a man. He was tall, ramrod straight, with a mane of lead-colored hair brushed back from his forehead. His long face was rawboned and hollow-cheeked, with knobby cheekbones and a prominent chin.

He had bushy gray eyebrows, a same-colored

mustache, and dark brown eyes. He wore a gray tweed jacket with elbow patches, a white shirt and thin black tie, a red sweater vest.

He had been introduced to Steve as Skye's uncle. From what Steve could gather, apparently both her parents were deceased.

Others of the family were grouped around the table.

Skye sat on Steve's left. She'd dressed for dinner, exchanging her riding clothes for a tight dark blue bolero-style jacket, red silk blouse, high-waisted gray flannel slacks, and red ankle boots.

Steve felt a tad self-conscious about his informal attire. He'd tried to beg off earlier from Skye's dinner invitation on the grounds that he was improperly dressed, but she would have none of it.

"Lord knows we Morays have our faults but snobbery isn't one of them," she had said.

To make a hasty exit after having enjoyed the pleasures of Skye's intimate amatory attentions would have been rude, Steve thought. Besides, he was still besotted with the loveliness of her face and form; her youth and beauty had filled his senses and he was hungry for more.

He was just plain hungry, too, having built up an appetite from the horseback riding and lovemaking. What the hell, he told himself, he had to eat someplace.

Steve accepted the invitation and went to dinner dressed in the same clothes he'd worn earlier to go riding: black cable-knit woollen sweater, faded blue jeans, hiking boots.

Not only Skye but the rest of her family intrigued him and he wanted to find out more about them. Now here they were, all assembled around the dinner table. *The gang's all here,* thought Steve.

And what a group they were.

In addition to Jules, seated at the opposite end of the table, two family members, including Skye, sat on Steve's left, three more on his right. It was a long table with plenty of elbow room for the diners and no danger of crowding.

On Jules's right sat Lillian Moray, a member of the family by marriage. She was in her mid-forties; tall, with the broad shoulders of a swimmer; full-breasted and long-legged. Straight bronze hair with gold highlights framed her face, its ends reaching her firm jawline. The hair gave an impression not of age but rather of strength. It was metallic like an armored skullcap or headdress. Amazonian.

Dark eyes glittered in a sharp-featured but not unattractive face. She was deeply tanned, nut brown. Her skin had the leathery look that comes to a woman of a certain age who's spent long hours under a strong sun.

Lillian was married to Olcott Moray, who sat across from her on Jules's left. He was about forty-five, heavyset, thick-featured, baggy-eyed, with thinning ginger-colored hair and a walrus mustache.

He wore a navy blue blazer, a white pin-striped shirt, and a red and tan paisley dickey, looking like he'd just come from a meeting at the yacht club. All that was missing was a nautical commander's cap.

Next to Olcott, on his right, sat Teela Moray. Thirtyish, she had brick-red hair, green eyes, a red mouth. A long-sleeved jade green dress made of tight-clinging jersey clung to her lush, full-bodied curves.

On Teela's left and Steve's right sat Skye's brother, Brett Moray. He was about Steve's age, broad-shouldered, athletic, with wavy black hair, sharp cheekbones, and ruggedly chiseled features. His pale glacier-blue eyes were the same color as those of an Alaskan malamute, thought Steve.

Hovering around the edges of the scene to make sure that the dinner proceeded properly and the wants of the family and guest were attended to was Pyne, the butler. Steve didn't know if Pyne was his first name or his last. That's how the others addressed him.

He was fiftysomething, balding, watery-eyed, chinless, and paunchy. The nostrils of his beaklike nose had quivered earlier with what could have been the faintest hint of aristocratic hauteur when he'd shown Steve to a bathroom where he could get washed up in preparation for dinner.

Pyne wore a kind of old-fashioned black coat with scissor tails, a starched white shirtfront, a black bow tie, gray striped pants, and shiny black shoes. He reminded Steve more of some of the old-time, old-school clubmen turned State Department diplomats than a butler, retainer, valet, or whatever the hell Pyne's title was.

His global assignments over the years as an undercover Dog Team assassin had put Steve in contact with more than a few members of the diplomatic corps.

Not that Pyne handled any real chores during dinner. They were handled by Margit, the serving maid, with occasional assistance from big Bertha, the cook. Pyne just sort of stood around in a supervisory capacity, telling the women when to clear away the dishes from a particular course or serve the next one, that sort of thing.

An attractive and personable bunch, this Clan Moray, thought Steve. They put on a fine feed and certainly did all right by themselves. They lived well.

The dining room was a rectangular space on the ground floor. The walls were wood paneled up to shoulder height; above that they were plastered and painted a rich cream color.

The table was spread with a crisp white linen tablecloth and laid with gleaming sterling silver utensils, fine china plates, and cut-crystal glassware. The floor was mostly covered by a richly patterned Persian or Turkish carpet. Where the carpet did not reach, the glossy dark brown planks of a highly polished wooden floor were in view.

An electric chandelier hung from the ceiling

over the table. It dispelled the late afternoon gloom of a dark, overcast day.

On Steve's left, a long wall was lined with a row of tall windows with pointed, arched tops. They looked out on a terrace on the rear, southern side of the mansion.

Beyond the edge of the flagged terrace lay sprawling grounds tufted with lifeless straw-colored winter grass. To one side on the northwest could be seen the corner of the stable. Gusty winds rattled the mansion's windows.

"A storm is blowing in," Steve said.

"Snow?" Skye asked.

"Rain, I think. We've had our share of snow and more up here this winter. Record snowfalls. Being in the mountains we usually get some snow, but this year we saw some real blizzards."

"Have you lived here long, Steve?" asked Lillian. Everyone was on an informal first-name basis, as dictated by Jules, the self-proclaimed arbiter of the table.

"A few years," Steve said. "But all the old-timers agree that this was the roughest winter in memory. Before the rains washed it away, the snow was drifted three feet tall in places. You've missed the worst of it, though."

"Too bad," redheaded Teela said, her voice rich and honeyed. "I like extremes—of weather, that is."

"And everything else, dear cousin," Skye said.

Teela chuckled throatily. "Look who's talking!"

"Now, ladies, no engaging in personalities

tonight," said Jules, gently admonishing the two women.

The Morays certainly set out a fine feed, thought Steve. The meal began with chicken consommé, meaty chunks of white meat floating in a savory, near-clear broth. The entrée was roast beef with roasted potatoes, fresh green beans, and salad, accompanied by a dark, rich Burgundy.

"I hope that cut of meat's not too rare for you, Steve," Jules inquired.

"Not at all; that's how I prefer it."

"So do we," Teela said. "We Morays have a taste for blood."

She ate well and heartily, clearing her plate. Clearly she had no concerns about dieting, at least not for this meal.

By contrast, Skye ate lightly, nibbling a few green beans and salad while ignoring the rest of the viands. Her roast beef remained untouched, the sharp cutting knife at her place setting unused. From time to time she refreshed herself with a few small sips of red wine. She gnawed on a breadstick, a row of little white teeth showing under the curve of ripe, red lips.

Olcott was a big eater and an even bigger drinker, frequently draining his glass of wine and refilling it. Little blue broken veins in his nose and cheeks betokened one who was overfond of alcohol.

He held it well, though. His eyes gleamed more brightly and his complexion reddened but otherwise he showed no signs of the wine's effect on him.

Brett drank not wine but beer with his meal. He was the first to call for it, an act for which Steve was silently grateful. Not much of a wine imbiber, Steve was more of a beer-and-a-shot kind of guy.

He'd wanted a beer but had felt a bit inhibited about requesting it, not knowing if it was the custom of the house to drink only wine with the evening meal. Once Brett broke the ice, Steve followed his example and also requested beer.

The brew was an amber-colored ale, fresh, tangy, with real taste. He and Brett drank out of long pilsner glasses.

Teela rested her elbows on the table's edge and leaned toward Steve's direction, her full, rounded breasts thrusting against the thin, clinging fabric of her dress. Pebble-sized nipples were clearly outlined beneath the garment.

Skye looked up from her plate, where she'd been moving food around without eating it, to glare at Teela.

"Do you do much shooting, Steve? Little Skye gave the impression that you're something of an outdoorsman, that's why I asked," Teela said. "You certainly look fit, with all those muscles."

"Stop drooling, Teela. Skye saw him first," Lillian drawled. "Teela's just trying to get a rise out of you, Skye."

"I'm more interested in getting a rise out of our guest," Teela said.

Olcott choked on a swallow of wine.

Jules cleared his throat to get their attention. "Mind your manners, Teela. Steve's unfamiliar with your brand of good-natured raillery and won't know that you're just having fun," he said drily. "In your fashion," he added. He smiled benevolently, his face lighting up.

"Getting back on track," said Brett, joining the exchange, "do you hunt, Steve?"

"Now and then," Steve said.

"How's the hunting hereabouts?"

"In season, good. There's deer, varmints—squirrels, raccoons. Sometimes the bear population needs thinning out and they have a controlled hunt. There's quail, pheasant. Even a few wild turkeys."

"The only 'wild turkey' I hunt comes out of a bottle," Olcott said, chuckling.

"Yes, and you never miss, do you, darling?" said his wife, Lillian, in a sweetly acid tone.

"No!" Olcott said, unabashed, then laughing loudly.

Steve spoke to Brett, "Like to hunt, do you?"

"My favorite sport," Brett said.

"You came to live in the right place, then."

"Maybe we'll go beat the bushes for some fresh game."

"It's a go," Steve said. "The fishing's good, too. Wild trout in the streams. Mirror Pond on the ridgetop has sunfish, perch, mackerel."

Brett shook his head. "Fishing's not for me.

I like to shoot." He added, "Of course, Rory's the real marksman in the family. Rory is Skye's brother. Didn't she mention she's a twin?"

"No, she didn't," Steve said.

"I didn't want to bore him with our family tree," Skye said sullenly.

"I'm sure you managed to keep him interested somehow . . . in your fashion," Teela said too sweetly.

"Rory's quite the sportsman. The best shot of all the Morays," Brett said. "Wouldn't you agree, Skye?"

"That remains to be seen," Skye said.

"O-ho! That sounds like a challenge, little sister."

"Take it any way you like, Brett."

"He generally does," said Teela.

"The question is, how will Rory take it? He's so jealous of his prerogatives . . . as you know," Brett said. "Pity he couldn't be here with us tonight to enjoy the fun."

"Yes, isn't it?" Skye said. She seemed uncomfortable, her manner evasive. Her face was flushed but she was white around the mouth, tight-lipped.

"Um, yes, Rory does everything well," Teela purred.

Skye gave her a dirty look.

A bit discomfited himself, Steve tried to change the subject. "I didn't catch what line of business you folks are in?"

The others looked to Jules, at the head of the table, for a response.

"You might say we're in the extraction industry. Taking things out of the earth," Jules said.

"Mining and such?"

"In a manner of speaking, Steve. The Morays originally hail from West Virginia, in the heart of the coal-mining country. One of the bleakest, most impoverished regions in the nation. By pluck and luck, we managed to bootstrap ourselves out of the black-lung country. Of course, it's been several generations since any of our people actually had to dig coal. . . . Still, we manage to keep busy," Jules said. "And you, Steve? What's your line?" he asked.

"I work for a private courier service hand delivering sensitive documents for the government and private industry," Steve said.

"Interesting," said Lillian, her tone implying it was anything but.

"Not really," Steve said. "But I get to travel a lot, so it has its benefits."

Teela leered at him. "Now that you've met our Skye, you might find it more beneficial to stay close to home for a while, hmm?"

"You might find it more beneficial to mind your own business for a change, Teela!" Skye retorted.

"Tsk-tsk, such a temper! Better watch out for Skye, Steve—she bites."

"Now, girls . . ." Jules chided them gently.

Margit, the serving woman, entered and began clearing away the dinner plates. She was too big to be called a serving girl. Twenty-five, she was tall with a good, solid figure, if a bit on the hefty side. Long dark hair was coiled and pinned up in a bun at the back of her head. Her features were good but a sullen expression kept them from prettiness. She wore a maid's uniform of some shiny gray fabric with white cuffs and piping. She had brawny arms, thick thighs, muscular calves, slender ankles.

She piled up a stack of dirty plates and silverware and carried them away, exiting into the kitchen via a swinging door in the wall behind Jules. She returned, cleared off the rest of the plates.

"I think we're ready for coffee and dessert," Jules said.

"You can bring out the coffee and dessert now, Margit," echoed Pyne, the butler.

"Yes, Mr. Pyne, sir."

The table was cleared; cake plates, cups, and saucers were laid out. Margit brought out a large silver urn, rich coffee aroma wafting from it. She moved around the table, filling the diners' coffee cups. Another server with cream and sugar was set out. Olcott pushed back his chair, crossed to a sideboard.

"Allow me, sir," Pyne offered.

"Quite all right, Pyne, it's no trouble," Olcott said. He picked up a cut-crystal decanter containing a quantity of golden-brown liquid and carried it to the table, set it at his place. He sat down, removed the decanter's teardrop-shaped faceted stopper, and poured the liquid into his empty coffee cup, filling it to the brim.

"Have some coffee with your brandy, Olcott," Lillian said mockingly.

He shook his head. "No, thanks—dilutes the stuff. Why waste perfectly good brandy by cutting it?"

"Perhaps someone else would like some. Our guest, say."

"None for me, thanks. I'm good," Steve said.

Presently the sated diners sat leaning back in their chairs, sighing, replete.

"We're not quite done yet. I understand Bertha, our cook, has something special for us all," Jules Moray said.

"I'll get her, Mr. Jules."

"Thank you, Pyne."

Pyne went through the swinging door into the kitchen. A moment later, Bertha emerged carrying a silver platter with a rounded cover in both hands.

"In honor of your visit, Steve," Jules said.

"Well . . . thanks," Steve said. He was full and didn't want to eat anything else, but he supposed that in the interests of sociability he'd have to go along with whatever they had planned.

Middle-aged Bertha, built like a prison matron, had short dark hair, black button eyes, and a pug nose in a moon face with a double chin. Red spots of color shone in her apple cheeks. She wore a white bib apron over a short-sleeved black dress uniform. Her arms were thicker than Steve's.

She circled around the back of Jules's chair

and moved down the table, pausing when she stood between Brett and Steve.

"This is for you, Steve," Skye said, all traces of her diffident manner during dinner having vanished. She was bright-eyed and enthusiastic.

"What is it?" Steve asked.

"It's a surprise. Specialty of the house," said Skye.

Bertha, good-naturedly beaming, eyes twinkling, set the warming dish–covered platter down on the table.

The Moray family leaned forward in their seats, animated by an air of expectancy. Bertha's hand was poised on the ringed handle on top of the silver half globe. She lifted the top, exposing what lay beneath on the platter:

A gun.

Skye suddenly rose out of her seat, gripping the sharp-edged steak knife she'd palmed earlier and savagely stabbing downward with it, impaling Steve's left hand and pinning it to the table.

The attack came without warning. Steve was distracted by the revelation of the gun under the warming dish, and the diversion created a split-second window of vulnerability that Skye took advantage of.

Her stroke fell hard, straight, and true. The sharp, slim blade pierced the back of Steve's left hand, driving through flesh, blood, and bone. Several inches of the point emerged from his palm, penetrating several inches deep into the wooden tabletop.

Steve roared with shock and pain. And outrage.

Brett nimbly picked up the gun from the platter, pointing it at Steve's head.

"Keep still—you'll live longer," he said. "Not much longer," he added.

Steve sat rigid, upright in his high-backed chair. His face was frozen in a snarl. That was no mean feat for him because the IED bomb blast in Somalia had disfigured his face, requiring extensive plastic surgery and skin grafts to restore it. The face changers had re-formed his face into a presentable if grim visage but the surgery and skin grafts had left his features largely incapable of expression, except in the case of moments of extreme emotional upheaval.

Such as now.

A circle of red blood expanded outward from under his left hand, soaking into the white linen tablecloth.

Steve's eyes were glazed, pain-stricken orbs. Veins stood out on his forehead and neck like snakes. He broke into a cold sweat. Breath hissed through clenched teeth; knotted muscles worked at the hinges of his jaws.

No other sound escaped him after that initial howl of rage and pain.

The others seated at the table reacted in various ways according to their natures.

Skye's yellow-gold eyes glittered. Red dots of color glowed in her cheeks. Her lips were parted; strong, shiny, upper front teeth nibbled on that ripe lower lip.

"Sorry, Steve," she said, not sounding sorry

at all. "I forgot to tell you—my real passion is for killing."

"A family tradition," Olcott said.

Brett lazily wagged the gun barrel at Steve Ireland. "Don't reach for that gun holstered in the small of your back, sport. Not if you want to keep that other hand intact for a while longer."

Steve sat stock-still, statuelike. So they knew about his ace-in-the-hole gun! Whoever these Morays were, whatever their purpose, they had done their homework.

Olcott, radiating boozy good cheer, arched an eyebrow. His index and middle fingers formed a V, the tips of which stroked his mustache, smoothing it down.

Lillian's smooth, bronzed face was immobile, her eyes narrow horizontal slits. Her lips pressed together, forming a taut horizontal line. Her chest rose and fell with slow, deep breaths.

Jules rested his forearms on the table's edge and leaned forward, surveying the situation. His expression was one of superficial geniality below which lurked avid, lip-smacking sadistic interest.

Teela seemed lazily fascinated, a cat contemplating the opening foredoomed struggles of a mouse in its clutches.

Brett was all business, intent, eyes narrowed. He rested the elbow of his gun hand on the table, careful to avoid bumping the nearby silver coffee urn. His hand was steady and unwavering as he held the gun pointed at Steve's head.

"Search him and relieve him of his hardware, Bertha," he said.

"Yes, Mr. Brett," Bertha said.

"Careful not to get between him and the gun," he cautioned.

"Yes, sir."

Bertha set the now-empty platter and rounded top down on the table. She went around the back of Steve's chair, approaching him from the left side, looming over him. Her meaty hands ran over his shoulders, patting him down, frisking him.

Every jarring movement that disturbed his pierced, pinned left arm sent pain waves rocketing through Steve, traveling up his arm to detonate inside his skull.

Bertha smoothed her palms along his sides, under his arms, continuing to frisk him. She grabbed a handful of Steve's sweater and the shirt underneath at the middle of his waist behind his back, lifted it up, baring his lower back.

Clipped to the belt in a holster pressed to the small of his back was a .32 semiautomatic pistol.

Steve never left home without it.

It would have been hard to find for someone initially unaware of it. That was why it made a good hole gun for tight spots like this.

But not when the opposition had been tipped off to it, as they must have been.

Earlier when he'd had sex with Skye in the

woods, it had taken some careful juggling and sleight of hand to fold the top of his jeans over his gun and holster to conceal them as he took his pants down to his ankles and then put it to the girl. He thought he'd done it rather well and she hadn't noticed it—a wrong guess apparently, he realized now.

Bertha took the gun from him, circled the table, and placed the holstered piece flat on the white linen–covered tabletop between Brett and Teela.

Returning, she bent over, running her hands along Steve's denim-clad legs, feeling for concealed weapons, finding none. She looked into the tops of his boots but no weapons were concealed there.

"He's clean, Mr. Brett," she said, straightening up and stepping away from Steve.

"You think so?" Skye asked.

"Yes, Miss Skye," Bertha said.

Skye shook her head. "Steve's more than a shooter, he's an artist with the blade, too. Or so I've been told. Let me prove it to you. Observe," she said.

Skye patted the back of Steve's knife-pierced hand in a gesture of mock sympathy. She gripped his wrist with one hand and with the other rolled his left sleeve back to the elbow, baring his forearm.

Steve exerted iron self-control to keep from crying out in pain. He could take it; he'd endured worse—for months at a time, during his painful convalescence in the hospital throughout a lengthy recovery. He'd be damned before giving his captors the satisfaction of seeing him suffer, he vowed.

A pair of thin tan leather straps encircled his left forearm, one several inches above the wrist and the other up close to and below the elbow. The straps secured a leather sheath to the inside of Steve's forearm.

The sheath contained a blade worn hilt downward.

So—the Morays knew about the throwing knife he also habitually wore strapped to the inside of his left forearm, Steve thought. He couldn't see how Skye could have known about that without outside information. The .32 was one thing; it was possible that she might have glimpsed it during their wild, frantic coupling in the woods—though he doubted it. But he was sure that the knife had remained undercover.

Could be—must be—that someone had tipped the Morays to his operational dossier. The pistol hidden in the small of his back and the throwing knife strapped to his left arm were secrets known only to a few besides himself, a very few; and of those few most were dead—except for the ones on his side.

The ones supposed to be on his side.

Did the Dog Team have a traitor hidden in its ranks? Hard to believe, but that's what the facts seemed to indicate.

Skye's strong, slim fingers undid a catch at the top of the sheath, opening it. She gripped the hilt between thumb and forefinger and pulled it out.

It was a long, slim, stiletto-like metal blade, gleaming with a mirrorlike finish that caught the light from the chandelier overhead, sending scintillant rays and gleams a-beaming. It was a flat blade resembling a die-cut pattern, its edges wickedly sharp, its point lancetlike.

"A pretty toy," Skye said, fascinatedly handling the toy.

"Like you, dear," Brett murmured.

Steve's masklike face betrayed nothing: no apprehension, relief, guile. Nothing but the strain of having his hand pierced and pinned to the table by a knife.

"That boy carries a lot of hardware," Olcott said.

"He's defanged now," said Jules.

A certain keyed-up tension seemed to go out of the Morays at this announcement. They were sure of their prey now, ready to relax and savor the enjoyment of the cat-and-mouse.

Skye balanced the midpoint of the flat of the blade on the tip of her finger, where it hung evened out like the scales of justice. "Perfectly balanced—a throwing knife," she said.

She gripped it, letting the blade protrude point first from the top of her fist. Eyeing Steve speculatively.

"Ahem," Jules said. "A little restraint, Skye, if you please. Hold in check your well-known proclivity for infliction."

"Why?" she asked.

"We're not done with our guest yet. He may be able to elucidate certain points of information vital to the successful completion of our current assignment."

Lillian barked a curt, mirthless laugh. "He won't talk," she said.

"No?" Skye said.

"They all talk under the treatment," Olcott opined.

"Not all," Lillian said. "This one won't. He's a stiff-necked bastard. You can tell just by looking at him. He'd rather die than give you the satisfaction. He'll make you kill him."

"We'll see," Skye said.

"He's tough," Teela said admiringly. "That's good. The tougher they are, the sweeter the sport. And it lasts all the longer."

Olcutt reached for the decanter, refilling his cup. "Sorry I can't offer you any, young fella, but you know how it is," he said to Steve.

"No. How is it?" Steve said. He took a deep breath and used it to keep speaking. "You people must have me confused with someone else," he said in a rush.

Agony underlay his words, rasping in the timbre of his voice. His stiff face was frozen, except for his glittering eyes.

Jules tut-tutted. "Mistaken? Hardly. You're Steve Ireland, the man we want. Captain Steve Ireland, United States Army, of the higher echelon's elite Dog Team assassination squad."

Steve didn't bother trying to deny it.

"Who are you?" he asked.

Jules smiled gently, laugh lines creasing around watery green eyes. "I suppose we owe you some sort of an explanation, under the circumstances. In a sense you could say that we're rivals of yours. Professional rivals. Seeing as how we're all in the same line of work."

"Only we don't stooge for the Pentagon," Brett said, "or any other government agency."

"Who do you stooge for?" Steve fired back.

"We'll ask the questions," Brett retorted.

Jules chuckled. "For now, call us . . . the Dog-catchers."

That drew knowing smiles and chuckles from his fellow family members around the table.

"Talk sense. Say what you mean," Steve said.

Jules shook his head in mock sadness. "I could almost admire your stubbornness if it weren't all so unnecessary. But that's the code, eh? Never give in, admit to nothing. Deny, deny, deny. But the time for dissembling is over, Steve. The noose hangs high. You're already one of the last of a dying breed. Most of the others of your team have already met their fate. The Dog Team, that is—now defunct."

"Never heard of it," Steve said.

"That's very good. But pointless. You see, we know who you are and what you are. And there'll be no last-minute reprieves. No cavalry riding in in the nick of time to save the fort," Jules said.

He went on. "My point is that the Dog Team has reached the end of its usefulness. You served a purpose back in the day but this is a new day. You're old-fashioned and out of date, boy. You and the hidebound Army mossbacks who sic you and your colleagues on those they deem an enemy to the republic.

"This is a new era. The republic such as it was is done. It was always more of a hope and a dream than a reality, anyway. Your handlers and fellow diehards have outlived their usefulness. The republic is dead, replaced by the corporate empire of money. Global capital beyond the nation-state.

"Simply put, the Dog Team got in the way of the real masters of the world. You tried to say no to supreme corporate interests. Dared to defy them and keep them from making more money.

"That's a crime, son. A capital crime punishable by death. You're attack dogs that don't have the sense to come to heel. You've got to be put down. Put to sleep."

"And that's where you come in?" Steve asked.

"That's right, boy," said Jules, "us and others like us. We're not hampered by any crazy notions like duty, honor, and country. Our allegiance is only to the highest bidder and we never double-cross the best offer." Then he added, "Well, hardly ever." That got a knowing laugh from some of the others at the table.

"The masters of society know they can trust us because they're the same way," Jules said. "It's you crazy idealists who're monkeywrenching the system. That's why you've got to go."

Steve's rigid face formed a sneer. "You talk big, but you're the real sucker. Once you've done the dirty work, the bosses will get rid of you, too."

Jules waved a hand in the air, a gesture of negation. "It's been tried. But we Morays have been around for a long, long time and we plan to be around for a whole lot longer. We've got a system and it works."

"Who fingered me to you?" Steve asked.

Jules shrugged. "What difference does it make? Nothing you can do about it anyway."

Steve tried his left hand to see if it was still workable. His fingers wriggled. They felt like they were over in another county, but some sensation, some utility, still remained in them.

He gathered his feet under him, bracing himself. His right hand still clutched the table's edge as if to endure the pain, fingers working convulsively, clenching and unclenching, clawing at the tablecloth.

Brett noticed Steve's unease and smiled thinly, savoring it.

A gust of wind blew up, rattling the windows. Raindrops pattered against glass panes, big fat raindrops that made wet splattering sounds. A minor distraction but—

Steve grabbed a fistful of white linen tablecloth and suddenly pulled hard on it.

Part of the tablecloth was pinned in place to the table, along with his left hand. That was on the left side of the table. Steve worked the right side, playing the tablecloth like snapping a whip.

It was a variant of the same principle as the magician's classic trick of whisking a tablecloth off a table so fast that it leaves dishes and place settings undisturbed.

Not so Steve's goal. He wanted the layout plenty disturbed. He threw some English into it.

The tablecloth humped up into a wave, sweeping across the near side of the table. Cake plates, cups and saucers, water and wineglasses, silverware were all tossed topsy-turvy.

Steve's eye was on bigger game: the coffee urn, which was set down near this end of the table between Brett and Teela.

He flicked the tablecloth with a snap of the wrist, upsetting the silver coffee urn and toppling it toward Brett.

The urn hurtled sideways, its hinged lid opening. It flew off the table and fell into Brett's lap, dousing him with the steaming brown brew.

Brett's shriek rose into falsetto as he threw himself back from the table, dropping his gun to free his hands to pluck the uncapped coffee urn from where it was spewing between his legs.

Steve stood up, his chair overturning behind him.

Each movement sent white-hot bolts of agony from his pinned hand lashing up the nerves of his arm into his brain. Like a dentist's drill tearing into a raw nerve.

A wave of sick weakness seized him and he fought to keep from passing out. The pain kept him conscious, focused, intent. He made it work for him.

His mind, his senses switched into hyperdrive. Hyperalertness. It was as if time were standing still.

A roaring sounded in his ears, oceanic. He didn't know it was his own wordless shout of rage and defiance.

He pressed his left hand flat against the table. His right hand gripped the hilt of the carving knife, fastening on it with a monkey grip. With a lurching heave he yanked it up, freeing the point from where it was planted several inches deep in the wooden tabletop.

Bellowing, he pulled the knife clear of the tabletop, wrenching it free from his maimed hand.

Adrenaline powered, Steve was irresistible, implacable. He slashed the blade at Skye, intent on cutting her throat.

She was too quick for him. Skye threw herself to the side, chair and all, away from him, overturning the chair as she tumbled sideways while still seated in it.

The knife blade slashed empty air where her long swanlike neck would have been.

Skye kept moving. With acrobatic agility she threw herself backward out of the fallen chair, somersaulting backward away from the table. Coming out of the roll, she got her feet beneath her and leaped up, plunging toward the kitchen.

Brett stood doubled over, howling, holding himself between the legs. There was a large, steaming, dark wet patch on his crotch and middle where the coffee urn had spilled its piping hot contents on him.

Teela rose, lunging, reaching across the table for the gun Brett had dropped.

Steve pivoted toward her, turning his upper body. He whipped the carving knife straight at Teela, letting it fly.

Momentum carried it straight and true. A meaty thunk sounded as it buried itself deep in Teela's chest between her breasts, sticking out by the handle.

Olcott threw the heavy crystal brandy decanter at Steve's head. Steve ducked and it flew over him to smash through a windowpane.

The swinging door swung back and forth, still agitated by Skye's flight into the kitchen.

Jules's face contorted. His body shifted—a shrugging motion. Suddenly a gun was in his hand. It happened so fast that Steve knew Jules must have been fitted with a spring-operated sleeve gun that popped the weapon into his ready hand.

Steve glimpsed something out of the corner of his eye—

Bertha bearing down on him, charging. Arms extended, oversized strangler's hands reaching for him.

She collided with him, almost knocking him

down. He fended her off as best he could with his right arm, favoring his maimed left hand. He was 180 pounds, and she outweighed him by a good forty.

Bertha slammed into him again, bulling him backward. Steve backpedaled to stay on his feet and lessen the impact of her charge.

Lillian followed Skye's lead, darting through the swinging door into the kitchen.

Brett crawled on hands and knees, picking up the gun Teela had dropped. She lay nearby in a heap on the floor.

Gun in hand, Jules circled around the head of the table angling for a shot. Bertha grabbed Steve's upper arms, sweeping him backward across the floor toward the windows. She stood between him and Jules, causing the latter to hold his fire as he tried to line up a clear shot.

Brett wasn't so scrupulous. Rising shakily to his feet, mouth open and moaning, he held his gun in both hands. He fired at Steve, not aiming, not caring who he hit.

A slug tore a chunk off Bertha's brawny left shoulder. A second tagged her in the middle of her broad back. Several other shots went wild, starring the windows in the opposite wall.

Bertha jerked forward, staggering.

"Stop shooting, you fool! You've hit Bertha!" Jules shouted at Brett.

Steve pressed close to Bertha now, using her for a shield. She was still going but dying on her feet, life running out of her with each step.

Steve held her upright, carrying her along with him.

The windowed wall loomed up behind him. The sill bumped against his hip.

Steve sidestepped, grabbing Bertha's arm and whipping her headfirst into one of the windows. The glass pane disintegrated with a whoomping sound, followed by the tinkling chimes of a cascade of broken glass.

Bertha was a big woman and the combination of her speed and weight knocked most of the glass out of the windowpane, spilling it on the flagstones of the terrace. Her body lay facedown, draped over the windowsill so that she lay half in, half out of the room. Her upper body hung outside, her middle was draped over the sill, and her lower body remained inside.

Bertha had served as a battering ram, clearing the glass out of the window. Contact with the jagged shards left her looking as though she'd been mauled by a tiger. She'd cleared the way for Steve.

He dove headfirst through the window, launching himself into empty air.

Brett's gun jerked in his hands, wildly pumping rounds at Steve, none coming close.

Jules did slightly better, one of his shots nipping the corner off Steve's left boot heel as he plunged through the empty window frame.

"Get him!" Jules shouted.

NINE

Steve hit the paved terrace, breaking the impact with a shoulder roll, still experiencing a bone-jarring thud.

The air was cold, fresh, raw. It helped revive him. Coming out of the roll, he got his feet under him and sprang upright.

He'd catapulted himself onto a flagstone terrace that aproned the rear of the house.

The terrace, long and wide, fronted south. Pieces of white-painted iron lawn furniture stood scattered on the patio. Several chairs grouped around a round-topped table, and there was a high-backed bench built for two.

It was good to be out of the death-trap room, but the outside was too open. Steve felt nakedly exposed.

He glanced back at the house. Moving figures showed behind the windows. The Moray group, moving to finish what they'd started. Moving to finish him.

The patio was thirty feet wide and stood

three feet above ground level. At its far end a curved flight of stone stairs slanted down to the lawn.

Steve darted left toward the terrace's western end, racing to get clear of the firing line from the window. A waist-high stone balustrade bordered the terrace. Steve rested his right hand on the rail as he threw his legs over it, vaulting it.

Bare thornbushes lay below, running along the terrace's edge. They broke his fall, spilling him onto the cold, hard ground.

Bullets cut the air overhead, whizzing past.

Lillian stood with her upper body leaning out the dining room window, shooting at Steve. "There he goes! Don't let him get away!"

Steve looked around. What next?

His Suburban was parked on the north, opposite side of the mansion. A long way off. The Morays could get to the front entrance and outside well in time to intercept him. The nearest buildings were the garage and the stable. The garage was closer to the house's northwest corner, where Steve was. One of the bay doors was open; inside it a fancy car could be seen. A man stood there peering out at him.

Steve recognized him as Ludlow, the family's chauffeur and handyman. Skye had introduced him to Steve earlier, when Ludlow had saddled up their horses prior to the ride.

Ludlow had been absent during the fun and games in the dining room, but considering the fact that the other household servants were all part of the Moray cabal, there was no reason to assume that Ludlow was any different.

This was the damnedest ménage that Steve had ever seen!

Ludlow ducked back into the garage, out of sight.

Steve looked back toward the stable.

A one-story shedlike structure, it had a peaked roof with light gray shingles; the wooden-frame building was painted battleship gray. A set of swinging barn doors in front was now closed. It was one of those modern show barns that looked like a real estate agent's office.

Steve made a beeline for it. His wounded hand ached, throbbing, feeling like a second heart pounding away at the end of his left arm. It bled steadily but not profusely. Gore covered his hand, making it look as if he wore one red glove.

Steve was a realist with no illusions. He knew he was running on adrenaline. Shock, pain, and loss of blood would all too soon take their toll.

Ludlow came out of the garage, gun in hand, and started after Steve. Lillian still leaned out of the window, shouting and pointing at the fugitive.

Where were the others?

Jules, Brett, Olcott, Pyne, Margit—and Skye. They wouldn't be sitting still waiting to see what Steve did next. They were direct actionists. They would take active measures to stop him.

The stable stood catty-corner to the northwest

corner of the house, its long front side facing it at an angle. Access was also provided by the side doors, one at each short end.

Steve went around to the far side door. It wasn't locked—the knob turned under his hand. That was a break.

Ludlow ran toward him, fast closing the distance between stable and garage.

Steve ducked inside. The stable was modern, better appointed than a lot of people's houses. It was electrically lit and heated. There was the mixed scent of hay and horse, a not unpleasant aroma.

Three stable stalls lined the rear wall, two of them occupied by horses: the gray mare and the brown gelding.

Steve's sudden entrance made them uneasy. They snorted, pawed the floorboards with their hooves. He looked around for something he could use as a weapon, something he knew was there because he'd seen it earlier. He found it in a corner leaning up against the wall, tines down:

A pitchfork.

Steve took hold of it, gripping it like a rifle with a fixed bayonet. He peeked out of a corner of one of the front windows, not showing himself.

A short, squat man running on stump legs, Ludlow was almost at the barn.

Steve ducked low, below the window sight line. He ran to the opposite end of the barn and opened the side door, leaving it ajar.

Still crouched low, he scrambled back to the other side.

He stood to the left of the door, hunched down with his back against the wall. Holding the pitchfork across his chest bayonet-fighter style.

Ludlow opened the door, entering. He held a 9mm Beretta leveled at his hip. He cursed when he saw the open door at the far end of the barn.

The diversion gave Steve the opportunity he needed. He stepped forward. Ludlow saw him out of the corner of his eye.

Steve struck out with the pitchfork, slashing the edge of the fork hard against the wrist of the other's gun hand. Knocking the gun from his grip. The pistol fell to the floor, not discharging.

Steve struck mostly one-handed, right hand clutching the handle, left arm bent at the elbow so he could guide the pitchfork across the top of his left forearm. He thrust the pitchfork into Ludlow's middle, the soft belly below the breastbone. Spearing him in three places with the tines.

The sharp-pointed tines penetrated with surprising ease. Steve pinned Ludlow against the wall. He was hampered because of his bad hand. He leaned into it, putting his weight behind it.

Ludlow opened his mouth to scream but the impalement took his breath away. All he could do was make choking, gurgling noises. Blood gushed out of his mouth.

Ludlow's legs buckled at the knees. He slid down the wall, leaving a bloody vertical smear to mark his path. He sat down hard, legs extended in front of him.

Steve bore down hard on the pitchfork, giving it a savage twist. Ludlow coughed, spasming, black blood pouring from his mouth as the light in his eyes faded away and died.

So did he.

Steve left the pitchfork sticking in him and picked up the pistol. It felt good in his hand.

The killing had spooked the horses. They stamped, pawed, whinnied, kicked against their stalls. Frantic hoofbeats clattering on the floorboards.

Steve inspected the gun, making sure that a round was in the chamber. It was. Lucky it hadn't gone off when dropped. The piece had safety functions built in to guard against such an accident, but you never can tell. . . .

Steve stuck the pistol into the top of his waistband so that it was securely lodged. He went to the stable's front double doors, which were secured by a bar mounted on a pivot and dropping into open U-shaped metal staples. He raised the bar, unlatching the doors.

He eased one open a few inches and peered outside. Covering, not showing, himself.

A group was gathering on the terrace.

Jules, Lillian, Olcott, Brett, and Skye. They were variously armed with rifles, small machine guns, and pistols.

Skye held a double-barreled shotgun. She

broke away from the group and crossed quickly toward the stable, well ahead of the others.

Jules was calling to her: "Wait for us, Skye!"

"No! This kill is mine!" she shouted back over her shoulder.

She hurried ahead, unheeding. Her sporting blood was up. The lure of the chase had her in thrall. She craved the thrill of the kill.

The hunt had turned interesting, taking an unsuspected twist. The prey was more resourceful and dangerous than expected.

No righteous rage at the death of Cousin Teela possessed Skye. The Morays were not that sort of family. She and Teela had hated each other since childhood days. Perhaps because they were so much alike.

The others' calls for her to wait fell on deaf ears. They only sought to deprive her of the credit and glory of the kill, Skye told herself. It was only fitting that she take the honors.

She'd already coupled with Steve and it had been good. To liquidate him would be sweeter still. To mate, then kill—truly, was that not the Moray way?

With figurative blood in her eye and real murder in her heart, Skye closed on the stable. She was out in front, far ahead of the others.

Her eyes shone; raw wind whipped color into her face. "Steve!—"

The stable's double doors swung outward and open, crashing against the wall.

The gray mare bolted into view. Steve was

riding her. Bareback. The gun was in his right fist, the horse's reins wrapped around his fist.

Skye was too close to evade the animal's charge; the gray was right on top of her. Wild-eyed, the horse checked, rising on its hind legs.

The horse's advent startled Skye, crowding her so that she was unable to swing the shot-gun up in time to throw down on Steve—or do anything else. Her feet got tangled up with each other.

She recoiled, losing her footing and falling backward.

She jerked one of the triggers as she fell. The double-barreled shotgun discharged one of its loads, firing harmlessly into the air. Further spooking with its booming thunderclap the already unnerved animal.

The horse danced around on its hind legs, almost throwing Steve, who somehow managed to stay on. The gray's front hoofs touched down.

He leaned over its right side and triggered a couple of rounds into Skye, drilling her in the chest.

It was like driving nails with a nail gun. Skye spasmed as the slugs tore into her.

"No!" Jules shouted.

Steve pulled hard on the reins wrapped around his gun fist, dug his booted heels into the mare's sides to urge her to speed. The animal needed no urging, frantic to leave the scene of blood and thunder. It trampled Skye as it fled.

Steve turned the horse, rounding the corner of the barn.

Lillian shouldered a .30-.30 hunting rifle and pointed it in Steve's direction, but too late; he was out of her firing line.

Steve raced the horse west across the fields toward the edge of the woods.

Riding bareback was a rough ride. Even for a horseman in full possession of his faculties. Damningly difficult for a man with one good hand.

Luckily the mare already had been haltered and bridled. Steve could never have made his getaway otherwise. He wasn't out of the woods yet.

Rather, he wasn't into the woods yet.

Back home in Arizona growing up on a ranch he'd mastered the art of bareback riding, like the bronco Apaches had done in frontier times. Even as a kid, he knew this: it was no fun. Easy to bust a bone in your seat or fall off. And back then it had been done with a saddle blanket between him and the horse.

This, now, was really riding bareback. He had an incentive, though: to keep from being killed. Mindful of where the rest of the Morays had been bunched, he tried to keep the barn between himself and them as much as possible.

Pops sounded. Bullets whizzed around him.

The woods neared.

With eyes going in and out of focus, he peered ahead, searching for a gap in the brush that would indicate the mouth of a trail. Spotting one on the left, he rode toward it.

His abrupt change in direction saved him from several well-aimed rifle shots that came his way. The slugs made sharp rapping wood-pecker noises as they tore into the trees.

Then Steve was in the trail and riding away, its winding course putting a screen of forest cover between him and the shooters.

TEN

Activity at the mansion:

In the aftermath of Steve's escape, the Morays and their staff assembled outside the house, moving purposefully and with decisiveness. Jules directed the cleanup operation.

Brett was shaky; he walked haltingly, spraddle-legged from the hot coffee scalding he'd received.

Pyne came out of the house. He wore a winter jacket, fur-lined cap, and fur-lined black leather gloves. He handed an overcoat to Jules, helped the patriarch to don it.

The group collected around Skye. She lay on her back, sightless eyes staring at the sky. Jules went down beside her on one knee, closed her eyes.

Pyne went into the stable to assess the damage. Olcott, Lillian, and Brett went into the mansion.

Pyne emerged from the stable carrying a horse blanket. He and Jules laid it flat on the ground beside Skye's body. Jules arranged her limbs, closing her legs, pressing them together. He crossed her folded arms over her chest.

Then he and Pyne rolled her up in the blanket, cocooning her.

Margit came out of the house wearing a winter jacket and gloves. A pickup truck hitched to a horse trailer was parked in the main driveway off the mansion's southeast corner.

Margit went to it. She got in the truck cab and started it up. She drove the truck and trailer along the driveway, up over the curb, and across the lawn to the back of the house, halting in the yard near the stable.

She switched off the engine and got out. She went around to the rear of the pickup and lowered the tailgate.

Jules and Pyne stood over Skye's blanket-wrapped body. They hefted her at either end, Pyne wrapping his arms around her chest, Jules gripping her around the ankles. They carried her to the back of the pickup and loaded her into the hopper.

Olcott and Lillian emerged from the house. They had changed their clothes; both now wore outdoor gear: winter jackets, pants, hiking boots. They carried hunting rifles and wore sidearms.

Brett remained inside, tending his scalded flesh.

Olcott and Lillian stood on the lawn below the terrace, conferring briefly with Jules. He did most of the talking, giving them their instructions. He could have used their help to dispose of the bodies but they had a more important task: stop Steve Ireland. Time was of the essence.

Olcott and Lillian went around to the front of the house, got into a black Land Rover with their weapons, and drove off. The Rover went down the driveway, turned right onto Crestline Drive, and proceeded south across the top of Hessian Hill.

Olcott and Lillian were charged with the mission to seek and destroy Steve. With luck they would intercept him on the road en route to his house. If not, they were to go to Steve's place and lie in wait for him.

Jules, Pyne, and Margit now put their heads together. Jules gave them their orders and went into the house, not looking back.

Margit and Pyne went into the stable. They came out ten minutes later carrying a second blanket-wrapped body: Ludlow's.

Margit was a big, strong young woman. She showed no signs of strain from her labors. Indeed, she was doing the lion's share of the carrying, bearing the heavy load of Ludlow's beefy upper body. Pyne had him by the feet and was huffing and puffing.

They heaved the body up onto the pickup's tailgate. Margit climbed up in the hopper and dragged the corpse so that it lay lengthwise next to Skye's. Then she climbed back down again.

Pyne went into the house.

Margit closed the tailgate, got in the truck,

and started it up. She drove to the foot of the terrace, stopped the truck with the empty double horse trailer still hitched to it, and got out. She lowered the tailgate.

She climbed the stone steps to the terrace, crossed it, and disappeared inside the house. After a while she emerged with Jules and Pyne.

They were carrying a body: Bertha's. Bertha wasn't wrapped; she was too heavy to carry in a blanket. They needed to get a grip on her limbs to haul her away. They could have used Brett's help, but he had begged off, saying he was hurting too badly from his burns to lend a hand. Jules fixed him with a coldly skeptical eye, but Brett wasn't budging.

Clan patriarch, butler, and serving maid lugged Bertha across the terrace. Jules and Pyne each gripped an arm, while Margit held each of the cook's thick ankles tucked under an arm.

Bertha was a heavy load. Her body drooped, hanging down in the middle like an overloaded hammock. The carriers had to pause several times to rest and catch their breath.

Finally, they managed to get her down the stone steps to the truck. They put her on the ground while resting up for the supreme effort of hoisting her body up onto the tailgate.

Margit went into the mansion, then returned with a blanket. She climbed in the hopper and laid the blanket on the truck bed.

She climbed back down. She, Jules, and Pyne each gripped one of Bertha's limbs and heaved. By dint of massive effort, huffing and puffing, they finally managed to get the body up onto the tailgate.

That was enough for Jules. He went into the house.

Pyne and Margit took a quick break, Margit smoking a cigarette. When she was done she climbed back up on the hopper. She and Pyne managed to wrap Bertha in the blanket. The corpse was moved around so that it lay lengthwise in the hopper. Margit stood at the head, bending over at the waist to take hold of the blanket-wrapped body. Pyne stood on the ground, pushing Bertha's swaddled feet. Together they managed to position the body alongside those of Skye and Ludlow.

Pyne was sweating. He mopped his forehead with a handkerchief. "This is rough," he said, wheezing.

He and Margit went into the house and came out bearing Teela's body. Teela was no lightweight, but compared to Bertha the job was easy. Teela was wrapped in a blanket. Her body joined the others in the truck bed.

Pyne and Margit went into the garage. They emerged carrying a rolled tarpaulin and a length of coiled rope. They unrolled the tarp, dragging it over the four bodies in the back of the pickup.

Margit adjusted it so that it covered all the corpses. Pyne used a knife to cut some smaller lengths of rope. He and Margit ran the lines through eyeletted holes in the edges of the tarp, then tied the ropes down to eyebolts on the truck bed and hopper to secure the tarp in place.

Margit closed the tailgate and locked it. She drove the truck into the driveway, backing it up to the horse trailer. She drove the truck with the trailer attached across the yard to the stable. She could hear the bodies thumping and bumping around in the hopper.

She opened the rear door of the horse trailer and hauled out the loading ramp.

It started to rain. It was full night now, dark and wet. The cold rain fell lightly but steadily.

Margit went into the stable. Presently she came out leading the brown gelding by a halter rope, coaxing the horse up the loading ramp and into one of the dual stalls. The animal seemed eager to be quit of the scene and cooperated without a balk.

Margit put the ramp in the trailer, closed and locked its rear door.

She got in the cab and started the truck. Since it was full dark, she was forced to switch on the headlights. Silver streaks of falling rain slanted through the beams.

She drove across the yard and into the driveway, parked, and went into the house.

Pyne drove a big black Continental out of the garage, then parked it in the driveway in front of the house. He went inside. The Continental, a Cadillac SUV, and the pickup with horse trailer were all parked in front of the mansion.

Pyne came out, carrying a suitcase in each hand. He placed them on the front stone stoop and went inside for more. He and Margit carried out a number of suitcases from the house. Presently the last of the suitcases was loaded into the car and SUV.

Lights in the mansion began going dark as they were systematically shut off, leaving most of the house dark except for the front hall and the exterior lamps mounted over the front entrance.

Jules, Brett, Pyne, and Margit exited through the front door. Margit got in the truck, Pyne in the SUV, and Jules in the Continental.

The Continental pulled out first, going down the driveway and turning left on Crestline Drive, heading for Shunpike Road, the route that would take them off Hessian Hill.

It was followed by Pyne in the SUV and Margit in the pickup with trailer. Red taillights faded in the distance, and then they were gone.

Gone but not forgotten by the unseen watcher who observed their departure.

Steve watched the three-vehicle convoy depart Crestfield.

He sat on the gray mare in the mouth of a trail at the edge of the tree line where the fields began. He was hidden by rain and darkness, able to see without being seen.

Yes, he had fled—but not far. The Morays would have expected him to flee far. Instead, he'd faked flight and quickly doubled back on the trail so he could keep the estate under observation.

He'd returned in time to see Olcott and Lillian load their weapons in the Rover and drive away.

No doubt they were going to his house several miles farther south on the road. If they were waiting for him to show—and he was sure they were—they'd have a long wait.

Steve was currently outnumbered, outgunned, and wounded. One of the few things—if not the only one—he had working for him was the element of surprise. The Morays wouldn't be expecting him to return to the scene of the trap.

He was in pretty bad shape. He'd torn a strip from the bottom of his undershirt and used it to bind up his wounded hand. The makeshift bandage was now sticky with dried blood at the site of the entry and exit of the wound.

No jacket protected him against the cold and the wet. All he wore were a sweater, shirt, undershirt, jeans, socks, and boots. The sweater was made of thick black wool.

It provided some warmth but not enough; it was sodden with rain.

Steve was weak from pain, shock, loss of blood, and exposure. The cold drizzle wasn't helping. Snow was starting to appear in the mix, with big fat wet flakes. He didn't like that so well; the snow would cause him to leave tracks for the pursuers.

On top of everything else, his tailbone was

numb and felt like it was busted. Riding bareback was no picnic. He didn't dare get off the horse, either. He might still need it for a getaway and he wasn't sure that he could get back on.

The gun in his belt was a comforting presence, but he had no knife and his cell phone had gotten broken sometime during his escape.

Not that Steve was one to call for help. Dog Team members were by nature self-reliant and used to doing for themselves, getting out of their own jams.

Besides, who could he call? The police? That would raise more questions than he was prepared to answer. The neighbors? Up here on Hessian Hill they were few and far between, and those who were here were mostly passing acquaintances. Steve didn't dare involve civilians in this mess. They'd be as helpless as toddlers trying to cross a high-speed freeway at rush hour.

His Dog Team handlers and contacts? They would have to be notified, of course, but not yet. Somebody had fingered him for a pro kill, someone who knew his modus operandi, his behavioral quirks, where he lived, what concealed weapons he carried and where, even what made him tick.

Maybe not that last. He was unsure himself of what made him tick, why he did the things he did.

He could take it, though, Steve told himself. This was a picnic compared to taking a bellyful and faceful of hot shrapnel, like he'd done in Somalia.

It looked like the Morays were clearing out. They'd taken their baggage, including their dead, and cleared off the property.

Unless they had another member or members of the group he hadn't seen and was unaware of staked out inside the house on the chance that he might come back.

That was a risk he would have to take.

As for Olcott and Lillian, what would they do when he failed to appear at his house? He might have escaped and gotten help, or he might have collapsed and fallen off the horse on some woods trail, for all they knew.

A simple plan would be for one to remain at the house in case he showed up and the other to go in search of him. Or both clear out for fear he would return with reinforcements: the police or other Dog Team associates.

Leaving behind a souvenir like a booby trap, in hopes he would be so careless and distracted, so much at the end of his tether, as to blunder into it.

Or would they return here to regroup? Steve somehow doubted the pair would return to Crestfield—the household's packing up and clearing out had an air of finality to it.

Steve shivered, his teeth chattering. He felt hot and cold. Waves of dizziness swept over him. He was grateful for the pain because it gave him a focus and kept him from blacking out.

The horse sidled nervously. It had been subjected to a great deal of stress. Horses dislike blood and death. More, the gray was surely unused to being ridden bareback. Steve talked to the horse, gentling her, stroking her muscular neck with his good hand. It helped, some, but the horse was still anxious. If it bolted or reared up on its hind legs it would be all he could do to keep from being thrown.

He dared not wait too long to make his move. He had to move while he still had something left.

Time passed. Darkness deepened and the rain increased. To Steve, few things were more miserable and lonesome than the feel of cold rain falling on his bare head.

That decided him.

He gave a touch of his heels to the horse's flanks, urging it forward. He rode out of the woods and downhill along the north side of the tree line edging the fields.

Eyes alert, scanning, ears pitched to keen alertness, he drew abreast of the north face of the mansion and the curving driveway fronting it.

His Chevy Suburban was where he'd parked it earlier that day. It seemed a lifetime ago, something that had happened to him in another existence.

Common sense said that the Morays had quit the mansion, that it was abandoned, empty. Survival sense told Steve not to play it that way, to expect the unexpected. Survival sense, which the foolish and uninitiated call "paranoia," won out.

Steve sighed, knowing he was going to have to do it the hard way. Like always, he said to himself sourly with a wry, twisted grin. Even at the best of times, a twisted grin was all the taut flesh of his reconstructed face would allow.

And this sure as hell was a long way off from the best of times.

Steve slid off the horse, getting down on its left side, keeping the reins wrapped around his right hand. He gentled the horse, talking low voiced to it, patting it. The insides of his thighs were raw and aching from having gripped the animal's flanks so long and so hard to stay on it.

Lights shone from two lamps mounted over the front door, and some footlights scattered along the curve of the driveway illuminated the road. Spotlights were mounted under the eaves on the front corners of the mansion. The big front lawn was thick with shadow, wet with slushy snow.

Steve tied the reins to the branch of a bush at the edge of the lawn. He might need the horse and didn't want to risk its escaping. Turning, he started across the lawn toward the Suburban.

He kept the big, boxy dark green machine between him and the house, using it for cover. He moved crouched forward, bent almost double.

It was nerve-wracking, though, to be exposed out in the open like this with minimal cover. If there should be an ambusher in the house,

or if Olcott and Lillian or any of the others
should return—

They'd get their damned heads shot off,
Steve told himself. To hell with those bastards!

The gun, a talisman of death-dealing po-
tency, in his fist, he closed unmolested on the
Suburban.

At first glance it looked okay. No tires shot
out, no bullet holes in the hood, sides, or rear.
The Moray group must not have thought he'd
be coming back for it.

He'd had the place under observation for a
fair amount of time but not always. There was
a chance they might have gimmicked it while
he wasn't watching. If so they wouldn't have
had much time to rig a complicated device to
the starter or under the hood. The likeliest
threat would come from a slap-on magnetic
explosive device or tracking apparatus. Something that could be attached behind the
bumpers or along the undercarriage.

The driver's-side door, locked, showed no
sign of having been tampered with. Neither
did the hood.

Steve sat on his heels beside the Suburban.
He eyed the house. No signs of movement in
the front windows. No shapes, silhouettes, blurs.

He felt around inside the left front wheel
well for a mine, bomb, tracking device, or anything else that shouldn't be there. Didn't find
any. He did the same for the left rear well, too,
with equal lack of results.

He wriggled under the rear of the Suburban

on his back and crawled underneath it. Light from the front of the house failed to dispel black darkness along the undercarriage.

He felt around for a bomb or tracking device, not neglecting the right-side wheel wells. His right hand was stiff with cold. He whacked his fingers against his side to restore circulation and rubbed his fingertips against his thigh to warm them and restore some feeling.

The underside of the vehicle seemed clean as far as he could tell.

Steve crawled out from under the Suburban and duckwalked around to the driver's side, crouching to avoid presenting a target. He dug into his pocket, pulled out his key ring.

Thick, too clumsy fingers went through the keys. He pressed the button of the electronic keying device, automatically unlocking the doors. Steve winced at the telltale *boink-boink* noise.

There was no worry about triggering the overhead dome light in the cab when he opened the driver's-side door. He routinely kept the dome light switched off to prevent its lighting automatically and outlining him in the cab at night. A safety precaution.

Steve got behind the driver's wheel, leaving the door open in case he had to abandon the vehicle in a hurry. He ducked low in the seat, keeping his head below the bottom of the window frames.

The ignition lock and dashboard seemed untampered with. Steve fumbled the key in the ignition to start the engine, half expecting to be blown sky-high by a bomb he hadn't found.

The engine turned over and came to life.

Steve's taut nerves vibrated from the strain of being pitched to maximum alertness in the breathless hush of anticipation. Not knowing whether his actions would cue a shattering barrage of gunfire from hidden lurkers.

He threw the machine into gear and stepped on the gas, steering one-handed. He reached reflexively with his left hand to pull the door shut. White-hot agony wired from wounded hand to brain set off fireworks inside his head.

Working mostly right-handed, he wheeled the truck around, driving up over the curb with a double bump onto and across the lawn.

Steve drove in a straight line to where he had tied the horse's reins to a bush. He halted, engine running, lights dark. He got out, looking back at the house. It looked empty, abandoned.

He got out of the pickup, leaving the engine running. He untied the horse's reins and slapped its rump. The gray took off running.

Steve jumped back in the cab and did the same.

The pale horse, misty breath streaming from its snout as it galloped across the mansion's front lawn in the wet snowfall, made an eerie, haunting image.

Let the horse run free for a while. There were enough evergreens for it to forage, so it wouldn't starve. Sooner or later someone would call it in. He'd do it himself as soon as he got the chance.

Horses, Steve liked. People not so much. Less now than ever.

He drove away, cutting across the lawn at a tangent to reenter the driveway near where it exited the property.

He turned left on Crestline Drive and drove north, going a quarter mile or so before turning on the headlights.

Like the pale horse, Steve was taking it on the run.

Clan Moray had put a hurting on him. They'd drawn first blood, maiming his left hand, appropriating his gun and knife.

But he'd hit back hard. Thanks to him the Moray group now had four members in the grave: Ludlow the chauffeur, Bertha the cook, Teela—and Skye.

A macabre notion came to Steve. He'd brought Skye to a climax twice today, once in lust and again in death.

The Final Climax.

What had Jules said?

"Call us the Dogcatchers."

He'd forgotten that sometimes dogcatchers get bitten.

Above all, now, a single burning question continued to plague Steve's mind:

Who the hell were the Morays, anyhow?

ELEVEN

"It's all clear. Come on up," Doc Wenzle said.

"I'm on the way," Steve said. He broke the connection and switched off his cell phone.

At eight p.m. Steve stood in the recessed doorway of a defunct shop watching the front of the Gall Building in downtown Washington, D.C.

It was now Wednesday of the week following the Saturday of his rumble with the Morays. In the time since then he'd lost weight; his face was a bit grimmer and the light in his dark blue eyes colder and more intense.

After escaping the death trap at Crestfield manor, Steve had gone black. He'd dropped off the board, arbitrarily severing all contacts with friends, associates, and officialdom.

It wasn't that hard for Steve to step into limbo. As an active-duty Dog Team assassin his life was already compartmentalized. He had few friends and only a handful of professional associates. His parents and kinfolk back in Arizona all believed he was dead, killed five years ago while on Army duty in Iraq.

His faked death was part of his Dog Team cover. It had been done to protect his loved ones from vengeful retaliation by terrorists, spies, warlords, international criminals, and other malefactors who'd been stung by the sanctioned killings he'd carried out as part of the Army's ultrasecret assassination arm.

Steve was a skilled clandestine operator. But going black now took him to a whole new level of secrecy.

The Morays knew too much—about him and the Dog Team. The killer clan weren't military but they had information that should have been restricted to a select handful of U.S. Army covert agents and their equally elusive enablers in the service's higher echelons.

The Dog Team's security was compromised. The team may have been penetrated, hiding one or more double agents within its ranks. So Steve feared, and that fear was not for himself.

It was for the team, the Army, and the dire consequences for the nation itself should the assassination unit's existence become public. Until he had sorted out the situation and gotten some hard answers, Steve knew he must tread very carefully.

Instead of immediately reporting the attack to his handlers and case officers in the team, Steve vanished, cutting all contact with them.

He had to assume that his dossier was in the hands of the enemy. The enemy's identity was a mystery. Their agents were the Morays, that much Steve knew.

But behind the Morays lay the hidden hand of . . . who?

To find out, Steve had to stay alive. To do that, he must for the moment cut all connections with his previous life.

He had not returned to his house on Hessian Hill since Saturday night, when he had fled Crestfield. The Morays knew where he lived. It was a sure bet that they'd have his place staked out in readiness for his return there.

That was only the beginning. Did the enemy have his dossier? Steve had to assume that they did. The Morays could not have learned the details of the hideout gun Steve routinely carried holstered at the small of his back, or the throwing knife he kept up his left sleeve.

That was inside stuff that someone had to have tipped to them.

If his dossier was compromised, then his pattern was known. All human beings, all living creatures, have patterns. Where they go, whom they know, what they eat and drink, whom they sleep with, what they wear, and countless other bits of information that make up the sum total of one's behavior.

The wise hunter first learns the pattern of the prey: whether the animal is social or solitary, whether it moves by night or day, where it nests, what it feeds on and how, what path it takes to the water hole, and so on.

Once the pattern is known, the hunter has a blueprint for a successful kill.

Steve, in his capacity as first a Special Forces combat soldier and second a Dog Team assassin, had certainly stalked and slain enough targeted men—and women—to know that the pattern is the key to the kill.

Now that he was the hunted, he must break his pattern. It was not enough for him to shun home, friends, and associates to evade pursuit. Not in today's high-tech, total surveillance environment.

The necessities of modern life were potential signposts betraying his whereabouts to the foe. The vehicle he drove, his bank card, cell phone, computer password, and Web address—all these things and more could be used to track and locate him.

The Dog Team had supplied him with sets of cell phones equipped with scrambling devices and hardened against electronic eavesdropping by outside interests. But who watches the watchers?

Steve knew that the team-supplied cells contained locator chips that could be activated by the higher-ups without his knowledge or control, even if the cell was set in the OFF position.

One needs money to live, but if he used his bank or credit cards the record of the time, date, and nature of his purchases could be flagged and accessed by interested parties.

One needs a car or motor vehicle to get around in, but his Suburban was known and its license plates subject to being seen by any one of the thousands of security and traffic-monitoring cameras scattered throughout Washington, D.C., and its surroundings.

Steve was not without resources, however. He hadn't been joking when he told the late Skye about his being prepared. Having Plan B to fall back on was second nature to him.

That philosophy extended to his career as a Dog Team assassin. Major Joseph Kilroy, the man who'd recruited Steve for the team and mentored him during his apprenticeship, had made sure to tell Steve the facts of life concerning their peculiar trade. Kilroy was ever mindful of the fate of Dog Team One, the original Dog Team.

Its origins were obscure, its antecedents murky. It may well have begun in the days of the American Revolution or even before, in the time of the French and Indian War. All armies need an assassination component.

The Continental Army in the era of the Founding Fathers had learned that there are some situations that demand not a combat-ready fighting force but rather a single individual skilled in the ways of sudden death.

And so the Dog Team had been formed.

Elite, secretive, necessary, it had existed ever since under various names and identities, seeing action through the nineteenth century, into World Wars I and II and beyond, serving during America's "police actions" in global hot spots in the mid-twentieth century.

Then something had gone wrong, drastically wrong.

The Vietnam War and its aftermath had generated a dangerous counterreaction in the nation's liberal political and media elites. These opinion leaders turned against the military, scapegoating it for a war that these same politicians and pundits had created in the first place.

The full truth about the extent and nature of Dog Team One's lethal activities had never become public knowledge, but enough of the truth had leaked out for the team to become a pariah for publicity-seeking congressional inquisitors and their cheerleaders in the media.

Dog Team One had been deactivated, disbanded, and denounced by the antimilitary crowd. The unit's high-ranking officers had been forced into retirement. Lower ranking personnel found themselves smeared by a stigma that resulted in career suicide, causing them to leave the service.

It was a disgrace, a shameful finish for a cadre of unsung heroes whose every covert mission held the risks of capture, torture, imprisonment, and death. Many of its members had made the supreme sacrifice.

Human nature being what it is, and politicians and war being what they are, it was not long before wiser heads in Congress and the Pentagon realized that having a military assassination unit was a necessity, and so the new Dog Team was formed.

But history has a way of repeating itself,

Kilroy had warned Steve. What had happened before could happen again. Especially in today's crazily overheated political climate, there was no telling when the reformed Dog Team might be exposed and sacrificed on the unholy altar of political correctness.

One of the first things a soldier learns is to never enter a building without first knowing where the exits are.

The same applied to the Dog Team, Kilroy had told Steve.

"You've got to have an exit strategy," Kilroy had said. "If the political winds change and the big shots decide to throw you to the wolves, don't be caught without an escape plan."

For a professional assassin, such an escape plan must encompass many eventualities. Following Kilroy's advice, Steve had assembled the components necessary to drop out of sight and begin a new life.

They included such things as a numbered offshore banking account with a hefty nest egg and papers and documents necessary for disappearing into a new assumed identity. Prudence alone dictated that such necessary precautions be kept secret from the team's handlers, case officers, and higher-ups.

Steve never knew that Kilroy's natural father was the legendary Terry Kovack, Dog Team One's supreme assassin, and that Kovack's descent into poverty, deprivation, and death following the public disgracing of the original team had informed Kilroy's thoughts regarding the wisdom of not putting too much trust in the politicians of the U.S. government.

Or some of the politically minded military careerists in the Pentagon, either.

But Steve knew good advice when he heard it and had acted accordingly. His leap into the black following the encounter with the Morays therefore found Steve not without resources.

Now, on this Wednesday night less than a week after surviving the attack, Steve was about to resurface.

Which is why he stood in the darkened doorway of a shuttered store across the street from the Gall Building in downtown Washington, D.C.

Steve had contacted one man he was sure he trusted in the organization, Doc Wenzle, his official Dog Team handler.

Tough as an old Army boot, Wenzle was a career officer who had gone undercover to serve as a key component in the Dog Team's clandestine infrastructure. Wenzle was no medical doctor; the sobriquet "Doc" by which he was known was a tribute to his cunning and professionalism.

In his midsixties, he looked like anything but a military man. Which was the point of the subterfuge. He was rumpled, shaggy, overweight, with a bushy walrus mustache and sloppy personal appearance. He was also a brilliant intelligence officer.

Wenzle operated out of the Gall Building, an

aging, slightly frayed office building located in a run-down business district of the nation's capital. His office was on the fifth floor, a suite of rooms operating under the name of the Holloman Research Institute. The institute was the publisher of "J. D. Holloman's Information Alert Bulletin," a monthly e-newsletter that went out over the Internet to subscribers. It featured timely investment and stock tips.

It was all a cover for a Dog Team way station.

There was no J. D. Holloman; rather, Doc Wenzle was J. D. Holloman. The "Information Alert Bulletin" was a real newsletter, incorporating stock market information and market trends that Wenzle gleaned from his intelligence activities. The IAB had several hundred legitimate subscribers, all unaware that it was part of the front of an ongoing covert operation.

The information must have proved accurate enough, though, since most of the subscribers stayed on the active list rather than dropping the newsletter.

Steve had had the Gall Building under observation off and on at irregular intervals for the last twenty-four hours. He detected nothing to indicate that it was the object of enemy activity.

A few moments ago he had phoned Wenzle, using an inexpensive cell he had picked up that afternoon in an electronics hardware store. The cell was unsecured, with no scrambler or encryption devices. Its featureless anonymity made it useful for Steve's purposes. No one could track him via it; when he was done he would just throw it away.

Steve had said that he had some important information to pass along. Wenzle assured him that the site was secure. Steve was across the street in a deserted doorway where he'd been keeping an eye on the Gall Building for some time as an added precaution. It looked okay, so he got moving.

This was a business district and most of the buildings had been cleared out of their workers by five p.m. It was now almost three hours later. The pedestrian traffic had thinned but not the street traffic, which remained heavy on the two-way street fronting the Gall Building. The nondescript cross street was a well-used artery for the steady flow of workers going home from their jobs in the capital's nearby extensive government office buildings.

Steve stepped out of the darkened doorway where he'd been sheltering for the last hour or so. It was the entrance to a furniture store that had gone out of business. The store was dark and empty, its display windows masked by brown paper and FOR RENT signs. A number of street-level stores and shops along the avenue were similarly shuttered. Times were tough.

Steve waited for a gap in the two-way traffic flow, then darted across the street. He wore a gray-green fur-lined trench coat, unbuttoned for quick access to the guns he wore under his sport jacket. An Army Colt .45 semiautomatic pistol, old but serviceable, was in a shoulder sling holstered under his left arm. A snub-nosed .38 revolver was in his left-hand jacket pocket. A couple of spare clips were in the right-hand pocket of his heavy tweed sport coat.

The weapons and ammo came from one of several dead-drop caches he'd prepared long ago in case of emergencies, caches hidden both here in the city and in and around Rampart County, Virginia. He'd unearthed one of the caches, supplying himself with the handguns, ammo, and several thosand dollars of cash money.

His left hand was wrapped in white gauze bandages. They left his fingers and thumb free but he didn't have much mobility in them.

In the aftermath of his escape from Crestfield, Steve had had the hand tended by a veterinaran, an acquaintance of his who owed him a favor and whom he'd kept isolated from his Dog Team contacts in anticipation of just such a situation as he now found himself in. After the veterinarian had tended the wound and patched it up, he'd pressed some pain pills on Steve despite Steve's initial reluctance to accept them. Steve had to stay sharp and didn't want to dull his senses and reflexes, but the vet convinced him that it was better to have the pills in case he needed them badly than to need them badly and not have them. Steve's Special Forces training had included learning first-aid treatment for wounds, allowing him to change the bandages and clean the wound with medical supplies the veterinarian had given him.

The bandages were a dead giveaway, so he kept the hand buried in his trench coat's deep left-hand pocket. He'd cut the bottom out of the pocket so that if he had to he could get to the .38 pocketed in his sport coat. He knew he had enough mobility in the wounded hand to work the gun; he'd already tried it out. It hurt like hell but it was doable. If it hurt that meant you weren't dead.

He missed the feel of the .32 he'd kept hidden at the small of his back, but now that that dodge was known he'd given it up. The gimmick with the .38 was new and might conceivably catch some foe unaware.

A long, slim, flat-bladed throwing knife once more reposed in a sheath strapped to his left forearm. The Morays were on to that dodge, too, but Steve said to hell with them and toted the blade. There were too many circumstances where a silent throwing knife might come in handy.

As Steve hustled across the street in the middle of the traffic flow, an oncoming car's right front fender brushed the edge of the tail of his open three-quarter-length trench coat streaming after him. The driver was halfway down the block before thinking to angrily honk his horn.

Steve liked weaving on foot through traffic; it tended to discourge shadowers. Not that anybody was following him as far as he was aware, but it was good tradecraft, just in case.

He crossed the pavement to the Gall Building lobby, went inside. It was pretty sad. The floor was covered with dirty linoleum in a faded green and pink checkerboard pattern, the walls were paneled to shoulder height in dark brown wood-looking plastic, and above that the plastered walls were painted mustard yellow.

A glass-fronted directory listed the tenants with white plastic letters on a black background. A glance told Steve that a lot of vacancies had opened up lately in the building. Another sign, as if any were needed, of the stinko economy.

The lobby was empty. No security guard or night watchman was on duty. Such amenities did not fall under the provenance of the Gall Building's cash-strapped management and owners.

That suited Steve just fine. It meant that there was no register to sign in with, even with a phony name, and no witness to remember his face and visit.

A pair of elevators stood on the right-hand side of the lobby. Steve decided to take the stairs. An elevator could be a confining metal cage; not where he wanted to be when he was on the dodge.

The fire door was on the left-hand side of the lobby. Steve went through it into the empty stairwell and started the long climb.

It was an effort. He was in top shape and ordinarily he could have scaled five floors' worth of stairs without much accelerating his heart rate. But his Crestfield ordeal and the succeeding days on the run had taken a lot out of him.

By the time he reached the fifth-floor landing he was breathing hard. His wounded hand throbbed fiercely. Each time it throbbed it sent pain waves hammering through him. He paused for a moment to catch his breath.

Steve reached under his sport coat, loosening the .45 in the shoulder sling under his left arm, in case he needed to get at it quickly.

Cracking the door open a hair, he peered into the fifth-floor hall, a long corridor lit by overhead fluorescent lights that were reflected as pale blurs in the linoleum floor. Offices lined the hall on both sides, their doors closed. Most of them had long since closed for the day, their occupants having gone home.

A light shone behind the frosted-glass door of an office at the end of the left-hand side of the corridor as seen from Steve's vantage point in the stairwell.

That was the office of Holloman Research Institute, the front maintained by Doc Wenzle to cover his covert role as Dog Team handler and case officer.

Steve started to open the fire door, then ducked back when he saw the HRI outer door open. He held the door open a hairline crack so he could see what was happening.

A man came out of the office. He wore a dark narrow-brim hat and a tan raincoat. He was a stranger to Steve.

The stranger left the outer door ajar. Steve's sight line from the landing would not permit him to see inside the office. The man in the tan raincoat crossed to the elevators, pressing the DOWN button.

A moment later, the door of one of the two elevators slid open. The man in the tan raincoat got in. He stood facing the hall, eyeing the HRI office, holding the elevator car in place by pressing its OPEN DOOR button.

A second man came out of the office. He wore a soft-fabric fisherman's hat and a brown leather jacket. He eased the outer door closed and walked briskly across the hall to the elevator and got in.

The door closed and the elevator car started downward.

Steve emerged from the landing and went down the hall to the HRI office. The outer door was open a few inches. Reaching for it, Steve smelled the reek of gasoline fumes.

He reached under his jacket, snaking out the .45. He opened the door wider, holding the gun leveled as he stepped inside.

The smell of gasoline was stronger now, choking, almost overpowering.

Beyond the outer door lay a small anteroom with a couple of plastic chairs and a side table with some magazines lined up alongside one of the walls. At the far end of the anteroom stood Wenzle's suite of offices.

Wenzle's office door was open. Inside, the lights were on.

Doc Wenzle was in. But he was out, too— permanently.

Steve had gotten there a little too late.

Wenzle sat slumped behind his desk, leaning forward, head and shoulders sprawled flat across the desktop. A bullet hole in his forehead had spilled a large quantity of blood on the desk.

The smell of blood was an undertone in the stink of gas fumes permeating the office. The reek of gas was so strong there that it stung Steve's eyes and burned his nostrils and the back of his throat.

The carpeted floor was stained dark with the stuff, saturated; visible fumes rose from it. It smelled like someone had emptied several gallons of gas in the room.

Steve started forward, stepping through the inner door. As soon as he crossed the threshold, a click sounded.

He jumped back behind the wall on one side of the doorway.

A spot of blue flame appeared on the carpet, spreading outward in a circle toward the edges of the room.

A whoomping noise followed, cueing the floor to suddenly burst into flame. Within seconds the inner office was an inferno, a fiery furnace.

Steve realized that upon entering the room he must have tripped some sort of electric-eye triggering device, causing it to detonate into flames that torched the gas-saturated space.

Heat from the conflagration poured out of the doorway. The inner office was a mass of yellow-red flames, blurring the image of the desk and Doc Wenzle's dead body slumped across it.

Nothing Steve could do for Doc now, the poor old bastard.

Greedy arms of flame reached beyond the door frame, seeking to make inroads on the outer office.

Steve scurried back into the hall. He was too late to help Wenzle but maybe not too late to stop Doc's killers.

No taking the elevators, not now when there was a fire. But he pressed the elevator's UP button anyway, as a kind of safety precaution.

Steve rushed to the fire door, hammered the palm heel of his right hand against the wall-mounted fire alarm, breaking the glass and triggering the alert. Shrill fire bells jangled throughout the building, filling it with noise.

Steve hurried down the stairs, all five flights. It was a nightmare sequence, one that seemed like it would never end. Down one flight of stairs, then another, then hit the next landing below to resume the process all over again.

No matter how good shape you're in, you can go down a staircase only so fast without running the risk of falling and maybe breaking an ankle or a leg.

The descent seemed interminable, but in reality it couldn't have taken a moment or more before Steve reached the ground-floor landing.

He reached for the knob of the fire door with his left hand, pain screaming along the nerves of the injured hand and arm as he unsealed it. He had to use his left—in his right was the .45, ready for action.

Steve kicked the fire door wide open, so that it swung back on its hinges and slammed into the outer wall.

Sure enough, just as he'd suspected, one of Doc Wenzle's killers lurked in the hall, waiting for him.

It was the guy in the brown leather jacket. He stood facing the elevator doors, gun in hand. He'd fallen for Steve's little trick of pressing the elevator button as if summoning the car to the fifth floor.

The guy turned around when the fire door crashed open but he was way behind the curve; Steve already had his gun in action and blasting.

Steve pumped a couple of slugs in the gunman, chopping him in the middle. The gunman spun and fell crashing to the floor.

It was a setup, Steve realized. The killers had come not only to eliminate Doc Wenzle but also Steve, a two-for-one play. They must have known Steve was coming up and gimmicked the scene to entrap him, too.

Too bad for them that Steve was shooting their ambush to pieces.

Gunfire boomed as a couple of slugs tore into the wall near Steve, missing him.

The second killer, the one in the tan raincoat, stood at the front of the lobby, throwing lead in Steve's direction. The gunfire was meant to cover the shooter's exit as he threw open the street door and exited the building.

Steve stopped long enough to put a bullet in the fallen gunman's head, splashing his face into wet redness—just in case he wasn't dead but still had enough life left in him to work the gun still clutched in his hand.

Steve crossed the lobby, throwing open the street door. He hesitated a beat before exiting.

Bullets ripped through the glass door, starring it in several places.

They'd been fired by the guy in the tan raincoat, who stood to the left on the sidewalk about twenty feet away.

A couple of paces away from him stood a passerby, a middle-aged woman in a brown topcoat who'd apparently happened by at the moment of the shooting. Wide, startled eyes were black buttons pasted on her doughy-white, double-chinned face.

Steve stepped outside, angling for a shot at the gunman, but the latter dashed behind the matron, sending her sprawling to the pavement in the process.

He ran, turning left and ducking into an

alley between the Gall Building and a neighboring structure.

The matron recovered from her temporary paralysis from fear to open her mouth and set to shrieking. She had a hell of a set of lungs on her and unleashed an operatic aria of screams.

Ignoring her, Steve rushed past her along the sidewalk, stopping just short of the alley mouth. Ducking low, he stuck his head and gun hand around the corner of the wall at about waist height.

The guy in the tan raincoat fired at him, blasting several shots.

He jumped back, hiding behind the cover of a Dumpster an instant before Steve returned fire.

A booming blast sounded high overhead.

The fifth floor of the Gall Building, already a mass of flames, suddenly erupted in a massive explosion.

Had the killers planted an explosive device as well as a firebomb in Wenzle's office? Or had the blaze touched off some built-in fail-safe device designed to protect the Dog Team's secret files from exposure by obliterating them?

Steve didn't know, and in either case the result would have been the same. The concussive bomb blast blew out all the windows on the fifth floor, raining flaming debris on the street scene below.

Chunks of fiery wreckage and glass shards pelted the sidewalk, none of them hitting Steve.

The terrified matron had stopped screaming long enough to crawl into a doorway and huddle there while the debris came falling down.

A few fireballs plummeted into the alley, lighting it up.

Above, oily black smoke poured out of empty window frames on the fifth floor of the Gall Building.

The debris stopped falling.

Footfalls sounded in the alley, the sound of the guy in the tan raincoat running away.

Steve ducked into the alley after him.

The alley was ten feet wide and sixty feet long, connecting to a parking lot in back of the building. It was lit by a few wall-mounted lights that left much of it in shadow.

Steve wanted to take the gunman alive. He was the only link available to the Morays and the hidden hand that lay behind them.

He blasted a shot at the fleeing man, who was at the midpoint of the alley. The guy flung himself to one side, swallowed up by a broad patch of darkness.

Steve didn't know whether he'd tagged the other or whether the guy was playing possum, lying low to lure Steve into his gunsights.

The shooter had used the Dumpster for cover earlier; two could play at that game. Crouched low, Steve entered the alley, using the blocky bulk of the Dumpster to stand between him and the shooter.

Black shadow engulfed the stretch of alley where the shooter had disappeared. No motion or sound came from it as Steve advanced soft-footed.

The scuff of shoe leather on concrete pavement sounded nearby behind Steve, raising the hairs on his neck.

Before he could turn around something punched him in the back between his shoulders, hard. Stabbing him.

Someone flipped a switch, zapping him with a massive charge of electricity. The jolt knocked Steve flat onto the paved alley floor.

The crackling charge ripped through him, paralyzing him. He couldn't move a muscle on his own will, not even to draw a breath!

He writhed in spasms on the pavement, helpless. The gun that had fallen from his hand had skittered across the concrete.

Electrified torment continued for a timeless, endless interval.

Footsteps approached, two figures nearing him, each coming from different directions.

One belonged to the guy in the tan raincoat. The other?!

The guy in the tan raincoat stooped, picked up Steve's fallen .45. He held his own gun pointed downward at Steve's head.

"He's tamed," he said.

The electric current was suddenly switched off. Steve sucked air, gasping for breath.

"Freeze, chum. Move an inch and you get another jolt," Tan Raincoat said.

The thing that had hit Steve between the shoulder blades was a plug with two sharp-pointed metal prongs. They had penetrated his garments and lodged into his flesh.

At the far end of the prongs was a pair of electric wires fifteen feet long. Their opposite end was connected to a square-shaped, boxy device with a handgrip and trigger.

A Taser!

A nonlethal weapon employed by police to subdue violent, unruly suspects by immobolizing them with a paralyzing electric charge. The Taser fired the dartlike plug with its two flesh-piercing prongs into the suspect. The wires were connected to the Taser, whose massive batteries delivered the man-stopping charge to the victim.

The Taser was now cradled in the soft, fat hands of the no longer screaming matron, the one Steve had mistaken for an innocent passerby. She'd been part of the setup, undoubtedly hiding the Taser under the voluminous folds of her topcoat.

"Nice work, Mabel," Tan Raincoat said.

"Gets 'em every time," she said, smirking. "Want I should zap him again?"

"Why not? It'll take some more of the starch out of him. Just don't give him a heart attack and kill him. We need him alive—for now."

"Too bad I can't say the same for you," a new voice announced.

It came from a dark figure who had entered the alley unobserved by Tan Raincoat and Mabel as they stood gloating over Steve.

"I don't need you alive at all, not one little bit," the stranger said.

He opened up with a pair of semiautomatic pistols, one held in each hand, pouring lead into Tan Raincoat and Mabel, filling the alley with gunfire.

Flashing muzzle flares created a strobe effect as the duo was blasted into oblivion.

The muzzle flares underlit the face of the shooter, revealing him as . . .

Kilroy!

TWELVE

The sights and sounds of Ward Thurlow being eaten alive by crocodiles filled the conference room of the penthouse suite at the top of the Imperium casino-hotel on the boardwalk at Atlantic City, New Jersey.

It was a hell of a show.

The footage was being imaged on a massive flat-screen LED TV hanging on the wall at one end of the conference room.

It was five o'clock on a Friday night, two days after Steve had somehow escaped the trap set for him at the Gall Building.

The Imperium, once one of Atlantic City's most stellar attractions, had recently fallen on hard times. It consisted of a shoebox-shaped casino building attached to a towering skyscraper hotel.

Like the rest of the gaming industry, the Imperium's receipts had fallen off drastically due to the depressed economy. Its fiscal woes were compounded by the inept management of its owner, real estate magnate and obnoxious TV personality Dudley Crimp. Dangerously overextended and already in Chapter 11 bankruptcy, Crimp had seen the recession ruin any last chances for him to recoup his fortune.

He had already been forced to take a loan from the White Tiger, a leading yakuza crime clan based in Osaka, Japan. The loan had long since been squandered, and the yakuza's oyabun, or godfather, was most rudely insistent that Crimp repay the outstanding debt.

The yakuza don't fool around. Crimp knew that if he wanted to retain possession of all his fingers and toes—and quite possibly his head— he'd better make full restitution to his White Tiger creditors, and quick.

Crimp had therefore been forced to sell his holdings in the Imperium for a song, for pennies not on the dollar but rather on the hundred-dollar bill.

The casino's new owner had moved into the casino, setting up headquarters in the luxurious penthouse suite that Crimp had built for himself in happier times.

The Imperium's new czar now sat in the penthouse conference room watching wide-eyed as rogue CIA agent Ward Thurlow was ripped to pieces by ravenous killer crocs.

The mighty master of capital, Simon E. Gunther, sat stiff-faced and motionless, eyes bulging as he watched the awesome carnage.

Gunther was in his late forties but looked

ten years younger. A mop of brown curly hair topped a face with a high, bulging forehead, brown eyes, an upturned nose, and a neatly pursed Cupid's-bow mouth. The snub nose and a scattering of pale freckles on his clean-shaven face added to his boyish aspect.

Gunther, one of Wall Street's golden boys, had scored notable achievements in the worlds of both high finance and criminal securities fraud. An investment banker for the prestigious brokerage house of Saxbee Mangold, he'd amassed a towering fortune by dint of twenty years of screwing the investors and stealing them blind. His instrument for this massive transfer of wealth from its rightful owners to himself was his overlordship of the Transworld Capital Fund, a Saxbee mutual fund that until recently had numbered among its client union and government pension funds, numerous corporate employee IRA and 401(k) plans and investments from various state treasuries, as well as thousands of mom-and-pop investors who'd trusted their hard-won nest eggs to the fund in hopes of growing them into retirement bonanzas.

The investors had finished out of the money, their Transworld mutual fund holdings now worth only a fraction of what they had been. Most of it had been transferred into secret off-shore banking accounts maintained by Gunther and the board of directors of Saxbee Mangold. The plundering had been accomplished with such complex sleight of hand and finesse that government investigators had no idea how and where the money had gone. Not that they were trying too hard to find it. The congressional legislators who'd taken office via huge campaign contributions from Saxbee pressured the investigators to cool it. The rot went clear up to the Oval Office of the White House.

By all rights Gunther should now have been sitting on top of the world. In a manner of speaking he was, occupying as he now did the palatial digs of the penthouse high atop the Imperium's lofty tower.

But there was trouble in Paradise. Gunther had the fear on him.

A few hours earlier, a small package had been delivered to him at the Imperium by private courier.

The package had been handled according to procedures set down by George Knight, Gunther's head of security. With hundreds of thousands of people having been defrauded of their life's savings by Transworld, Gunther might well become the target of a vengeful sorehead who didn't have the sense to go lie down and die.

Underlings had examined the package, inspecting it and its contents for an explosive device, even for indications that biological or chemical agents had been employed.

Once cleared, the package had been hand delivered by Knight to Gunther. Its contents consisted of a DVD in a hardened plastic case and, still more oddly, a picture postcard.

Puzzling . . .

The label had provided no clues to the sender's identity. The sender was identified as one "Peter Collinson." The name meant nothing to Gunther or Knight. The return address was a numbered room in Atlantic City's main post office building. The room was revealed to be the dead letter office, the final resting place of letters that for some reason or another never reach their intended recipients and are returned to the postal system to be filed, forgotten, and ultimately destroyed.

The picture postcard held a still more ominous aspect. It was from Lagos, Nigeria, of a sort that could be picked up at the counter of any hotel gift shop. Considering Gunther's recent shady dealings in that area and the setbacks he had suffered, he had summoned a business associate and partner in crime into the conference room for the first viewing of the DVD.

Blaise Carrollton was the founder and owner of the private security firm MYRMEX. He was middle-aged with wavy silver hair, a rosy, clean-shaven face, and the shiny, hard, dark eyes of a shark.

Only Gunther and a few trusted associates knew that rather than being safely ensconced in the tiny West European extradition-free principality of Lichtenstein, to which MYRMEX's corporate headquarters had been relocated,

Carrollton was back in the United States, in the Imperium penthouse, in fact. A number of Treasury Department agents and process servers would very much like to know that Carrollton was back in the States, where he could be subpoenaed and detained.

Gunther and Carrollton had sat down to view the DVD. Knight had loaded the DVD into the player. A big man built like a pro football lineman running slightly to fat, he had thinning, wispy blond hair and a jowly, hang-dog face enlivened by shrewd blue eyes.

The DVD had started playing, the picture bursting into view on the flat-screen TV mounted on the wall.

The footage had opened without preamble, explanation, or opening credits. A handheld cell phone camera had apparently been used to capture the sequence. It depicted a scene on the water, where a screaming man secured to the end of a long rope thrashed about in a cloudy, greenish-brown river.

Now, Carrollton started in his chair at the sight. He leaned forward, goggling, his mouth hanging open.

"Stop! Freeze the image!" he cried

Knight worked the remote, freezing the frame. Carrollton peered disbelievingly at the face of the man in the picture.

"My God! It's Thurlow!" he said.

"Thurlow—that's our man in Lagos, isn't he?" Gunther asked.

"He *was*," Carrollton said. "He disappeared

two weeks ago during that business in the Vurukoo fields. He headed the mission to, er, neutralize the two survivors who'd escaped the crash of the DIA flight."

"Let's see the rest of it," Gunther told Knight. Knight resumed playing the DVD.

The scene shifted for a moment as the camera panned to the black mud beach, showing the mass of crocodiles crowding it. The sound track was uninterrupted, Thurlow's shrieks and sobbing pleas for help continuing unabated.

The crocodiles picked themselves up from where they were lolling around in the mud and began streaming down the shore into the water. They moved surprisingly fast.

The camera returned to imaging Thurlow thrashing and screaming in the water as the crocodiles closed in on him. Surprising, too, was the amount of blood contained in a human body, as demonstrated by the red clouds that tinted the water as the crocs took Thurlow apart piece by piece.

No less surprising was how long and loudly Thurlow continued to scream even when there was so little of him left. He kept bellowing right until a crocodile bit off his head.

The DVD ended, the flat-screen TV going blank.

"Want to see it again?" Knight asked, after a pause.

"No, thanks," Carrollton said crisply, biting off the words.

Gunther, white-lipped and shaken, got up

and crossed to a sideboard where a minibar had been set up. He was so upset that he got himself a drink instead of having Knight fetch it.

Gunther splashed some bourbon in a glass and tossed it back straight, shuddering. He poured another and gulped that down. Some of the color came back in his face. He went to his chair and sank into it, staring at the blank screen.

"Well, now we know where Thurlow disappeared to—into the belly of a bunch of crocodiles," Carrollton said grimly.

"Who could have been responsible for that atrocity?" Gunther asked.

"Thurlow was hunting two men, Kilroy and Raynor. We know he got Raynor because he reported it in. Looks like Kilroy got him, though," Carrollton said.

"And how!" Knight exclaimed.

"Kilroy—that's the one who shot our Nigerian deal all to hell when he blew the head off of Derek Tayambo," Gunther said.

"We think so. There's no concrete proof but the circumstantial evidence certainly points to it," Carrollton said.

Having recovered from his initial fright at viewing the snuff footage, Gunther began to get angry. When he was angry he looked like a sullen, pouty child; he looked that way now.

"That was sloppy work, Blaise, very sloppy! Your MYRMEX people in Nigeria were responsible for getting Kilroy and you failed, costing us a great deal of money!"

Carrollton's face stiffened. "The preliminary intelligence failed to detect the fact that Kilroy was a member of the Army's Dog Team unit, a trained professional killer. That was Thurlow's fault. We were relying on him and his sources in the CIA for the background material. He was the one connected to the agency, not us. He made the mistake."

"He paid for it," Gunther said.

"Kilroy's Dog Team involvement prompted us to contract the Moray family to eliminate as many active-duty members of the unit as possible. As you well know, Simon."

"I ought to," Gunther muttered, scowling. "I had to give them a solid minority shareholding in MYRMEX before they would accept the deal."

"A small price to pay. You're still the majority stockholder in the company. You control it outright with ownership of fifty-one percent of the shares. I'm the second largest single shareholder," Carrollton said.

"Which is why you're still MYRMEX's chairman of the board. But remember, Blaise, that chairmanship is predicated on success."

"I'll stand on the record. Since contracting the Morays, they've managed to eliminate eighteen active-duty members of the Dog Team, out of twenty-five members whom we know of. Eleven members here in the States and seven members abroad. It's a small unit and it's been virtually decimated, effectively put out of business."

Carrollton went on, "What's more, by using

our Washington connections to wield the threat of public exposure of the team's activities, we've managed to checkmate the Army from retaliating in kind against us. What more do you want?"

"I want Kilroy dead!" Gunther said.

"We're working on it, Simon."

"How so, Blaise? By dangling me as live bait to flush him out into the open?"

"Frankly, yes. Here in the Imperium you're safer than the president in the Oval Office."

"That's not saying much."

"Well, maybe that was a bad choice of words," Carrollton said, shrugging. "But you've got nothing to worry about. You're here at the top of the Imperium tower, guarded by a small army of MYRMEX's finest—fifty heavily armed trigger-pullers. What's more, as your own personal private bodyguards, you've got the Morays right here at your beck and call. And no one is better motivated to want to finish off the Dogs. Remember, they've lost family to the team."

"Is that supposed to reassure me?" Gunther snapped. "I'd feel better if they were all hale and hearty and the last remaining Dogs were dead."

"This is war, Simon. You can't have a war without casualties. Besides, what do you care if some of your hired guns get smeared while protecting your interests? That's what they get paid for," Carrollton said.

That last comment caused Knight to look up from what he was doing at the DVD player and cut a hard side glance at Carrollton. Knight was unaffiliated with MYRMEX; he was directly in Gunther's employ, and he had little love for Carrollton and his private army.

Neither Gunther nor Carrollton took any notice of Knight, any more than they did of the furniture.

Gunther picked up the picture postcard from Lagos and examined it. It depicted the pink and white Arabian Nights fantasia of the presidential palace. Written in block letters on the back of the card was the message:

WISH YOU WERE HERE.

"Kilroy sent this, didn't he?" Gunther asked accusingly, as though Carrollton were responsible for the postcard and DVD.

"We think so," Carrollton said.

"So he's in the U.S.?"

"That's a fair assumption."

"Not just in the U.S. but near. Here—in Atlantic City. That's where it was sent from," Gunther said. "'Wish you were here.' That's the palace in Lagos where Kilroy shot Tayambo dead with a sniper rifle."

"Apparently."

"When he says he wishes I was there, he means he wishes I was in the same spot as Tayambo so he could shoot me dead, too."

Knight chimed in, "It could mean that he wishes you were where Ward Thurlow was."

"That's a cheery thought. He'd like to feed me alive to a bunch of crocodiles," Gunther fumed.

Knight looked away in order not to betray the glimmer of pleasure that came into his eyes at the thought of his tempermental boss being devoured by killer reptiles.

"Don't get hysterical, Simon," Carrollton soothed. "Kilroy is doing just what we want. Finding him and his last few remaining associates in a nation of 333 million is like searching for a needle in a haystack. We want him to come to us. Then we'll have him. No lone handful of ragtag Dogs, cut off from all official Army assistance, can ever get by the MYRMEX guards we've got posted all over the Imperium."

"They'd better not, because if they do you're going to be right here with me," Gunther said.

"That's why I'm here now instead of in Lichtenstein. I'm betting my life along with yours and I say it's a no-lose wager, no gamble at all," said Carrollton.

"It'd better be," Gunther fumed. He examined the mailing label on the envelope the package had come in. "What's this business about the return address being the dead letter office?"

"Some of Kilroy's twisted sense of humor, I imagine. Apart from any negative connotations a dead letter suggests, it also refers to the fact that for some time the Dog Team operated under the cover of Mercury Transport Systems, a private courier company."

"And the sender's name, 'Peter Collinson'? What's that all about?"

Carrollton scratched his head. "Beats me.

None of my people have been able to figure that one out yet. The name doesn't track with any of the known Dog operatives or aliases."

"I can shed some light on that," Knight offered.

The other two looked at him.

"'Peter Collinson' is a piece of slang from the late nineteenth and early twentieth centuries, used primarily by railroading men. It means, simply, 'nobody'—a phantom, someone who doesn't exist," Knight said.

"Where'd you pick up that nugget of information?" Carrollton demanded.

"I searched for it online," Knight said, smiling meaninglessly.

Carrollton scowled.

"Some joker, that Kilroy! A real funny man," Gunther said, his voice dripping sarcastic venom. "You could die laughing."

"Let's hope not, sir," Knight said.

The other two gave him dirty looks. A knock sounded on the conference room door. It was one of Gunther's executive assistants. Gunther told him to come in.

"Phone call for you on line five, sir," the assistant said.

"What are you bothering me with that for? I'm busy. That's what I keep you around for, to screen my calls," Gunther said.

"This sounded important, sir. It's a Dr. Dunkel."

"Dunkel? What does he want?"

"I don't know, Mr. Gunther, he wouldn't tell me. Says he'll only speak to you. An emergency, he says."

"All right, I'll take it," Gunther said. "Get out!"

The assistant exited. Gunther picked up the phone, pushed the button for line five.

"Gunther here. Who's this? Dunkel? What do you want? I sent you the check for this month—"

Gunther fell silent as the caller relayed his information. The news rocked him. He reeled, as if struck by a physical blow. Already pale, he took on a deathly white pallor.

The receiver slipped from his hands to fall clattering on the conference table. Gunther's legs folded at the knees. He sat down hard in his chair.

Carrollton went to him. "What is it, Simon? What's wrong?"

Gunther forced himself to respond:

"My wife—she's been taken!"

THIRTEEN

Earlier that Saturday afternoon, Steve sat in the passenger-side seat of the cab of a Polar Pride laundry truck parked to one side of the Dunkel Wellness Center in the township of Mantoloking in south-central New Jersey.

Blazoned on both sides of the truck was the Polar Pride logo along with its motto: "Laundry White as the Driven Snow."

Steve wore a white commander's cap with stiff black visor, a long-sleeved white tunic and pants, and a pair of black boots. He held an M-4 carbine cradled in his lap, out of sight of anyone glancing at the truck.

"They've been in there a long time," he said to the driver seated beside him.

The driver, Fred Osgood, rested his hands on the steering wheel. The truck idled, motor running.

"I don't hear any shooting yet," he said. "So far, so good."

Like Steve, Fred was a Dog Team member,

one of the last few such left alive. Since returning to the United States from Nigeria, Kilroy had managed to assemble a squad of veteran Dogs. In addition to Ireland and Osgood, he'd also collected team members Jessie Toler and Reuben Diaz, Jr.

The group had made its headquarters at a safe house in the town of Egg Harbor at the Jersey shore. Kilroy had laid out the whys and wherefores of the unprecedented onslaught that had been leveled at the Dog Team.

Behind it lay the hidden hand of financier Simon E. Gunther. Using his complete and unlimited control of brokerage house Saxbee Mangold's Transworld Capital Fund, Gunther had assumed majority ownership of private security contractor MYRMEX. Gunther kept MYRMEX founder and owner Blaise Carrollton on as company CEO.

The Transworld Capital Fund and MYRMEX worked in concert with Nigerian strongman Minister of Defense Derek Tayambo to cut a billion-dollar deal to build an oil transshipment port in Lagos. Central to the deal was the understanding that the completed port would be bought by the People's Republic of China. Rich, resource hungry, the PRC made its primary foreign goal in the Third World locking up future supplies of oil and rare minerals. The PRC had involved MYRMEX as a cutout to hide its part in the arrangement from U.S. intelligence. Once the completed port was in

Red Chinese hands, Tayambo would ensure that Nigeria's vast oil reserves would be sold exclusively to the PRC, cutting the United States off at the oil spigot.

The Defense Intelligence Agency sent an investigative team to Nigeria to probe the murky doings. The investigators had unearthed the Transworld/MYRMEX/PRC triumvirate and was about to head back home to Washington to make a full report to the Pentagon.

Rogue CIA agent Ward Thurlow, MYRMEX's man in Lagos, alerted the Gunther interests to the DIA team's threat. Gunther had ordered that the investigators be neutralized, that is, killed. Their homeward-bound plane was blown up in midair, slaying eight investigators and destroying their painstakingly amassed evidence. Kilroy and Raynor escaped the slaughter by virtue of their being away in the Vurukoo oil fields following up some investigative leads.

Raynor was killed but Kilroy escaped the net, feeding Ward Thurlow alive to the crocodiles. Kilroy had his own connections in Lagos, contacts and friends unknown to his Dog Team handlers and the CIA. They enabled him to surface in Lagos and assassinate Minister Tayambo with a sniper rifle.

Tayambo's death monkeywrenched the Transworld/PRC oil deal. Vice President Johnny Lisongu, pro-Western in sympathies and aware that Tayambo had been killed by an American assassin, thereby securing his place as the new power center in the Nigerian governing cabinet, threw out the MYRMEX contract to build the new port and the PRC oil deal, negotiating a new arrangement with Washington.

Unaware of the extent of the Dog Team's knowledge of his dirty dealings and fearing their vengeance, Gunther authorized MYRMEX CEO Blaise Carrollton to contract an elimination operation against the Dog's strike force, the active-duty field operative assassins, who numbered about two dozen in all.

Carrollton farmed the contract to Clan Moray, a family dynasty of private assassins who'd been in the murder-for-hire game for more than a century. The Morays were paid a substantial sum along with a large block of stock shares in MYRMEX, allying their fortunes with that of the company.

A traitor inside the Dog Team apparatus gave the Morays detailed inside information about their targets, the active-duty operatives. Using the arts of subterfuge, deceit, and sudden death, the family killed some eighteen Dog Team members, all of them unaware that they had been fingered for death.

Gunther's go-betweens communicated to Pentagon bigs the message that the Army's assassination unit's existence would remain a secret as long as the military took no action against Gunther, Transworld, or MYRMEX. Otherwise the explosive information would be leaked to Transworld's many friendly contacts in the media, who would splash it all throughout the mainstream media, creating a firestorm of negative press that would adversely impact not only the Army and the U.S. military but the nation's vital national security interests throughout the world.

The Army's high command seethed at the blackmail but was forced to go along, at least until it could find some way of neutralizing Gunther and MYRMEX that would not unleash a torrent of damaging revelations about the Dog Team.

So much Kilroy had learned from his extensive contacts in the military and intelligence worlds, all of them confirmed patriots like himself who chafed at the bonds of unholy blackmail being forced on them by the Gunther/Transworld crowd. Many of them quietly, covertly helped Kilroy to gather the personnel and material for a counterstrike.

Having assembled Steve Ireland, Jessie Toler, Fred Osgood, and Reuben Diaz, Jr. and gathered them in the Egg Harbor safe house, Kilroy detailed the situation to them. When he had finished, Osgood said, "I get it—we've got to kill Gunther and his pals."

Kilroy shook his head. "First, we've got to hit them where it hurts, in the source of their power—their pocketbooks." He then added, "Then we'll kill them."

Which is why Steve and Fred were disguised as Polar Pride laundrymen early Saturday afternoon.

So were Kilroy, Toler, and Diaz.

They had stolen a Polar Pride truck and

uniforms to invade the precincts of the Dunkel Wellness Center, an exclusive private clinic in New Jersey. The center was a place where rich folks sent their alcoholic, drug-abusing, or otherwise dysfunctional relatives and loved ones to be dried out and cleaned up.

Its founder, Dr. Ernst Dunkel, was none too particular about medical ethics when it came to the care and release of his charges as long as the checks from their relatives cleared. Families who had problem members best kept out of the public eye for one reason or another could pay and pay well to have the offending parties committed to the clinic and kept as prisoners under virtual lock and key for an indefinite amount of time—years even—with no hope of escape or release.

Such a captive was Faye Blaylock Gunther, the estranged wife of Simon E. Gunther. An attractive and intelligent woman of a certain age, she had made the mistake of too strenuously objecting to her husband's countless infidelities. Worse, she had protested his appropriation and misuse of her own family funds, a mountain of money and assets that was the source of Gunther's sudden and dramatic rise to the ranks of the superrich.

Faye was a Blaylock, an old-money dynasty that had made its pile back at the turn of the nineteenth century in the days of the robber barons, using railroads and timber and mining interests to acquire a multi-million-dollar fortune. In the twentieth century, shrewd management and investments had pyramided that sum into a billion-dollar bonanza.

As the last living heir of the Blaylocks, Faye was the inheritor of that fabulous wealth. As such she had been wooed and wed by Gunther. But when she made the mistake of objecting to his plundering of her family bequest, he took steps to neutralize her.

It was a tricky problem. Faye's death would provide no solution. Her fortune was bound up in trusts and legal instruments that ensured that no spouse could profit by her death. If she died, the money would go to a tax-free charitable foundation created by the Blaylocks. Not only would Gunther fail to collect a red cent, but he would also be forced to provide an accounting of how some of those monies had been spent, a disclosure that would send him to a federal penitentiary for the rest of his life.

But if Faye was declared not of sound mind, her husband could force a power of attorney that would let him control her fabulous megafortune without having to account for it to any probing outsiders.

Enter Dr. Dunkel. Working in connivance with the corrupt medico, Gunther had his wife virtually abducted, imprisoned in the clinic, and declared insane, allowing him to take control of her assets.

That had happened five years ago. For five long years Faye Blaylock Gunther had languished as an inmate at the Dunkel Wellness Center. The first year went by in a chemical haze, as Dunkel and his minions kept her sedated with large doses of mind-numbing tranquilizers, the sort given to psychotically violent patients.

After that first year or so, Faye was sufficiently tamed so that the dosages were lessened. She was kept in a locked room but allowed the minimal comfort of books, music, and television. Several foredoomed escape plans resulted in the revocation of privileges and the renewal of massive drugging.

In the last two years, she had given up all attempts at escape, although the hope of ultimate freedom someday helped her keep her sanity. Which wasn't easy, being surrounded as she was by genuinely disturbed if not crazy inmates.

When an orderly arrived this Saturday afternoon to escort her to Dr. Dunkel's office, Faye had no idea what it was all about. She asked no questions, submitting meekly as the brawny orderly gripped her upper arm as he led her through winding fluorescent clinic corridors to Dr. Dunkel's office.

Surprisingly Ms. Prymm, Dr. Dunkel's receptionist, was absent from her post in the medic's office. In her place was a young woman who looked like she was barely out of her teens.

She was Jessie Toler—thirty, but looking ten years younger than her actual age. She was five and a half feet tall, weighed about 115 pounds, and had curly brown hair, a youthful freckled face, and a slim physique. She was a trained Dog Team assassin.

The next deviation from standard routine came when the orderly balked at handing over Faye without an okay from Dr. Dunkel. Apparently the proper forms and protocol had not been followed.

When the orderly became obstinate, Jessie produced a gun and shot him. It was a dart gun, shooting a tranquilizer dart. The orderly took a few steps forward, staggered, reeling, and fell unconscious to the floor.

"Do you want to get out of this place?" Jessie asked.

"Yes," Faye said.

"Do exactly as I say and you'll walk out of here in ten minutes."

Jessie locked the outer office door, leading a dazed and bewildered Faye into Dr. Dunkel's inner office, where another surprise awaited.

Dr. Dunkel and his receptionist, Ms. Prymm, were handcuffed and gagged with strips of duct tape pasted across their mouths. They were being guarded by two white-clad men whom she would subsequently learn were Kilroy and Diaz.

Not only was Ms. Prymm gagged and handcuffed, she'd been stripped down to her underclothes and stocking feet. Jessie handed Faye a pile of folded garments that belonged to Ms. Prymm.

"Put these on," Jessie told Faye.

"Who are you people?" Faye asked.

"Friends."

Kilroy had designated Jessie as Faye's handler, not knowing the woman's mental state after years of confinement and thinking that Faye would feel less threatened if her primary contact was a woman.

Faye proved to be surprisingly resilient. Recovering from her stunned surprise, she quickly pulled on Ms. Prymm's blouse, jacket, and skirt. The shoes were too large but Faye solved that by stuffing wadded paper into the toes and heels.

Kilroy and Diaz herded Dunkel and Prymm into a supply closet and locked them in. Then they, Jessie, and Faye exited the office, locking the outer door behind them. The three Dog Team members were armed with real guns that they kept concealed as they escorted Faye across the hall and down the stairs to the front entrance. They were prepared to use them but didn't have to, because none of the few passing staffers took any interest in them.

Seeing the group emerge from the building, Steve went around to the back of the stolen laundry truck, opened the door. Faye, Jessie, Kilroy, and Diaz got inside, and Steve shut the door behind them.

The laundry truck rolled down the long drive to the main gate. The guard raised the electronically controlled bar gate, opening it. He responded with a cheerful wave to driver Fred Osgood's two-finger salute.

The truck drove away with Faye inside it.
It was as simple as that.

At ten p.m. that same Saturday night, Steve
breezed into the Imperium casino-hotel.

He was in pretty important company. Seated
in the back of a chauffeured stretch limousine
with Steve were General Lucian "Vic" Vickery,
U.S. Army (Ret.) and C. August Villard, Esquire.

Vickery, a much decorated military man
who'd served in combat in the first and second
Iraq wars and Afghanistan, was a member of
the MYRMEX board of directors. He'd been
put in as a figurehead and kept out of the loop
regarding the company's nefarious doings.

He was back in the loop now. Big-time.

Villard was one of the nation's leading corporate lawyers, specially recruited for the occasion. A briefcase filled with legal documents
rested across his knees.

The limo was followed by a second, similar
vehicle. In it were six smart lawyers from Villard's blue-chip Manhattan legal firm.

Anticipating a foray from Kilroy, the Imperium had been closed to the public, its staff
given the night off. The casino swarmed with
heavily armed MYRMEX guards. None of whom
dared resist the entrance of General Vickery
and Counselor Villard. The combination of a
MYRMEX board director and a high-powered
New York City lawyer baffled the gun-toting
brigade.

Following in the wake of the twin dynamos was Steve and Villard's battery of six lawyers.

They were deep into the casino when their approach was temporarily balked by Tom Bland, head of the security detail.

Villard had his lawyers serve Bland with legal papers.

"To save time I'll explain them to you," Villard said. "What they mean is that control of Transworld Capital Fund and all its assets, most definitely including MYRMEX, has been assumed by its rightful owner, Faye Blaylock. Formerly known as Faye Blaylock Gunther. She no longer wishes to be known by her married name."

"MYRMEX being one of her assets, she further deposes Blaise Carrollton from his position as CEO of the company and installs General Lucian Vickery in his place. That means you're taking orders from me from now on, sonny, and if you want to keep your overpaid post, you'll do as I say and damn quick!" said Vickerly, clearly relishing the assumption of command and the authority that goes with it.

It was all sewed up neat, proper, and legally. Faye, currently being guarded in a safe house by Jessie and Diaz, as well as a cadre of retired Special Forces and SEAL team members, had signed the paperwork, all of which had been prepared well in advance by Villard's law firm. Once she'd affixed her signature to the documents, they'd become legal and binding.

The higher echelon of Army brass at the

Pentagon, not without its own set of powerful friends and assets and resentful of Gunther's blackmailing, had worked with Kilroy and friends to lower the boom on the financier and his creatures.

Counselor Villard handed the dazed MYRMEX security chief another set of documents.

"This is an injunction freezing all Simon E. Gunther's assets, revoking his control over them and reverting all rights to their original and legal owner, Faye Blaylock," Villard said.

"Gunther, Carrollton, and their crowd are going to the federal pen for the rest of their natural lives. Unless you want to join them, you'll fall in line and hop to it," General Vickery said.

Bland, no one's fool, knew which side of his bread had the butter on it. Snapping to attention in a rigid brace he hadn't held since his days as a West Point cadet, he said, "Yes, sir! Awaiting orders, sir!"

"Now you're talking," the general said, smiling wolfishly.

A short time later, an unusual scene developed in the Imperium penthouse tower as the squad of MYRMEX guards posted there to reinforce the Morays in protecting Gunther and Carrollton deserted their posts and thronged in front of the penthouse elevator.

Gunther stood there in slack-jawed disbelief, the Morays in simmering, seething rage.

"Stop! What the hell do you think you're

doing?!" Carrollton screamed at the MYRMEX squad.

"We've been ordered to stand down and report to the lobby," said the squad leader.

"Ordered? By whom?"

"By Tom Bland, our unit commander."

"Bland? Bland works for me, you idiot! I own this company!"

"Not anymore. You've been fired. We're working for General Vic Vickery now. And I don't mind telling you that after some of the stuff I've seen around here, it'll be a pleasure," the squad leader said.

"You're fired!"

"You can't fire me. You're the one who's out of a job, bub," the squad leader said.

He and his men got into the elevator car. Carrollton was still shrieking obscenities at them after the door closed and the car started its high-speed plunge to the lobby.

Gunther put a hand against the wall to steady himself and keep from falling.

"I think I'm going to be sick," he said.

Clan Moray—Jules, Olcott, Lillian, and Skye's twin brother, Rory—exchanged significant glances.

"The world's gone mad!" Carrollton frothed, spewing saliva from his lips, his face beet red. He looked like he was going to have a stroke. "What's happening, Gunther?"

"It's Faye," Gunther said in a near whisper, his face expressing a look of stunned incredulity mingled with dawning realization. "That's why they snatched Faye from Dunkel's clinic," he said.

"I don't understand—"

"Don't you see, Carrollton? Everything I own was bought with Blaylock money! As long as I had power of attorney while she was safely locked up in the nuthouse, nobody could touch me! But now that's she's loose and able to get her own lawyers, she's moving to retake control of her property!" Gunther shrieked.

Carrollton staggered as if struck, reeling like a drunken man.

The Morays went into hasty family council, standing off by themselves, away from Gunther and Carrollton.

In the lobby, the elevator disgorged the MYRMEX squad who'd been guarding the penthouse. The squad leader reported to Bland for further orders.

Catching Steve's eye, General Vickery nodded significantly.

"All clear," Steve said into a radio handset, transmitting his message.

"Acknowledged," was Kilroy's response.

Several minutes later a black helicopter flew in from the west, closing on the Imperium tower. It was a modified Apache chopper bearing no identifying markings or registry numbers.

It had been "borrowed" from a nearby Army base whose personnel had been ordered to stand down and do nothing after their commander

had received a scrambled phone call from a
high-ranking officer attached to the office of the
Army's Chief of Staff. No record of the message
existed; officially it had not happened.

The result was that the copter, containing a
pilot, Kilroy, and Osgood, was now closing on
the Imperium tower.

In the penthouse, Clan Moray was restive,
sullenly rebellious. The Morays darted hard
looks at Gunther and Carrollton.

Gunther reached a decision.

"There's only one thing to do: Faye must
die! With her dead, my attorneys can legally tie
up ownership of the assets long enough for us
to acquire enough funds for a getaway!" he
declared.

"Before we do that, we have to know where
Mrs. Gunther is," Jules said, his voice omi-
nously gentle. "Do you know where she is, Mr.
Gunther?"

"I can find out! I've still got sources left,
there's still time to save the situation—"

Gunther had to shout to be heard over the
racketing drone of the approaching helicopter.

Suddenly the black helicopter dropped into
view, nose pointed at the long rectangular plate-
glass window set in the penthouse's west wall.

Seen from the cockpit, the penthouse was
like an exhibit under glass, a well-lit dollhouse
where Gunther, Carrollton, and the Morays
stood out in clear view.

Kilroy said, "Do it!"

The pilot thumbed a red button in the control handle, loosing a blast from the copter's bow-mounted chain gun.

The devastation was enormous as the chain gun streamed high-velocity rounds through the plate-glass window and into the penthouse.

Glass disintegrated along with flesh and blood as the chain gun scoured the penthouse with hundreds of rounds in a matter of seconds.

A scythe of lead harvested the Morays and Carrollton.

Gunther was turned into hamburger and the hamburger turned into holes and blue smoke.

The fusillade ended; the penthouse had become a slaughterhouse.

Rising, the black helicopter touched down on a helipad on the tower's flat roof. Kilroy and Osgood, outfitted with flak jackets and armed with M-4s and grenades, stormed the rooftop entrance, descending to the penthouse for the mopping up.

Quick reflexes and sheer luck had combined to spare Jules and his nephew, Rory, from the slaughter; the rest of the clan was dead, shredded and pulverized. Jules and Rory crashed through a fire door, raced down the stairs in search of escape.

They hadn't gotten very far when they met Steve on the landing, where he'd posted himself to forestall any such escapees.

Steve opened up with the M-4, cutting them down.

Jules spun, falling sideways over the handrail and dropping into the stairwell to plummet several hundred feet, bouncing off rails and stair edges before pancaking on hard concrete at the bottom of the shaft.

An instant's realization of how much Rory resembled his twin sister, Skye, flashed through Steve's head even as he fired into Rory's face, obliterating it.

In the penthouse, Kilroy and Osgood prowled the scene, examining the bodies. Some were beyond recognition; all were in a complete state of death.

"Don't shoot; I think this belongs to you," a voice said from inside the conference room, which had been out of the firing line and escaped the devastation.

Kilroy and Osgood covered the newcomer with their M-4s. The speaker was George Knight and he was not alone. He led out another man at gunpoint.

"No tricks, mister. Lose that gun," Kilroy warned.

"I'm putting it down now that you've got him covered. This is a very tricky fellow here," Knight said.

"Who're you?"

"George Knight. I used to work for Gunther, but I quit."

No need for Kilroy or Osgood to inquire the identity of Knight's prisoner. They knew him all too well.

Emerging from the stairwell, Steve entered.

He stopped in amazement when he saw the captive.

"Doc Wenzle!" he gasped.

Wenzle stood there with a hangdog look on his face, eyes downcast, mustache drooping, the corners of his mouth turned down.

"I saw you die," Steve said, amazed.

"You saw a look-alike," Kilroy said. "I thought something wasn't kosher about the setup at the Gall Building. The ambushers could have killed you, but instead they went to great pains to take you alive. Why?

"It all makes sense now. You were going to be turned over to the authorities so you could testify that you'd seen ol' Doc here die. If he was thought dead he wouldn't have to worry about the Dogs or anybody else looking for him. That's the way you worked it, eh, Doc?"

"Pretty much," Wenzle admitted.

"He's been stooging for Gunther and Carrollton all along, feeding them inside information," Knight confirmed.

"We'll take him from here," Kilroy said. "You go downstairs and report to General Vickery—and tell him Kilroy sent you."

"Will do, and thanks," Knight said.

Kilroy, Osgood and Steve, along with their prisoner, Wenzle, climbed the stairs to the rooftop helipad and boarded the black helicopter. It lifted off, flying out to sea.

When it was a couple of miles out and a thousand feet above the ocean, it hovered in place, waiting.

"I trusted you, Doc. Why'd you do it?" asked Steve.

"It was that damned investment tipsheet I was running as part of my cover. Everybody was making money on it and I fooled myself into believing my own bullshit. I invested everything I had and lost it all when the stock market crashed. I would have had to retire with nothing but my Army pension, to live in some trailer park eating off food stamps," Wenzle said, as if that explained it all.

"Millions of people live in trailer parks with little money without betraying their friends, teammates, and country," Steve said.

"But you won't be one of them, Doc," Kilroy added.

Wenzle shrugged. He didn't start pleading for his life until Kilroy opened the helicopter's side hatch, unsealing an exit to empty air, a black sea, and oblivion.

Wenzle babbled, sobbing and shrieking, shouting that he knew plenty about Gunther's dirty deals and hidden assets and how they could all be rich if only they'd spare his life.

Kilroy, tiring of his noise, stuffed a grenade in Wenzle's mouth. He had to shout to be heard over the rotor's propwash.

"Go to hell, Doc! And tell 'em Kilroy sent you!"

Kilroy pulled the pin of the grenade crammed between Wenzle's jaws and kicked him out of the hatch into eternity.

It was a long way down but Wenzle blew up before hitting the water.

The black helicopter flew west.

The battle was over, but the war against America's enemies abroad—and, more dangerously, at home—will never end as long as the republic endures.

Eternal vigilance, and death to the foe!

There's a new President of the United States . . . a virulent left-wing socialist who's dismantling the military . . . decommissioning America's anti-missile system and our nuclear weapons. . . .

He orders all domestic drilling and refining of oil to stop. . . . He also orders that no oil can be imported so as to "force scientists to develop a new source of green energy. . . ."

His plan is a massive failure. The United States is plunged into darkness. . . . Airplanes, cars, trucks, trains are idled. Supermarkets are empty. Three quarters of Americans are facing starvation.

But the worst is yet to come.

Islamic terrorists, exploiting the republic's weakness, detonate three nukes. When the government totally collapses, the extremists take over, renaming America the "Islamic Republic of Enlightenment." The people's choice is simple: submit to radical Islam or die.

Army major and helicopter pilot Jake Lantz is not going down without a fight. With a band of eight loyal soldiers, Lantz will fight off bands of roving thugs and an "Army of Allah" who attack them by land and by sea.

Jake Lantz is going to take back America. No matter what the cost.

ONE

Major Jake Lantz was thirty years old. A helicopter pilot and flight instructor in the Army Aviation School at Fort Rucker, Alabama, he was in the peak of physical condition, recently scoring a perfect 300 on his latest PT test, maxing out on the three required events: push-ups, sit-ups, and two-mile run. A not too prominent scar on his right cheek, the result of a shrapnel wound in Afghanistan, ran like a bolt of lightning from just below his eye to the corner of his mouth. He had blue eyes, and he wore his light brown hair closely cropped, in the way of a soldier.

Jake, who was a bachelor, lived alone in a three-bedroom ranch-style house on Baldwin Court in Ozark, Alabama, the town that proudly bills itself as the "Home of Fort Rucker." He had kept the heat down during the day to save on his gas bill. Now he shivered as he turned it up.

After stripping out of his flight suit, Jake pulled on a pair of sweatpants and a red sweat-shirt, emblazoned with the word ALABAMA across the front. He had not gone to school at Alabama but had become a big fan of University of Alabama football.

Checking the digital clock on his dresser, he saw that he had but one minute left until the program he wanted to watch came on, so he hurried into the living room, settled down on the couch, picked up the remote, and clicked it toward the TV.

The initials *GG* appeared on the screen, and then the voice-over introduced the show.

From New York! It's the George Gregoire show! And now, here is your host, George Gregoire!

The *GG* monogram moved into the back-ground and George Gregoire, with his signature crew-cut blond hair, slightly chubby face, and toothy smile, greeted his television audience.

Hello, America!
You are not going to want to miss the show today. I have information that—if I had been able to verify before the election last November—might have saved our country the anguish, turmoil, and trouble we are going to go through over

the next four years under President-elect Mehdi Ohmshidi.

In fact, I will say it here and now, this could be grounds for impeachment. Can a president be impeached, even before he assumes office? I don't know, but if the men and women in the House and Senate would put our country ahead of party, they might just want to think about this.

Here is a video, recently surfaced, of President-elect Mehdi Ohmshidi giving an address to the OWG. The OWG stands for One World Government. Ohmshidi is— well, let's just let the video speak for itself.

The video was somewhat grainy, obviously taken not by a camera for broadcast, but by a small, personal camera. Nevertheless, it was quite clearly President-elect Mehdi Ohmshidi standing at a podium addressing a rather sizeable crowd. Many in the crowd were holding signs, saying such things as:

U.S. Is an Obsolete Concept

One People, One World, One Government

No More Flags, No More Wars

Patriotism Is Jingoistic.

Ohmshidi began to speak and because the sound wasn't of the best quality, his words were superimposed in bright yellow, over the picture.

I see a world united! A world at peace! A world where there are no rich and there are no poor, a world of universal equality and brotherhood.

Such a world will surely come, my friends, but it will never be as long as we are divided by such things as religion, patriotism, the greed of capitalism, and the evil of so-called honorable military service. There is nothing honorable about fighting a war to advance one nation's principles over another's. One people, one world, one government!

Ohmshidi's closing shout was met by thunderous applause and cheers from the audience.

The picture returned to George Gregoire on his New York set.

The question of Ohmshidi's membership in the OWG was raised during the election, but spokesmen for Ohmshidi said that it was merely a flirtation he had entered into when he was in college.

Really?

Ohmshidi graduated from UC Berkeley twenty-one years ago. I'm going to bring the video up again, in freeze-frame. I want you to look at the sign on the curtain behind him.

In freeze-frame, on the curtain behind the speaker's stand were the words WELCOME TO THE GOVERNMENT CONVENTION.

Beneath the welcome sign were the opening and closing dates of the convention, June 6— June 10. The year was two years ago.

"Jake, are you in here?" a woman's voice called from the front door.

Jake picked up the remote and muted the TV. "In here, Karin," he called back.

Karin Dawes was a captain, an Army nurse, who was still wearing her uniform. She had short black hair, brown eyes, an olive complexion, and the same body she had when she was a college cheerleader. She was also a world-class marathoner who had just missed qualifying to represent the United States in the last Olympics. Seeing George Gregoire on the silent TV screen, Karin chuckled.

"You're watching Gregoire. Of course, it's six o'clock. What else would you be watching?"

"You should watch him," Jake said. "Maybe you would learn something."

"I do watch him," Karin said. "As much time as I spend over here with you, how can I help but watch him?"

"Ha! Now I know why you spend so much time over here. Here I thought it was my charm. Now I find out it's just so you can watch George Gregoire."

"I confess, you are right," she said. She leaned over to kiss him, the kiss quickly deepening.

"Damn," Jake said, when they separated. "That's what I call a greeting. Do I sense a possibility that this could go further?"

"How can it go any further?" Karin asked. "It's at least half an hour before Gregoire is over, isn't it?"

Jake picked up the remote again, and turned the TV off.

"You're sure I'm not taking you away from George Gregoire?" Karin teased. "I certainly wouldn't want to be accused of alienation of affection."

"Woman, you talk too damned much," Jake said, kissing her again. "Besides," he said, "I've got a TV in the bedroom. I can always watch him while—"

"You try that, Major, and you'll have George Gregoire in bed with you before I split the sheets with you again," Karin said, hitting him playfully on the shoulder. Jake laughed out loud, then put his arm around her as they went into the bedroom.

There was an ease in their coupling, the assurance of being comfortable lovers who knew each other well, and yet their relationship was not so stale that it couldn't still be fresh with new discovery. Outside, the wind was blowing hard, and Jake could hear the dry rattle of the leafless limbs of an ancient oak.

* * *

Afterward they lay together under the covers, her head on his shoulder, his arm around her, his hand resting on her naked thigh. It was, as always, a feeling of total contentment.

"Jake?"

"Yes, my love?"

"Will we always have this? I don't mean are we going to get married, or anything like that. I just mean, will we always have this sense of joie de vivre?"

"Is there any reason why we shouldn't?"

"I don't know," Karin admitted. "I know I tease you about watching George Gregoire all the time, and about listening to all the right-wing radio shows. But, what if they are right? What if the country has made a big mistake in electing Ohmshidi?"

"There is no what if," Jake said. "We did make a big mistake. Well, we didn't. I'm not a part of the we, because I didn't vote for him."

"I didn't either."

Jake raised his head and looked down at her. "What? You, Miss Liberal Incarnate? You didn't vote for him?"

"I couldn't bring myself to vote for him," she said. "Not when I knew the way you felt about it."

Jake kissed her on the forehead. "Maybe there is some hope for you yet," he said.

"But you didn't answer my question. Will we always have this?"

A sudden gust of wind caused the shutters to moan.

When there was an uncomfortable gap in the conversation that stretched so long that Karin knew Jake wasn't going to answer, she changed the subject.

"I wonder if it's going to snow."

"Don't be silly," he said. "It never snows in Ozark, Alabama."

There were three inches of snow on the ground the next morning as Jake drove the ten miles into Fort Rucker. Because snow was so rare here—it had been fifteen years since the last snow—neither Ozark nor Dale County, had the equipment to clean the roads. As a result, Jake drove slowly through the ruts that had been cut in the snow by earlier cars. He returned the salute of the MP at the Ozark gate, then drove down Anderson Road, which, like the streets in Ozark, was still covered with snow.

As Chief of Environmental Flight Tactics, Jake had his own marked parking slot, though the sign was covered with snow. He exchanged salutes with a couple of warrant officer pilots as he covered the distance between his car and the front door of the building, which held not only the offices of the faculty but also classrooms for the ground school.

"Major, I thought you told me that it never snowed in Southern Alabama," Clay Matthews said. Sergeant Major Matthews was Jake's right-hand man, the noncommissioned officer in charge of EFT.

"It doesn't," Jake said. "Disabuse yourself of any idea that this white stuff you see on the ground is snow. It's just a little global warming, that's all."

"Right," Clay said with a little chuckle. "Oh, Lieutenant Patterson called from General von Cairns's office. The general wants you to drop by sometime this morning."

"What's my schedule?"

"You don't have anything until thirteen hundred."

"All right, maybe I'll drop by his office now. I'm not surprised he wants to see me. I told him he wouldn't be able to run this post without my help."

"Yes, sir, that's what I tell everyone about Environmental, too," Clay said. "You couldn't run the place without me."

Jake chuckled. "Yeah, well, the difference is, I'm just shooting off my mouth when I say that about the general. But when you say that about me, you're right."

Like Ozark, Fort Rucker had no snow removal equipment. But it did have a ready supply of manpower, and there were several enlisted men, under the direction of a sergeant, clearing off the parking lot and shoveling the sidewalks at the post's headquarters. Because of that, Jake was able to walk from his car to the building without getting his boots wet.

Lieutenant Phil Patterson was on the phone when Jake stepped into the outer office, but he hung up quickly, then stood.

"Good morning, Major," he said. "Just a moment and I'll tell the general you are here."

"Thanks."

First Lieutenant Phil Patterson was a West Point graduate who had recently completed flight school. Jake remembered him as bright, eager, and well coordinated when he was a student going through the Environmental Flight Tactics phase of his training. Patterson had wanted an overseas assignment out of flight school, and was disappointed when he was chosen to stay at Fort Rucker as the general's aide de camp. But, he was a first lieutenant in a captain's slot, so the assignment wasn't hurting his career any.

Patterson stepped back out of the general's office a moment later. "The general will see you, sir."

Jake nodded his thanks, then stepped into the general's office. Major General Clifton von Cairns was pouring two cups of coffee.

"Have a seat there on the sofa, Jake," the general said. Jake had served in Iraq with von Cairns when he had been a captain and von Cairns had been a colonel. That was von Cairns's second time in Iraq; he had also been there during Operation Desert Storm.

"As I recall, you like a little bit of coffee with your cream and sugar," von Cairns said as he prepared the coffee.

"Yes, sir, thank you."

Carrying the two cups with him, von Cairns handed the one that was liberally dosed with cream and sugar to Jake. "I'm sorry I don't have any root beer," von Cairns said. "That is your drink, isn't it?"

"I like a root beer now and then," Jake said.

"Yes, I remember your 'beer' run when we were in Iraq," von Cairns said.

Jake's preference for root beer was well known by everyone who had ever worked with him. What the general was referring to was the time Jake had made a run to Joint Base Balad for beer and soft drinks. Beer wasn't actually authorized due to cultural concerns and was officially banned by the military, but the civilian contractors weren't constrained by such rules and were a ready source of supply for the army. But Jake had come back with only one case of beer and nineteen cases of root beer in the helicopter. He was never asked to make a beer run again.

"How many students do you have in your cycle right now?" the general asked.

"I have twelve."

"Can you expedite them through? Double up on the flight hours?"

"Yes, sir, I suppose I could. It would mean rescheduling some of the ground schooling."

"I want you to do that," von Cairns said. He took a swallow of his coffee before he spoke again.

"Jake, I'm not much for politics—I've always thought that as a professional soldier I should leave the politics to others. But I don't mind telling you, this new man we're about to swear in scares the hell out of me. I've heard some disturbing talk from some of my friends at DA. They're afraid he's going to start cutting our budget with a hatchet. If we don't get this cycle through quickly, we may not get them through at all."

"Surely he wouldn't halt flight training, would he?" Jake asked. "So much of the Army is now oriented around aviation."

"Did you watch George Gregoire last night?" von Cairns asked.

"I rarely miss it."

"You might remember when Gregoire showed Ohmshidi speaking to the OWG group he said, and I quote, 'the evil of so-called honorable military service.' This man doesn't just distrust the military, he hates the military. And he is about to become our commander in chief."

"I understand, General," Jake said. "I'll get schedules revamped as quickly as I can."

"You are a good officer, Jake. Would that I had a hundred just like you. It's a pleasure to have you in my command."

"And I am honored to serve under you, General."

General von Cairns stood up then, a signal

that the meeting was over. Jake stood as well and started to leave.

"Jake, are you still seeing that nurse? What is her name?"

"Karin Dawes, sir. Captain Karin Dawes."

"Yes, she's the one I pinned the Bronze Star on last month, isn't she? She's a good woman. You could do worse."

TWO

Hello, America.

On this last night before we swear in our new president, I would like for us to take inventory of just where we are in this country.

Four decades of social engineering have begun to accrue in such a way as to presage disaster for the U.S.

Gregoire held his hands over his head and waved them as he rolled his eyes.

This is not just the ravings of "mad" George Gregoire. No, sir, and no, ma'am. Events over the last several years have borne me out.

Consider this. Stringent environmental laws have inhibited drilling in new fields for domestic oil. Those same laws have also limited refining capacity and dictated exotic cocktail blends of fuel for certain parts of the country. Even during times of critical fuel shortages, these blends cannot be transshipped from region to region.

Automobile companies are mandated CAFE standards and unnecessary safety features that add thousands of dollars to the base price of cars.

Do you remember when we were young, how eagerly we looked for the new cars each year?

Gregoire changed the tone of his voice, mimicking the excitement:

"Have you seen the new Ford? Yes, but wait until you see the new Chevy."

He was silent for a moment, masterfully playing his audience.

Tell me, America, when is the last time you greeted the new models with anything more than a yawn?

And have you noticed that fewer and fewer models are being introduced now? Proud names such as Plymouth, Oldsmobile, and Pontiac Trans Am—cars that we once lusted after, cars with style and performance, are no more.

He began to sing:

What a thrill to take the wheel, of my brand new Oldsmobile.

America, we have had a century-old deep and abiding love affair with cars, but now we find them boring. We look back on the cars of the fifties and sixties with a reverent nostalgia, and like most nostalgia, this is an unrequited love—we will never return to those days. Do you remember those yesterdays when we were young? Do you remember the sweetness of life then, like rain upon the tongue?

He began to sing Roy Clark's "Yesterday, When I Was Young."

Oh, and how is this for intelligence? In California, federal courts, in order to preserve a two-inch inedible fish, have restricted the flow of water into some of the most productive agricultural areas in the country. And since California produces nearly fifty percent of the nation's fruits, nuts, and vegetables, this water restriction is already having a drastic impact on the market price.

Government interference with bank lending has caused the housing market to go bust, resulting in the loss of billions of dollars in personal equities across the country.

Gregoire, who was standing now, stuck his hands in his pockets and looked at the floor, silent for a long moment before he spoke again. The camera came in tight on his face so he could give the audience his most sincere look.

My friends, this is the country that elected Mehdi Ohmshidi, a naturalized American born forty-seven years ago in Islamabad, Pakistan. I can only pray that we survive this monumental mistake.

Thursday, January 19

"All right, Candidate Lewis," Jake told his flight student. "We've just received word from previous flights that the LZ is bracketed by small-arms fire from your two-seven-zero, and shoulder-launched ground-to-air missiles from your nine-zero. How are you going to avoid the ground fire?"

"Make the approach below their field of fire, sir," the warrant officer candidate replied.

"Make it so," Jake said, mimicking Captain Picard of *Star Trek.*

As WOC Lewis started his descent, Jake saw a flock of geese approaching from the right.

"Watch the geese on your ninety," Jake said.

"I see them," Lewis answered. Jake pulled collective to try to go over them, but the geese were making the same maneuver.

"Damn!" Lewis shouted as several of the geese collided with the helicopter. Blood and feathers from those that hit the main rotor suddenly appeared on the windshield. There was also a sudden and severe vibration at the same time they could hear the high-pitched whine of the tail rotor driveshaft spinning without any resistance.

"I've got it!" Jake shouted, taking the controls.

There was a loud bang as the tail rotor and a part of the tail fin separated from the aircraft. The center of gravity pitched forward and, without the antitorque action of the tail rotor, the helicopter began to spin to the right. Instinctively, Jake depressed the left antitorque pedal to halt the spin, even as he knew that without the tail rotor, it would be ineffective.

The spin was much faster than anything Jake had ever experienced, and earth and sky blended into a whirling pattern that made it impossible to separate one from the other.

Out of the corner of his eye, Jake saw Candidate Lewis start to grab the cyclic.

"Hands off!" Jake screamed.

They were about seventy-five feet above ground and had already spun around at least fifteen times. Jake knew he needed to kill the engines in order to lessen the torque, but the engine controls were on the cockpit roof and he had to fight the centrifugal force in order to get his arm up. Finally he managed to kill both engines. The whirling main rotor blades continued to generate torque but, mercifully, without the engines, the spinning slowed.

Then, just before impact, Jake jerked back on the cyclic and the nose of the helicopter came up. Now, with the spin rate down to half what it had been, and with the helicopter level, the Blackhawk made a hard but somewhat controlled landing.

Jake sat in his seat with dust streaming up around the helicopter and the rotor blades still spinning. He waited until the spinning was slow enough that he knew they would not generate lift, then pulled the collective up, putting enough pitch in the blades to slow them until they finally stopped.

"Are you okay?" Jake asked.

"What the hell happened?" Candidate Lewis asked.

"You got hit by an RPG," Jake said.

"What?"

"A goose, or some geese, took out the tail rotor," Jake said. "It was the same effect as being hit by an RPG."

"Damn. I'm glad I wasn't flying solo," Lewis said.

"Funny you would say that," Jake said. "I was just thinking I wish the hell you had been flying solo."

Although neither pilot was hurt, they were required by SOP to report to the hospital for a physical evaluation. Jake was in the examining room just zipping his flight suit closed when Karin came in with a worried look on her face.

"I heard you were in a crash!" she said, the tone of her voice reflecting her worry.

"I resent that. I made a controlled landing," Jake replied. "A hard landing, yes, but it was controlled."

Karin threw her arms around him. "Oh," she said, "when I heard you had been brought in I was scared to death."

"It's nice to be worried about," Jake said. "But really, it was no big thing."

"Hah, no big thing my foot. I heard some of the other aviators talking about it. You lost your tail rotor but were able to land. Everyone is calling you a hero."

"A hero?" Jake said. He smiled. "Yeah, I'll accept that."

"Well, now, don't let it go to your head," Karin teased. "You are hard enough to be around as it is."

"Really? How do you manage to be around me so much?"

"Because I'm a saint. Didn't you know that?" Karin asked. She kissed him.

"Careful, what if one of the other nurses came in now and caught you cavorting with a patient?"

"I'd tell them to get their own patient," Karin replied with a broad smile.

"I'm off tomorrow," Jake said. "Because of the aircraft incident, I'm supposed to take a forty-eight-hour stand-down. What about you?"

"I'm not off until next Tuesday, but I can trade with one of the other nurses."

"Come over to the house. We'll watch our new president be sworn in."

Friday, January 20

The pictures on the TV screen, taken from cameras stationed all through the nation's capital, showed throngs of people ecstatically cheering as the car bearing President-elect Mehdi Ohmshidi drove by, headed for the Capitol steps.

> It is estimated that the crowd gathered in Washington for the inauguration of our nation's first-ever foreign-born president numbers well over two million people.

The television reporter was speaking in breathless excitement.

> The excitement is contagious and the atmosphere electric—enough to send a tingle running up this reporter's leg. History is being made here today. President-elect Ohmshidi is the first person ever to take advantage of the Twenty-eighth Amendment to the Constitution repealing Section One, Article Two, and making any naturalized citizen eligible to be president of the United States. Think of it. America is now the world, and the world is now America.

Jake was in his living room, eating popcorn and drinking a root beer as he watched the inaugural proceedings.

Jake had not voted for Ohmshidi, but then he had not really been enthusiastic about the other candidate either. His vote, as he had explained it to Karin, had been more against Ohmshidi than it had been for Admiral Benjamin Boutwell, the former Chairman of the Joint Chiefs of Staff. Jake had often declared that if he had omnipotent power he would replace everyone in government, regardless of their party, with someone new.

Ohmshidi was born Muslim, but long ago renounced the faith of his birth. He had risen to national prominence as the federal prosecutor who tried the case against Masud Izz Udeen. Izz Udeen was an Islamic terrorist who released sarin gas into the ventilation system of Madison Square Garden, killing more than seven hundred Americans.

As Izz Udeen received his sentence of death, he pronounced a fatwa against Ohmshidi, whom he denounced for abandoning Islam, and implored Muslims of the world to martyr themselves if need be in order to kill Ohmshidi. The fatwa against him, along with his successful prosecution of Izz Udeen, propelled Ohmshidi to national prominence, resulting in his election to president of the United States.

Jake watched as Ohmshidi stood on the steps of the nation's Capitol building with his right hand raised, and his left hand very pointedly not on the Bible, but hanging by his side. The Chief Justice of the United States administered the oath of office, then concluded with, "So help me, God."

Ohmshidi responded with, "And this I, Mehdi Ohmshidi, affirm."

"Damn," Jake said aloud, speaking to himself. "What was that about?"

Ohmshidi moved to the microphone to present his inaugural address.

My fellow Americans. As your new president I make you this promise. It is not a campaign promise, it is not a mere statement of ambition, it is a promise that will be fulfilled. On this day we are embarking upon a world-altering journey that will bring about a new paradigm in American culture. This fundamental change will enable the poorest among us to share in the bounty of this, the wealthiest nation in the world. I will accomplish this goal by requiring more from those who have greatly profited by the opportunities offered them.

That means that the wealthiest among us will have to do their fair share in order to make all our citizens truly equal. But from their sacrifice will emerge a new order. Think of it—no more will there be people with no place to lay their head, with no food upon their table, without adequate health care, and with none of the finer things that make life worthwhile.

Such a thing has long been the goal of compassionate people, and in the past we have introduced welfare programs, food stamps, aid to dependent children, Medicaid, Medicare, and yes, even Social Security, to move in that direction. But any economist will tell you that all those programs have failed. I will not fail. We will have, before I complete my first four years, a universal program of shared wealth.

There was a light tap on the door, and when it was pushed open Captain Karin Dawes stuck her head in.

"It's me," she called.

"Come on in, Karin," Jake invited. "You're late. I've eaten almost all the popcorn already."

Karin walked over to the refrigerator and opened the door. "Don't you ever buy any kind of soft drink except root beer?"

"There is no soft drink except root beer."

"What a deprived life you have lived," Karin said as she grabbed one. "What have I missed?" she settled on the sofa beside him, pulling her legs up and leaning against him.

"Not much. Ohmshidi just admitted that he was a communist."

Karin popped the tab, and the root beer can spewed a fine mist. "You're kidding me!"

"Well, he as much as did. He's talking about sharing the wealth."

"Oh, that's all. Now, tell me the truth, Jake. Wouldn't you like to have some of Bill Gates's money?" Karin asked as she took a swallow of her drink.

"Not unless I did something to earn it. I believe in a fair wage for honest work, but I certainly don't believe in taking money from the successful to give to the losers who voted for this bozo."

"Come on, give him a chance. He hasn't been president for more than an hour, and you're already picking on him."

"It took him less than fifteen minutes to show his true color," Jake said. "And forget the people who were calling him a pinko during the election. He isn't pink; he's red through and through."

Karin laughed. "Jake, I can't believe you are such a troglodyte. Just calling you a right-wing wacko doesn't quite get it. You are to the right of Attila the Hun. Are all Amish that way?"

"If you mean do they want to do for themselves, the answer is yes. And I agree with them. I didn't abandon everything the Amish believe in when I left the life," Jake said. "I'm still a strong believer in the idea of individual self-reliance, rather than depending on the government for everything."

"He can't be all that bad," Karin said as she turned her attention to the TV screen. Ohmshidi was still talking.

"I thought you told me you didn't vote for him."

"I didn't vote for him, but millions of Americans did."

"I know, that's what frightens me."

"You will share the wealth tonight, though, won't you?"

"What do you mean?"

Karin laughed. "Pass the popcorn. Unless part of your self-reliance means I have to pop my own."

Jake passed the popcorn bowl over to her. "Just listen to him," he said. "Every time he opens his mouth, he sticks his foot in it."

During my campaign, I promised you a transparent presidency and, in adhering to that promise, I will keep you informed of my every action. So I am issuing now, in this inaugural address, my first executive order.

"Damn," Jake said. "An executive order in the inaugural address? I don't think that's ever been done before."

"You can't say he isn't up and running," Karin replied.

For too long the United States has been perceived by the rest of the world as a nation with an intrusive military presence. Since World War Two we have maintained a significant, and for much of the world, an intimidating force in other countries.

Therefore, on this day, as my first official action as president, I am ordering all American troops, wherever they may be, to return to the United States. From this date forward, we will have no deployed forces anywhere in the world.

"Whoa!" Jake said, leaning forward. "What did he just say?"

"He said he is bringing all the troops back home."

"And do what with them? Where are they going to go?" Jake asked.

"I guess that means I won't ever make it to Germany," Karin said.

"It's pure insanity," Jake said. "If this is the first thing he does, where do we go from here?"

Karin picked up the remote and turned off the TV. "I'm getting concerned about you. I'm afraid you are going to get so mad watching this guy that you may well have an intracerebral hemorrhage."

"A what?"

"A stroke. It is my medical recommendation that we forget about him and go out for dinner."

"You're right. Even if I don't have a stroke, watching this commie bastard is going to make my head explode," Jake said. "We'll go out, but I choose."

"What do you mean, you choose? I'm the one who suggested we go out."

"That's just it, you suggested it," Jake replied. "That's like being challenged to a duel; the one challenged gets to choose the weapons. In this case the one invited to go out gets to choose the restaurant."

"I've never heard that. Is that some Amish rule?"

"Don't be silly. I never ate in a restaurant in my life until I was an adult. It's just the rule of common sense. You made the suggestion we go out, I get to choose where we go."

"Don't tell me," Karin said. "You are going to choose Bubba's All You Can Eat Catfish Heaven, aren't you?"

"It is a great place, isn't it?"

"Oh, yes, it's just wonderful," Karin said, rolling her eyes.

"I'm glad you like it too," Jake said, purposely disregarding her sarcasm as he reached for his car keys.

"Jake, have you ever thought of maybe going to a quieter, more traditional restaurant where they have real silverware, elegant crystal, fine china, good wine, and maybe a strolling musician? You know, something romantic?"

"You know what's romantic?" Jake asked.

"What?"

"Catfish fried golden brown, steaming hot hush puppies, a plate full of French fries liberally doused with hot sauce, a side of sliced onion, a dill pickle spear, and an ice-cold root beer."

"How can you possibly say something like that is romantic?"

"Because it is beautiful," Jake said. "And isn't romance supposed to be beautiful?"

"You are incorrigible."

"Not really. I'm just hungry," Jake replied as held the door open for her.

She laughed. "All right, Bubba's All You Can Eat Catfish Heaven it is, then."

The restaurant was noisy and filled with customers, many of whom were soldiers from Fort Rucker. Half a dozen waiters scurried among the tables carrying trays upon which there were platters piled high with fried fish. Over in one corner a group of soldiers were doing their rendition of "All Out of Love," the singing discordant and loud.

"You wanted music," Jake said, nodding toward the table of singing soldiers. "You've got music."

"Oh, that's lovely. You think of everything," Karin said.

"I try."

"Any aftereffects from your incident yesterday?" Karin asked.

Jake took a swallow of root beer before he answered. "He tried to kill me, you know."

"What? Who tried to kill you?"

"The flight student I had yesterday. Oh, he might pretend that those geese hit us, but I know better. He went out looking for them. Every student I have ever had has tried to kill me. Oh, yeah, they all say they are just making honest errors, but I know better. I sincerely believe it's a conspiracy."

"I'm sure it is. A left-wing conspiracy, no doubt,"

Karin said. "Every flight student you have ever had has been a part of a left-wing conspiracy."

"That's true. But it isn't just the flight students. I mean, think about this: Ever since I got my wings, people have been trying to kill me. Did you know that in Iraq and Afghanistan, they were actually shooting at my helicopter?"

Karin laughed. "As I recall you were flying an Apache while you were in Afghanistan, and doing quite a bit of shooting of your own. You didn't get your Distinguished Flying Cross for making sightseeing trips."

"Still, you would think they would have more respect for a disparate collection of oscillating parts that, somehow, manage to levitate." Jake held up his right hand to call one of the harried waiters over, even as he was using his left to push another piece of fried catfish into his mouth.

"We'll need another platter full," he said when the waiter came over.

"We don't need another whole platter unless you are going to eat them all yourself. I'm absolutely stuffed," Karin said.

"No sweat, I'll eat them."

"Do you ever fill up?"

"Eventually," Jake answered.

THREE

General Clifton von Cairns, the commandant of Fort Rucker, used one of the larger classrooms to have an officers' call for all department, division, and section chiefs to talk about the troops that would be returning to the States. He admitted, during the meeting, that he had no idea what this would portend. The problem would be in finding billets for all of them.

"We don't have space for them, not in our CONUS TO&E units, and not in our training commands. Department of Army has asked every post commander to inventory their facilities with an eye toward absorbing the influx."

"General, will we be able to handle such an increase?" a colonel asked.

"Yes, of course. We had much larger numbers of troops in garrison during World War Two. Of course, we also had a lot more military posts then. The problem now is that so many posts have been closed down in the last several years."

"How long has DA known about bringing all the troops back to CONUS?" another colonel asked. "What I mean is, why didn't they give us prior warning?"

General von Cairns looked at the colonel with an expression that mirrored his frustration. "Colonel Haney, from what I was told by the Army Chief of Staff this morning, Department of Defense learned about this at the same time we did: when the president announced it during his inaugural address."

Monday, February 27

Hello, America.

In his inaugural address, Mehdi Ohmshidi stated his intention to bring back to the United States every uniformed American stationed overseas. Well, he has done that. So, let's take a look at what has happened.

All military training in America has come to a complete halt. The bases are overcrowded, there is no place to put the returning military, not in any training capacity, nor in any operational unit. Morale has sunk to an all-time low as officers and men and women report to work daily, but with no real work to do.

And what has happened overseas? With America's withdrawal from NATO, all

NATO operations have come to a halt. Terrorism has increased in Europe and in the Middle East.

Since 1953, U.S. troops in Korea have helped support the South Korean military, providing the security needed to lift that country from the Third World to one of the economic giants of the world. But with the withdrawal of American troops, North Korea has become much more adventurous, last week sinking two South Korean fishing vessels and, just yesterday, penetrating the buffer zone that separates the two countries and killing three South Korean border guards.

But it isn't just Ohmshidi's foreign policy that is failing. Let me ask you this. How is this universal program of shared wealth working out for you?

Let's do give Ohmshidi credit for establishing a degree of equality in the nation. He has not been able to improve the plight of the poor, but he has been quite successful in bringing down the living standards of the rest of us. And I'm not just talking about the wealthy, I'm talking working Americans. In barely over one month, the value of the dollar has fallen by eighteen percent.

I don't mind telling you, friends, I don't see this situation getting any better. In fact, I see it getting worse, much worse. I will do

my part: I will ask the bold questions and
I will always tell you the truth.

Just over one month after Ohmshidi ordered all overseas military to return to
CONUS, Fort Rucker was filled to capacity
with returning soldiers, and in order to accom-
modate the influx, all training activities were
suspended. It would have been difficult to continue training activities anyway, because in a
cost-cutting measure Department of Army was
now regulating the total number of hours that
could be flown in any week. Once Fort
Rucker got its allocation it would hold the
hours in a pool and pilots who needed flight
time for pay purposes would have to apply for
that time. The problem was, there weren't
enough hours allocated to the fort to enable
all the pilots to make their minimums, and as
additional rated officers arrived, the situation
grew even more critical. General von Cairns
had been correct in anticipating difficulty in
completing the flight program, and his recommendation to Jake to expedite the last
cycle barely enabled the twelve students to
complete their course.

At the post hospital, Karin was having her
own problems. Reductions in Medicare and
Tricare denied civilian health care to military
retirees and their families, so they were re-
manded to military base hospitals. As a

result, the caseload at the hospital was greatly increased. VA facilities all across the country were closed, and those who were eligible for VA benefits were instructed to go to active-duty military hospitals, which accepted them only on a space-available basis.

This increased patient load meant that Karin was working longer, harder hours each day and was often too tired to visit Jake. But tonight she came by, bringing hamburgers and French fries from a local drive-in.

"Do you have any idea how much two hamburgers and two orders of French fries cost?" she asked. Then, without waiting for a response, she answered her own question. "Thirteen dollars! Can you believe that?"

"Everything has gone up," Jake said. "In order to have enough to meet all the new projects, the government has begun printing money hand over fist. Gregoire says that the presses are running nonstop. Obviously the more money you have in circulation, the less value it has, so things that have real value, like food, are seeing drastic increases in price. I bought two twelve-packs of root beer this afternoon on the way home from work. Thirty-two dollars."

"You might want to think about giving up your root beer," Karin said.

"I'll give up my root beer when they pry the last can from my cold, dead fingers," Jake teased.

"Jake," Karin said, the smile on her face replaced by an expression of concern and even a hint of fear. "Where is all this going? What is going to happen to us?"

"I don't know, Karin. God help us, I don't know."

"That's not what I wanted to hear."

"What did you want to hear?"

"I wanted to hear you say that everything will be all right."

Jake was quiet for a moment, then sighed. "Karin, for us—for you and me—everything will be all right. But there is no way the country is going to get through this without serious, serious consequences."

"How can you say, then, that it will be all right for you and me?

"Because I will make it all right for you and me," Jake said. "That is a promise."

"Get the drinks. Let's eat," Karin said, wanting to change the subject.

"How about root beer?" Jake suggested as he started toward the refrigerator.

"Root beer? I don't know, let me think about it. Ummm, yes, I think I would like a root beer."

Jake brought the drinks into the living room and put the cold cans on coasters on the coffee table in front of the sofa.

"Did you fly today?" Karin asked as she handed a hamburger and fries to Jake.

"Nobody flew today," Jake answered as he unwrapped his burger. "I haven't flown in two weeks. We are limited to one thousand hours per month, and as of now there are only six hours remaining in this month's flight-hour pool. You know how many rated aviators we have on this post?"

"A lot," Karin replied.

"We had almost a thousand before the influx of troops from overseas, and that added at least two hundred more. That means there are twelve hundred pilots who are now in queue for six hours. That breaks down to eighteen seconds of flight time apiece."

Karin laughed, spewing root beer as she did so. She wiped her mouth with a napkin.

"It's not funny," Jake said. "If aviators can't keep up their minimums, aircraft are going to start falling out of the sky because the pilots aren't going to be safe."

"I know it's not really funny, Jake," Karin said. She laughed again. "But I'm just picturing someone getting into a helicopter for eighteen seconds." She hopped up from the couch. "I'm flying," she said. She plopped back down on the couch. "Oops, time's up."

"It's not funny, damn it," Jake said, but despite himself, he laughed as well.

"I'm going to turn on the TV," Karin said. "Kentucky is in the finals and they're playing Missouri tonight."

"What do you care? You're not running cross-country for Kentucky anymore," Jake said. "And as far as I know, you are no longer a cheerleader."

"You think I'm not?" Karin said. Getting up from the couch and standing flat-footed on the floor, she did a back flip, tucking in her legs at the top of the flip because she went so high that her feet would have hit the ceiling. Landing on her feet, she thrust her pelvis forward and held her arms over her head.

"Now, imagine me in my cheerleader outfit," she said.

"You're making me blush. Be nice now," Jake said.

"Are you sure you want me to be nice?" Karin asked, seductively.

"Maybe not that nice," Jake answered, pulling her to him for an openmouthed kiss.

Gulf Shores, Alabama, Wednesday, March 1

Bob Varney, Chief Warrant Officer 4, U.S. Army (Ret.), got a cookie and a cup of coffee from the welcome counter at the bank, then had a seat until he could speak to one of the bank officers.

"Bob?" Joel Dempster called, sticking his head out of his office.

Having finished both the cookie and the coffee, Bob dropped the paper cup into a trash can, then went into Joel's office.

"I read *Slack Man: Death in Dallas*. It was great," Joel said. "When is your next book coming out?"

"Within a month. It's *Slack Man: Ambush in*

Amarillo. I'll be signing at the Page and Canvas in Fairhope when it comes out."

"Don't know if I'll be able to get there, but I'll for sure buy it."

"Thanks."

"I think Hollywood should make a movie out of one of your books."

"From your lips to God's ear," Bob said.

"Now, what can I do for you?" Joel asked.

"I was just wondering. I went online to check my account; I didn't see the deposit for my army retirement."

"Yes, I thought that might be why you were here. If it's any consolation to you, it isn't just you, Bob. There was no deposit for anyone. We got a notice from DFAS that all transactions are being halted while they undergo reorganization."

"Wow. Really? Everyone?"

"Everyone. You are lucky; with your writing you have another income. A good income, I might add. But as you know, there are a lot of military retirees here, and many, if not most of them, depend entirely upon their military retirement and Social Security."

"I didn't even check for Social Security."

"Don't bother, there was no deposit for it, either."

"That's not good," Bob said.

"I'll tell you something else that isn't good. We have been ordered to submit a report to the federal government providing information on the amount of money every depositor has in all accounts."

"Are you going to do that? Do they have the authority to make you do it?"

"As long as we participate in the FDIC program, we have no choice but to comply."

"Maybe I should take out what I've got in there," Bob said.

"You can't."

"What do you mean, I can't?"

"You just deposited a royalty check earlier this week, didn't you? A rather substantial check?"

"Yes, it was for signing four contracts, and delivery and acceptance of a completed book. A little over twenty-two thousand dollars."

"At this point, any withdrawal, or check, in excess of ten thousand dollars must be approved by the federal government."

"Why?"

"I'm sure you have noticed that the economy is a little shaky now, and is getting worse almost by the day. I think this is to prevent a run on the banks."

"Is the money safe?"

"It is as safe as money is safe," Joel said. "The problem is, how secure is the American dollar? I've been hearing things through the grapevine that make me wonder."

"Now you are getting me scared," Bob said. "First you say there is no retirement or Social Security payments; then you say I can't get the money I do have out of the bank. Joel, what the hell is going on?" Bob asked.

"I wish I could tell you, Bob, I really do. I've talked to all the other bankers. We are very worried about this. Banks are only as good as the service they are able to provide to their depositors. When you start breaking that trust, then you are putting into jeopardy a bank's ability to function. If I were you—and I'm cutting my own throat by telling you this—but if I were you, I would withdraw nine thousand, nine hundred and ninety-nine dollars and ninety-nine cents. As long as you don't go to ten thousand dollars on any one transaction, you are safe."

"Thanks, Joel, I guess that's the route I'll take."

"Then come back tomorrow and do it again. Keep doing it until your account has just a few cents in it."

"I appreciate you telling me that, Joel," Bob said. "I'll do that, too."

"Just write the check here. I'll cash it. There's no sense in causing anyone to get curious. And, if you would, be careful about whom you tell this to."

"I will," Bob promised. "And again, thanks."

Bob wrote the check and handed it to Joel. Joel left the office, then returned a few moments later with the cash in a bank envelope.

"Are you going to rent your house this summer?" Joel asked as he handed the cash to Bob.

"I don't know if we are or not," Bob replied.

"By this time last year, we had eight weeks rented already. So far this year, not so much as a nibble."

"I guess folks are a little frightened of what's ahead," Joel said.

"Yeah, it sure looks that way."

Bob got up and stuck his hand out toward Joel. "I appreciate what you are doing for me, Joel."

"You're a good customer and an interesting guy," Joel said. "And, I wouldn't worry too much about things. I'm sure it's all going to work out."

"If not, we'll just whistle past the graveyard, eh, Joel?"

Joel laughed out loud. "Sounds like a good plan," he said.

Fort Rucker, Alabama, Thursday, March 2

```
From the Office of the
Commanding General
Fort Rucker, Alabama

Subject: Flight Time
Suspense Date: With immediate effect

1.All facility aircraft are
  herewith grounded. No flight
  will be authorized unless it
  is an emergency flight.
```

a. Emergency refers to national emergency only.
b. Authorization for emergency must come from Department of Defense.
c. Said authorization will require authenticator.

2. All aviators are hereby ordered to submit flight logbooks showing most recent flying time for analysis of flying patterns.

3. All aircraft maintenance logbooks will be surrendered to flight operations, and all aircraft will be rendered unflyable by removing lines from fuel tank to fuel controls.

4. Flight school students who have less than 200 flying hours will be dismissed from the course and reassigned to nonflying billets.

5. Flight school students with more than 200 flying hours will be subject to flight instructor's evaluation for further disposition. If

recommended by flight
instructor, they will be
awarded the wings of a rated
aviator.

Distribution:
150 copies to each Department
of U.S. Army Aviation School
100 copies to each TO&E unit
15 copies to each Army airfield
under Fort Rucker control

For the Commander MG Clifton von
Cairns

Joseph A. Wrench,
LTC Avn Adjutant

"What is this nonsense, Major?" Captain Greenly asked. Greenly was one of the instructor pilots in Environmental Flight Tactics. "All aircraft are grounded?"

"That's what the DF says," Jake replied.

"For how long?"

"That, I can't tell you, Len," Jake replied. "But I can tell you, it doesn't look good."

"I've only got one student who meets the two-hundred-hour requirement, but hell, that's because he's so uncoordinated he had to fly extra hours just to keep up. My two best students are still fifteen hours short. What am I going to tell them?"

"Tell them the truth," Jake said. "At this point

it doesn't matter whether they have their wings or not. Nobody is flying."

"Have you thought about where that leaves us?" Greenly asked.

"What do you mean?

"I mean if nobody is flying, there isn't much need for flight instructors, is there?"

"I see your point."

Greenly sighed, and ran his hand through his hair. He was a veteran of two tours in Iraq and one in Afghanistan.

"Jake, I've got forty-five days of leave time accrued. If you have no objections to it, I think this might be a good time to take leave."

"Why burn your leave time?" Jake asked.

"What do you mean?"

"Why don't you just take off? Check in with me every week or so and let me know how to get hold of you if anything comes up."

"You think that would be all right? I mean, to just leave without leave papers?"

"I don't know where all this is going, Len, but I seriously doubt that the Army will even know you are gone. I'm certainly not going to tell them."

Greenly smiled. "All right," he said. "Maybe I'll just do that. Drop in on the folks back in Kansas, unannounced." Greenly started toward the door, then stopped and looked back toward Jake. "Jake, what would you say if I told you I've been thinking about resigning my commission?"

"You're a good man, Len. You've been a fine

officer and an asset to Environmental Flight. I hate the way things are, but, with the way they are, I would say that I would understand."

Greenly stepped back toward Jake, then reached out to shake his hand. "Good-bye, Jake," he said.

"Good-bye, Len."

Greenly came to attention and snapped a sharp salute. Jake returned it, and then Jake did a crisp about-face and left the room.

Jake stared at the empty door frame for a moment, then sat down and looked up at the wall. It was filled with photographs of army helicopters, from the H-13s and H-19s of Korea, to the Hueys, Chinooks, and Cobras of Vietnam, to the Blackhawks and Apaches of Iraq and Afghanistan. There was also a picture of a CH-47 Chinook in Afghanistan, and under it was a caption:

Yes, the Chinook is still here. Nothing can ground this bird.

"Nothing except a dumb-ass president," Jake said aloud.

THE LAST GUNFIGHTER SERIES BY
WILLIAM W. JOHNSTONE